AF396476

Fin is a newly qualified broadcast journalist who wrote 'Deck of Cards' in the summer before his final year of university.

Having always had an interest and passion in history and the World Wars instilled in him by his grandmother, Fin created a documentary during his final year at university, exploring the life of one of the last remaining Lancaster Bomber Veterans.

He is currently balancing journalism work with the writing of his next book.

This book is dedicated to Auntie Pat, Auntie June and the real Sergeant Parker. I hope this story makes you proud.

Fin Brown

DECK OF CARDS

AUSTIN MACAULEY PUBLISHERS®

LONDON * CAMBRIDGE * NEW YORK * SHARJAH

Copyright © Fin Brown 2024

The right of Fin Brown to be identified as the author of this work has been asserted by the author in accordance with sections 77 and 78 of the Copyright, Designs and Patents Act 1988.

All rights reserved. No part of this publication may be reproduced, stored in a retrieval system, or transmitted in any form or by any means, electronic, mechanical, photocopying, recording, or otherwise, without the prior permission of the publishers.

Any person who commits any unauthorised act in relation to this publication may be liable to criminal prosecution and civil claims for damages.

This is a work of fiction. Names, characters, businesses, places, events, locales, and incidents are either the products of the author's imagination or used in a fictitious manner. Any resemblance to actual persons, living or dead, or actual events is purely coincidental.

A CIP catalogue record for this title is available from the British Library.

ISBN 9781035873135 (Paperback)
ISBN 9781035873142 (ePub e-book)

www.austinmacauley.com

First Published 2024
Austin Macauley Publishers Ltd®
1 Canada Square
Canary Wharf
London
E14 5AA

I'd like to thank my parents for without their unwavering love, support, and financial care this publication would not be possible – and also for allowing me to take over the dining room table for four months!

I'd like to thank Lily for being the first person to hear my ideas for the book and always giving me the confidence, love, and belief it was good enough to write.

Also, a big thank you to my grandparents for all your love and support. From museum trips to the first physical copy of the book I am forever grateful for your support.

1

Thwack! The cane rattled across the boy's knuckles, the pain sharp and harsh, sending tremors through his body. Again. And again. The teacher showed no signs of remorse as he struck the boy multiple times, the anguish written all over the young boy's face despite his stellar determination to fight back salty tears stinging his eyes as he stood there.

The torment ended and he made his way slowly out of the dingy classroom out into the courtyard, where a small crowd of twenty or more children of a similar age were huddled around the door anticipating his exit. One particular youngster waded through the group clutching the hand of the caned victim pulling him out of the way, leading them out of the gate and away down a cobbled path.

The sun rode high in the sky, streaming down beams of light, illuminating the Norfolk skies. Cromer was a small Norfolk coastal town, home to few but a community with a strong beating heart. The local children had just one school, no doubt preparing all the boys for a lifetime of farm labour or fishing.

That was not the goal for Archie Baxter though. Archie, now sporting streaking cane marks across his knuckles, wanted to follow in his father's footsteps in running the family bookshop. His grandfather opened the shop in his early years passing it down to his son who planned on doing the same. Archie was of a small, slight build, with messy brown hair ruffled into small curls, his face adorned with freckles.

Archie had always been a lover of books, his father and grandfather before him had been one of only a few in the local community who knew—and rather cared—to read, an ability that Archie's father and grandfather were both keen to pass down to him.

They would always read to Archie and teach him the meaning and value of great literature. Archie, for this reason, had always had the advantage over his small class in school who had very little ability when it came to reading.

This often left him in the firing line of the school's toughest bully Samuel Butcher. Samuel would often steal and take Archie's books away from him and mocked him for having no friends who didn't live behind the pages of the books he read and his imagination which gave them life.

However, to Archie, Samuel only ever stole his books or made fun of him because he was jealous that he didn't know how to read. In the way that bullies do, Samuel would assert his force over the far smaller Archie and the two would end up locked in each other's arms, pushing and scrapping with each other.

A long, ropey arm reached into the melee and pulled Archie from the crowd, trying hard not to rip his sleeve as he removed him from trouble. The crowd of boys around them jeered as Archie, red-faced and messy-haired stood on the edge of the rabble panting heavily.

"What this time?" a voice said, as Archie's rescuer looked down on him a smile across his face.

Just as Archie began to break out into a laugh, a tall, domineering figure bellowed from the edge of the courtyard.

"Baxter, Butcher, now."

Three spine-chilling words rang out across the courtyard as the crowds instantly dispersed leaving Samuel, Archie, and his rescuer stand there like sitting ducks. The two boys, who had only a few minutes ago been embroiled in a fight were now walking, heads low and sunken trailing behind their teacher, Mr Wright, as he led the way back into their classroom, the large oak door slamming behind them.

"Many children have been on the receiving end of this cane master Baxter and none more frequently as you," he would say, on a regular occurrence.

The teacher was a man of rugged appearance. His hair was wispy and thin in his ageing state, with his nose hooking over his top lip as he often towered over his pupils.

He was a teacher who taught through discipline, with his customary cane a staple of his day's outfit as it sat comfortably in his right hand as he would pace the classroom with his arms behind his back, wearing his same suit of Irish tweed as he did every day.

Archie had indeed become no stranger to maiming, with this day being no different as he ambled back along the dusty path on his way to his small family cottage.

To his side was the young boy who pulled him out of the crowd, a boy much taller than Archie, with hair as black as the night, pale skin and large dark rings around his eyes. He was a thin, gangly boy who smiled as he walked. With a name that suited his stature, Henry Longley had been friends with Archie ever since they were small children.

Their mothers had both worked as housemaids in the big house before getting married and having children, remaining friends after they left and bringing their children up as close friends as they were. Henry lived with his mother and older sister. His father passed away when Henry was just four years old, he died fighting in the Boer War, leaving his widow alone with a poor soldier's pension to raise their small family.

This meant that ever since he was old enough Henry used to help out as a paper boy. He would get home from school and ride his bicycle around the town delivering enough newspapers to make enough money to help his mother put food on the table for him and his sister. His sister, who was three years his elder, found work in a textile factory as soon as she could sew.

Archie and Henry had known each other all their lives and had been inseparable that whole time. Archie had always been quiet and was six months his friends younger. He always found a way into trouble; his father had always taught him to stand up and fight for what he believed in.

At times, he took that a little too literally, hence why Mr Wrights's cane had become well acquainted with Archie's hand. For someone who always got into trouble, he was never very good at getting out of it, Henry was the one for that. He was like his knight in shining armour whenever he needed one. Everyone liked Henry, everyone wanted to be his friend.

As the tallest in the class, all the children wanted to spend play time playing games with him and wanted to be seen leaving school with him, but that had never phased Henry, nor had he let his school popularity get to his head. He still valued Archie above any other, not just any other child but any other person.

He was very close with his mother and his sister, but he protected Archie like an older brother if ever there was any trouble, he was the first one on the scene, and as had happened on this very day, he was the first one to pull him out of the rabble. This day had been no different, another day of Henry playing peacekeeper and trying, but often failing, to keep his friend out of harm's way.

"You need to keep yourself out of trouble Arch, I keep having to pull you out of bother," said Henry, looking down on his friend as they walked, the beams of sunlight bouncing off Archie's face as he looked up, an ashamed look drawn across him.

"But I'll always be here for you," he said, wrapping his arm around Archie's shoulder and pulling him in tight to his waist, ruffling his curly locks with his other hand.

"Best friends stick together like glue," he smiled down at Archie who looked up into his friend's eyes, seeing the warmth and love radiating from them, and smiled back.

The pair walked the rest of the way home chattering and laughing, arms around each other, ambling down the Norfolk path.

In those moments, with the warm weather and blue skies blanket over the coastal town, the boys felt as free and as happy as possible. They would often deviate off the path, find their way into a field running around scaring away birds, or running to the beach and skimming stones.

They walked to Henry's house where the two parted ways, it was another 10 minutes down the stone track to Archie's house where he would often meander along the path in his own thoughts, making up stories in fantastical worlds until he reached his house and came back down into reality.

"I'm home," Archie called through the door, as he discarded his jacket by the chair in the hallway.

The Baxters lived in a small cottage, with quite enough space for what they needed. They never found themselves in a position of poverty or needing more than they could afford, so felt privileged in their community. They were a tight-knit family, Archie lived with his mother, father, and grandfather. His father had taken his own into their home after Archie's grandmother passed away when he was just a baby.

"In the kitchen," called Archie's mother, who was elbow-deep in flour as she was baking a fresh apple pie for the family.

"Smells amazing that does," said Archie, who planted a soft kiss on his mother's cheek and pulled up a chair next to his grandfather who sat, head sunken into his shoulders in the corner of the room.

"Alright, Grandpa," Archie placed a hand on his grandfather's shoulder.

He was an old man, who was very frail and had a tendency to stay in the same place for the duration of every day that passed. He would hang his head low, for the fatigue of lifting it any higher was too exhausting for him. He would speak very few words, but most of those were to his grandson, with whom he cared for, immensely.

"Set the table, your father will be home in a minute," Archie's mother said, as she turned to face him, her ginger hair catching the sunlight bursting through the window as she faced her son.

The door opened and Archie's father entered the room.

"That smells lovely my dear," the man said, gently kissing his wife as she served their dinner, "alright son, alright old man," he said jokingly as he patted both his son and father on the shoulder as he went to hang up his jacket.

Archie had always looked up to his father. He was a tall man with a strong build. His dark curly hair merged into his thick rugged beard, which would deceive many into thinking he had a scary, bear-like appearance. But Archie was one of the few to know the soft interior of his father.

Archie had always been amazed by his father's wisdom and wanted nothing more than to follow in his footsteps. He felt very lucky to have a father and a great one at that. Regardless of how much he looked up to him, he would never mention him around Henry.

He never wanted to make his best friend upset that he couldn't experience the same things and have the same bond that Archie had with his father. Henry would never show any sadness around the subject however, he barely knew his father so had very little to cling to now. The boys were closing on 12 years old, with their birthdays separated by one month and a day, so Henry had very few memories of his father left to cherish.

Archie sat at the dinner table infatuated as his father would tell stories of his day to the family as they tucked into their dinner. Stories of customers and what books he would sell along with what books he would bring home.

Archie's favourite part of the evening was when his father would bring him home a book or two every week for them to read and look at together. It was a tradition they had always had since Archie was old enough for his father to read to him.

It would then be Archie's turn to talk about his day and disclose the information about being on the receiving end of Mr Beadle's cane once more. His father would always sympathise with his child's cause and greet him with a soft smile and a wink, but his mother would always tell him off for it without fail.

"He's growing up Margie," his father said, "you need to be tough in this world and fight for what you believe in. No one else has got your back so you gotta look out for yourself."

Archie's dad would repeat this monologue almost every time Archie was on the receiving end of a telling-off from someone.

"He's growing up too fast that's the problem, Robert," his mother replied to his father, as her eyes were locked onto her son, "before you know it, he'll be out into the world for himself, then who knows the trouble he'll get himself into."

She wiped a solitary tear from her eye as she brushed her hand through her son's hair and the family of four sat in the quiet of the Cromer evening to eat their dinner all together.

Archie's mother was not able to have any more children, and because of that had always taken special care to look after her only son in every way she could. She struggled with the concept of time as all parents do.

She struggled with the knowledge that one day soon her son would no longer be the little boy who longed to hear stories in bed and play with his toy soldiers on his bedroom floor for hours on end.

Spending the days in the house on her own, except for the silent company of her father-in-law, she would occupy her time by baking and cooking her family's favourite foods, trying to savour the moments as long as she could, as if trying to capture them in a glass bottle and store them forever.

Archie was very close with his mother, when he was younger, before he could spend his weekends shadowing his father in the bookshop and building dens in the woods with Henry, they would spend days together exploring the surrounding countryside and sitting on the beach, looking out at the sunset across the horizon.

Those memories held special places in both of their hearts as Archie's mother would often sit and ponder to herself, wondering and hoping that she had given her son all she could to allow him to succeed.

2

The mist rolled over the hills around them, the solitude and peacefulness of the countryside offering a serene escape from the day's proceedings. Archie stood by his mother's side, his eyes welling up, the tears building into small pools of water ready to be released. He bit into his lip to put on his brave face as the church bell chimed.

And again. And a final time. Archie and his parents made their way into the church and sat waiting until Archie's grandfather was carried in by four large men and placed at the front of the church.

Archie had always had a special relationship with his grandfather. He was always someone he could turn to in times of hardship, someone who always protected and cared for him.

His stories used to be an escape from the world, a place where Archie could go to be in his own eutopia in his head. Now as he sat at the front of the church, he wondered what he would do now. Where would he get his stories from? How could he face the world without his grandfather by his side?

As he sat there in the silence of the church, his mind wandered back through all the years of memories he had made with his grandfather. From the first time he took him round the book shop, their weekly trips to the fun fair, when it rolled into town. His grandfather—Albert—had always been a warm, loving grandfather.

Although his final years were spent in the same chair day after day, in his grandson's early years he was a large man, as round as he was tall but with a warming smile, rarely seen without a pipe between his teeth. He would always walk with his hands behind, swinging a walking stick behind him which he would always carry but never used.

When out and about, he would never be seen without his baker boy hat firmly fixed on his head, with his gold pocket watch protruding from the pocket of whichever stripey shirt he had elected to wear on that day. His shirts always looked as though they were one deep breath away from a button bursting at the seam due to his ever-growing belly getting harder to conceal. This round stature made him all the cuddlier for Archie who would bury his head in his grandfather's stomach to hug him at the end of every day.

Their relationship had changed over the last few years as Archie got older as did his grandfather. He began to talk less, and the more time went on the more his eyes that once saw such wonders and told such stories began to fade, the loving look he so often would give his grandson turned to one of distance and his favourite person became nothing more than a stranger in his eyes.

The old man had fallen ill and spent his last years and months surrounded by those he loved most. Despite not being able to communicate much with Albert towards his end, not having his chair permanently occupied, or having the sound of his snoring on a quiet afternoon fill the silence had left a massive hole in the family home.

It was the happy memories of his youth that Archie was clinging onto and clawing to the front of his mind as the grief attacked him that morning in the church.

Archie had already left school a couple of years ago, like all the other children around him and he had started helping his father to work in the bookshop, while also helping the gardener at the big house to earn extra money for his family. Part of the reason he worked with the gardener was also to do with the fact that Henry worked at the big house too.

He, himself started work as a hall boy as his mother had got them a job and he worked long hours every day, running down the same cobbled streets he used to run as a small child to see Archie in the evenings when they both finished their work.

Archie enjoyed the gardening work, his mother had always taken pride in her rose garden that she would often prune on the weekends, and Archie had always taken an enthusiasm in helping, something he transferred when he worked for the big house. He would rarely see Henry while working but he would often sneak into the servant's hall for dinner when Henry was seated with the other hall boys and servants.

Both of the boys had higher aspirations for their current positions in life, but they knew they had to be patient. They were both 14 and change was in the air in 1911, they could all feel the next few years would breed change and they wanted to be ready for it the older they got.

Archie looked up at his father sat next to him in the church. Even as Archie got older his father always seemed a giant to him. His big, broad frame and round stomach always made Archie see him as warm and comforting and he had never seen him show emotion really in any way.

He looked up into his father's sad eyes as a solitary tear rolled down his cheek, lingering in his beard as it dropped. His father had always been a strong man, he had fought in the African wars and had seen sights that he never spoke about but could be read from the scars and expressions that sometimes shadowed his face.

He was a hard man, as soft as he was to Archie and his mother, he could be harsh. The experiences of war had hardened him and no matter how deeply he tried to conceal the effects it had, Archie had seen him sometimes lose his temper in the bookshop and a fiery look of fury would dart across his face.

He had lost many friends and two brothers in those wars; he had been one of the lucky few to return physically unscathed but the emotional and mental injuries he had sustained were clear to see.

Archie had seen signs of distress across his father's face before today, but the anguish written over his sullen expressions was the worst, the young boy had ever seen.

The priest finished the sermon and the family rose as they left the ancient building to bury Archie's grandfather in the grounds of the church. The fresh breeze whipped around the family as they stood, arms interlocked, in the cemetery as his beloved grandfather was lowered down.

His mother lovingly placed one of her precious roses onto the coffin and kissed her hand before placing it on the wood. They stood there for a moment. No one said anything. A couple of birds chirped in the distance but other than that subtle noise it was as if the world stood still. The family stood there together reflecting on their loved one before wiping away a final tear and turning to walk away.

Archie took one turn back as the grave was being filled before heading home to get used to a life without his grandfather. As his head came back round, he caught sight of someone standing by the church gates, arms folded and leaning against the wooden framing.

Dressed all in black, like the rest of the congregation, was a much taller, scruffy-looking Henry. He had turned out to be there for his best friend when he needed him most, and Archie separated from the group to head in his direction.

"At least, you got good weather for it," Henry joked, as Archie got closer, and specks of rain began falling around them.

"It's cos you've turned up, it was sunny before you got here," Archie replied, sniffling and wiping a tear from his eye as the two embraced each other.

"How'd you get away from the big house?" Archie asked, a puzzled look on his face.

"Ah, they won't notice if I'm gone for an hour or two. Besides, I think I've cleaned those bloody chamber pots and old boots enough for one day," he quipped, with a smile.

"How are you holding up, Arch?" he asked sincerely.

"It's weird, you know, you always know these things will happen, yet you approach every day never thinking about it, and yet it happens everywhere all the time."

"Even though we couldn't do much together, it was his presence, the fact he was the one that'd been there and seen it all and still knew everything was alright, he'd had to go to war and still come home to open the bookshop."

"He would always be the one to give people hope. With that gone, I don't know what'll happen."

"You crack on Arch, you step up," Henry said, both boys stopping in their tracks as they started walking down the road back to the big house.

"Your grandad led your family, and your father under him. Now it's your time to be a man. Everyone around you is growing up, we're not children anymore."

"Life isn't as easy as running into the forest and skimming stones anymore, you know that. Your grandad knew that you have to work hard to get what you want. Look at me, you think I want to stay a hall boy?" he said, raising his arms, shrugging his shoulders, and shaking his head with a smirk drawn across his face.

"I'm butler material." he said, puffing his chest and standing tall over his far smaller friend.

"And one day you'll lead the book shop, or you'll go on to do whatever you want to do. Your grandad knew you were capable of that and so do I. I never really knew my father, but I know if I ever have a kid, they're gonna know they can be anything they wanna be if they chase it."

"I'm gonna be head of this household, I'll be the tale of the hall boy to the butler. And you'll write your own version, and we stick together like glue you know that. You'll be just fine boy."

Henry finished talking, ruffled Archies hair, and wrapped an arm around him as they both continued on their way to the big house.

As they walked Archie stayed in silence, he was going over and processing everything Henry had said. He loved his bookshop, it was the only place he wanted to work, but as long as his father was there, he'd only be a helper and nothing more. He thought his father had many more years of leading the business without Archie needing to be any more involved than he already was.

He didn't have a plan like Henry. He would watch Henry's ambitions every day, knowing exactly what he wanted to do, but Archie always felt as though if he stayed waiting for his time to come at the bookshop, to run it, to have it be his, he'd spend years plucking rose bushes with no further goals in his life.

***

Two summers had come and gone, and much change had been brought on by the changing seasons. As the years had grown in number so had Archie and Henry, in both age and stature. At 16, Henry was one of the tallest boys in the community, he'd felt like a man for some time, but now everyone started to view him as one.

For Archie, he was far off Henry's height but the sideburns and stubble coming through on his face made him feel as though he too was coming of age. As ever, the time that passed had brought the two closer together and had also brought a new position in the house for Henry.

The big house was situated on a tall hill with a swirling driveway, that mazed through trees and finely pruned bushes up to the front of the house to reveal the splendour of the manor. Huckerby Hall was home to Lord and Lady Sheppherd, the figureheads in the town.

Lord Sheppherd was an elderly man, about 60, or at least that was how old Henry said, he looked. Archie never had much dealing with what went on inside the house and rarely saw its residents, but Henry would often boast about his daily dealings with them.

His Lordship was, on the whole, rather a friendly man, he always made the effort to speak to his staff. He would enjoy going down into the local communities or spending time by the harbour. He was a portly man and was always immaculately dressed, not a single hair was out of place on his head, where he had sported the same parted hairstyle with his hair slicked down on either side of his middle parting.

He had a thick, bushy, white moustache that sat above his top lip, almost walrus-like. He fashioned a monocle over his left eye with a string that would swirl over his ear to hold it in place. He was rarely seen without a cigar, the moment he finished one he would dive into his breast pocket to take out a gold case containing a fully stacked set of log-like cigars to light the next one.

It was always a mystery to everyone he met how he could smoke a dozen cigars in their company, yet the case would always look as though it had been untouched, with the contents never diminishing.

Most days, he would spend flicking a quill in the library, writing letters to other members of the nobility, organising dining events, or attending dinners dressed in the most pristine army uniform, with all his medals brandished across his chest, polished and glistening.

He would be involved in the running of the estate, and the running of the rest of the town, how it would be managed, how it would be overseen. He was a very clever man who had gone to Eton as a child and had made the most of his position to the benefit of the people of Cromer.

Lady Sheppherd, on the other hand, was a stern and fierce-looking woman. She was very pointed and angular, with her nose and chin coming to a sharp point, as though her face was made up of a series of triangles. Even her eyes had a spikey nature about them.

Socially, Lady Sheppherd had been born above her husband and married down and would often display that this was the way she felt. She never cared for the company of soldiers or other such characters, she preferred the finer taste of London and palaces, travelling the world and attending some of the biggest balls on the continent. They did not speak much inside the house; all the staff would witness it but keep their muttering about it to the confines of the servant's quarters.

The servant's quarters were a dark series of rooms, very little light was let in, and very little life was allowed either. Any signs of laughter were deemed a sign of giving up on working duties and quickly stamped out by the butler like a cold jug on a fire.

The butler, Mr White, was a very harsh man. He seemed like a giant to all who served under him, even Henry felt intimidated by the size of the man, and he was taller than him. Mr White disliked almost everyone.

He idolised the family upstairs as he had spent his life in servitude in Huckerby Hall and was very proud to be the head of all the staff, and there were very few people under his employment who he even viewed as humans rather than workhorses.

One of those, however, was Henry. Though Henry never understood why, Mr White had always appreciated Henry's work ethic and his determination to serve the family and climb the ranks in service. It was as though he saw some of himself in Henry, which would have been a terrifying thought for him to think about.

Following the Lord and Lady's annual summer trip across the East Anglian landscape to Suffolk to visit her Ladyship's cousins, which was the highlight of her year since their level of travelling had decreased, their second footman had left his job leaving the post vacant.

Ambitious as he was, Henry spotted an opportunity he didn't want to miss. He knew becoming a footman would be the first real step on the ladder to be a natural successor to Mr White. As soon as news filtered around the servant's hall that the footman had left, Henry made his way to the butler's quarters and knocked on the door.

He took a deep breath as he made a point of fixing his stance and standing upright as the door began to open slowly.

The ominous figure of Mr White answered the door, "Is there something, I can do for you?" he asked, a permanent sneer fixed upon his face.

"A…A word if you don't mind, Mr White," he stuttered, as he made eye contact with his boss.

Without saying a word, Mr White, opened the door wide and ushered Henry in with his hands, his palm guiding him into the room, towards the chair across from his desk.

Mr White's pantry was quite as dark and dismal as you would expect. It was fully furnished with dark oak wood furniture and had a small window in the corner of the room which allowed fractions of light to shine down on his desk which was the centrepiece of the room.

On his desk was a stack of letters and papers discarded to the side, with a bottle of fine wine being distilled into a decanter—which was clearly the job he was doing before Henry came to interrupt his day.

Henry entered the room and perched himself on the edge of the seat and Mr White sat comfortably down across the desk from him.

"So, what is it I can do for you Henry?" He asked, in a dull, monotone voice, which it was hard to believe anyone had ever heard any note of enthusiasm come out of that man's mouth.

"Well Mr White, you see, the thing is, I know we're now a footman down, and well you know, I've been here for a good few years now, as you know, and I feel ready to take the next step up the ladder and give being a footman a right good go."

Henry had got very into his pitch for the job as he got into it and had forgotten himself by the end with his professionalism slightly waning.

"A right good go…do you indeed," Mr White replied, raising a thick bushy eyebrow.

"Well, I've been under your guidance for a while now, and I feel I'm ready. I won't take any more money, not for now, I'll show you I can do it first, and then when you believe I'm ready I can be paid like a footman, but only when you think I'm ready," Henry said, with a smile drawn across his face.

"Oh, and now you're going to be telling me how I should pay my staff are you?" The smile quickly faded away as Henry tried to stumble some words out of his mouth, but they fell out in a jumbled stutter.

"Alas," Mr White continued, cutting off the stumbling before it got any worse, "while you're here, it does save me posting an advertisement for a new footman. The position is yours, as long as you understand fully what's expected of you."

The smile began to creep back onto Henry's face.

"I do, Sir…Mr White, I know, I'm the man for the job."

"The rest of the silver needs polishing and we are hosting a dinner for his Lordships' cousins tomorrow so you must make sure you represent this house with an exemplary standard of work."

"I won't let you down, Mr White," Henry picked up his cap that he had brought in with him to keep his fingers occupied to take the nerves away from requesting his new job and tipped it to the butler.

Mr White nodded at Henry to leave who got up and scurried out of the door with a beaming smile and a swing in his step. Mr White sat back in his seat taking a big deep breath and watched Henry leave his pantry, a small smile breaking out of the corner of his mouth before he got back to work.

Henry finished his day's work and no sooner had his fellow hall boys returned to their rooms for the night had he swung his jacket off the coat stand

and ran out of the back door, straight down the cobbled path and not stopping until he got to Archie's house where he used any remaining energy he had to relentlessly bash on the door until Archie came to answer the door to see what the commotion was all about.

"I got it, Arch," Henry spluttered, "the new footman jobs mine, I told you I'd be climbing, I said to you before too long I'll be serving dinner to the royals and regals that come to the big house, and now I've got it," he said, puffing his chest out.

Archie shook his hand vigorously and congratulated him. For Henry, where he had come from with very little prospects without having a father around, his quick rise to the role of footman showed his ambition and dedication and he felt as though he was only just starting his journey.

After a few congratulatory moments, Henry returned back to the big house and Archie closed the door, quietly and stuck in his own head. He was always constantly wondering what was out there for him to do to achieve more with his life. He was so used to seeing Henry put his mind to something and achieving it.

He wasn't sure what his best path was, but he knew he would have to find something soon otherwise he felt he would only ever live in the shadow of his best friend, whom he loved like a brother, but often felt very envious towards.

He went to bed restlessly that night, he lay awake staring up at the ceiling in the darkness his mind whirring. He knew he needed a change in the tide, he wanted to find his purpose, even if his purpose lies beyond the comforts of his beloved bookshop.

3

Another winter had come and gone, the leaves had fallen off the trees, and wilted away into nothing before returning full of life and colour in the spring months that followed.

The year was 1914, and Archie had just turned 17, he was a real man in the eyes of the society around him and had been for some time. For the past few months, he'd been working all day Monday to Friday with the gardener up at Huckerby Hall, pruning the bushes and trimming trees, planting flowers and sowing seeds for the summer ahead.

The spring months brought about a busy time of work for Archie, there was always the most to do in the garden during those months, the old crop of winter had to be cleared out before the fresh and brightly coloured flowers could take their place.

Archie was always fascinated by spring, a period of time where everything found life, where skins were shed, and beauty returned to the world. He had always found it a natural brilliance how from the depths of darkness and cold, every year without fail the beauty in the natural world would always prevail, bringing new hope to the world.

Despite his increasingly busier working life, the ageing gardener, Mr Humphrey, would allow him to spend several weekend hours at the bookshop, helping his father and preparing for a future beyond the big house.

Mr Humphrey was as kind a man as you could be willing to find. He loved gardening and being the man who looked after the renowned gardens of Huckerby Hall was his life's pride.

He was getting on though there could be no denying that, he was well into his seventies and despite the constant work keeping him fit and busy, his legs would often give up on him. There had been many times Archie would have to haul him up from the flower bed where his legs had buckled planting the roses.

Mr Humphrey had never been able to have children of his own, and had taken Archie under his wing, and to Archie he had often played the role of the grandfather since Archie no longer had one.

They would spend many long afternoons out in the Norfolk sun with Archie, piling his problems of life's countless confusions to the elder man who would always hand him pearls of wisdom no matter what the conundrum was. Archie valued the old man very highly, in fact, considering he did not share nearly the same passion for gardening as Mr Humphrey, he was the only reason Archie continued working at the big house.

Mr Humphrey was aware that Archie did not equal his enthusiasm, as was he aware that Archie was constantly on the search for his calling in life. He encouraged him to work at the bookshop when he had the time, so he could feel more connected to his passion, but he could see the excitement Archie once had about the bookshop was fading.

For all of Archie's life, it was all he had ever wanted to do, to run his grandfather's bookshop. He had such a deep love of stories and fiction that he had always wanted to share it with the rest of the town. However, as he got older and read more of the adventure books he valued so highly, he began to wonder where his life could take him. Where he could live a life worthy of his own adventure book.

Archie had spent so long surrounded by Henry whom he felt could never do any wrong in anyone's eyes and seemed destined to run the hall one day, and after some time it had started to rub off on Archie, he had started to be quite envious of his best friend. Despite the love he had for him, all he ever seemed to do was watch him succeed as he stayed in the same place year after year.

Henry certainly was thriving inside the house, being footman for over a year now he was an established member of the house staff. He was a favourite among the servants' quarters, always being the first one to make a joke and get out a deck of cards for a game, while also being the first one polishing the silver and setting the table for grand dinners.

Henry, on the eye, looked 27 rather than 17, he had grown into his height and his shoulders had become broader, and he seemed to puff out his chest a lot more ever since becoming a footman. His hair was jet-black and he had it set to one side, swept over, with the occasional strands falling over his forehead that he would have to brush away.

He always gained much attention from the maids and local young ladies in the town, but he never cared for it. He was incredibly content with the life he had built; he had the job he had always worked towards and a best friend who was by his side, while being able to help provide for his ageing mother.

Life in Huckerby Hall was as busy as ever, most nights there were dinner parties of one fashion or another. They were either welcoming family guests around, hosting parties of aristocrats, or hosting gatherings of high-ranking army officials.

Lord Shepherd had been in service in the South African wars and many wars before that. He had seen action many times and sometimes kept his arm in a sling due to an old army wound. While fighting the Boers in South Africa he was caught in a guerrilla attack from the Boers and a small bullet ended up striking his upper arm.

Being the stubborn man that he was he refused being sent home and relied on the treatment at the front. Because of this his arm never properly recovered and every now and then, and coincidentally every time there was a military event in which he was attending, he would tie his arm up in a sling to rest his aching war wound.

Lord and Lady Shepherd were renowned amongst all the neighbouring counties for putting on the most spectacular dances and balls. All the nobles from far and wide would travel down to sample the fine Norfolk surroundings and be treated to a night of regal entertainment.

Lady Shepherd thrived off a good reputation. She valued the image of her family and her house more than anything else. She would order Mr White to have the staff work tirelessly day after day to keep the house to her standards, a standard that was considerably higher than anyone else you were ever likely to meet. This never troubled Henry though, he was always used to hard work, so he never complained about what was expected of him.

As the month of July came around the family embarked on their annual summer trip to Suffolk. The family would usually spend all of July and August in the East Anglian County. However, this year, on the August 2, the butler of the Norfolk house came into the joint servants' quarters to inform the Huckerby Hall staff they would be leaving that day, but he had no reason why.

Henry, as a footman, was never needed for the Suffolk trips, the house would use their own and the Huckerby Hall footman would remain in Norfolk with Mr

White and the hall boys and maids to ensure the house was fully maintained for the families' return.

On the morning of the August 2, Mr White called all the servants together in the servant's hall and informed them of the imminent return. No reason was given but they were ordered to ensure the house was spotless for their arrival. When the family turned up in the evening after a long day of travel, Henry was in the grand hall with Mr White and the first footman, welcoming them into the house.

No sooner had they entered the house had Lord Sheppherd's valet emerged with a small overnight bag, and the two of them made their way out into the motor to catch the last train to London. Without another word said, business resumed as normal.

That night, the servant's hall was rife with confusion and questioning. The papers were full of news of European unrest, only the day before, Germany had declared war on Russia, and a few days before that Austria Hungary had declared war on Serbia. The servant's hall was full of speculation that the return had to be because of this.

It was common knowledge among all people that Germany wanted to compete with Britain, but it had never been taken seriously, especially by those working at the Hall. As they all sat around their table discussing the day's events, there was a growing feeling that something big was on the horizon and that would explain why Lord Sheppherd had been in such a rush to get down to London to see what was going on.

Henry stayed out of the conversation, he had always hated talk of war, it was how his father was taken from his family, and he hated entertaining talk of it. He got on with his daily jobs without paying attention to the hubbub around him, as far as he was concerned everything would blow over and the family would even return back to Norfolk within a few days.

Two days later all the papers in the country were covered in one simple statement: Britain declares war on Germany. It was clear that Lord Sheppherd had travelled to London to hear of the impending news before it was released to the public. He had been down at the House of Lords when Germany had sent its ultimatum to Belgium on the August 3, all but securing the fate of war between the nations due to Britain's alliance with Belgium.

Fresh from the news of the war, many people were supportive and welcomed the idea due to the fear realisation of a German threat of expansion.

Archie didn't know what to make of the news. He knew he didn't want any threat of invasion from the Germans, but he also failed to see how this war really impacted him. To him, his life was very small with very little significance, and he wondered what something of global politics could have to do with him. The day after the announcement he was talking over the news with Mr Humphrey as they were planting a new bed of dahlias.

Mr Humphrey was telling Archie that war affected everyone, even if it didn't feel that way.

"I've lived through more wars than is good for you, Archie, and one thing you learn is that even if that war doesn't touch the soil you walk upon, it'll touch the people in your community one way or another."

"You might go to the bakers and it's a different baker to the one you're used to because he was killed in the war, or you'll hear your neighbour's tears through the wall as they get a telegram about their son not returning home."

"Even though you might not think it'll touch you, war touches all of us, not just those who fight it."

Even after hearing what Mr Humphrey had to say, Archie, still couldn't make sense of what impact it would have on his own personal life, as far as he was concerned, he'd be where he is now for many years.

The next couple of weeks went by no different to most for Archie. Naturally, there was a hubbub of chit-chat about the outbreak of war around but on the whole, everyone felt the way he did, and anyone who wasn't convinced it would be over in no time because of the infamous strength of the British army.

Other than catching glimpses of war talk, Archie's life was unchanged by the declaration, and the next Saturday, he was spending the afternoon, as always, in the bookshop with his father.

His father had grown wearier with age, his eyes sunk deeper into his face and his hair was turning greyer with the turn of every year. Despite his rising age, he felt he had many years ahead of him in his beloved bookshop. He thrived for the weekends when Archie would come and work with him, where he could show him the ropes.

Of course, working with his father for as long as he had done, Archie knew all the ropes by now, but his father liked to think he could still impart new wisdom to his son. He loved the idea of Archie taking over from him one day and owning the book shop, he had never seen there being any alternative and knew nothing of the way his son was feeling as he was reaching his own adulthood.

That particular afternoon the bookshop started business quite busily. There were many customers coming in to purchase new releases and old classics to spend their weekend hours enjoying. The shop was located in the wealthier end of the town, where upper-class families would come with their children to set them up with the best books for their education.

Archie went about his business stacking shelves with the latest deliveries and selling books at the counter while his father was taking breaks. He would wear a white shirt like his father with brown corduroy trousers, and a dark green apron completing the uniform.

The day was drawing to a close and Archie was feeling exhausted. They were closing in half an hour and his father had just handed him a new delivery of books that needed alphabetically stacking on the shelves on one side of the store. As Archie was climbing the old, wooden ladder to reach the top shelf, the door opened, and the bell chimed.

It was one of their most frequent customers, Mr Fisher. Mr Fisher was well-known among the town and was rather well off. He was the owner of the only automotive dealership in Cromer and the only one within a few towns' radius. He was a tall, skinny man who always looked very strict and serious.

He had a pointed nose and a thick bushy moustache underneath it that cushioned his top lip. He had a sharp chin and wore very thin-rimmed spectacles. His outfit would always be topped off with a bowler hat, which he would tip to Archie's father when entering the shop.

"Ah, Reginald, long time no see," Mr Baxter greeted him into the shop, a surprised look across his face.

"We haven't seen you for a couple of weeks, was started to wonder whether you'd taken your business elsewhere," he continued.

Mr Fisher would be in the shop to buy more books, browse the latest deliveries, or reminisce over old classics most days, so his recent disappearance had been of great shock to Archie's father.

"Yes, my apologies," Mr Fisher said, removing his hat and giving Mr Baxter his customary hat tip.

"You see the thing is, we've been quite short at work recently, a lot of work for me to do, far more than normal," he explained.

He had a posher voice than most around Cromer and Archie had always wondered if he always spoke in a fake voice, or if he had somehow made his way east from the bright lights of London.

"A lot of our boys that we had working for us, you know boys that would fix up engines, or even just polish the vehicles have gone and signed up for the army," he continued.

"Oh no, that doesn't help you out though. Have you found any replacements?" Archie's father replied, pulling up a stall behind the counter to sit down as he spoke to his customer.

"No, none as of yet, but Robert I must say I haven't minded the extra work, after all, I encouraged them to sign up. Once the first lad came and said he had thoughts about it I told them all, if any one of you wishes to fight for their country, I would not stand in their way," he exclaimed, with a strong sense of patriotism in his tone.

"I can't say I share your passion, Reg," Archie's father shook his head subtly as he replied.

His mind could never escape what he went through, and he found it hard to support another war.

"Well, Robert," Mr Fisher started, before taking a momentary pause to look in the eye of the shop owner.

"There is no greater honour than to travel overseas and fight for your king and country. There is no greater pride and privilege, you know it you've been there yourself and your service for your country is something that can never be taken away my friend," he continued, as Robert sat there silently listening.

"Those young boys going off to France, packing up their lives to fight for their country, why they're nothing short of heroes," he exclaimed triumphantly.

On those words, Archie's ears pricked up. He had been partly listening in on the conversation, but when Mr Fisher described the boys going overseas as heroes he stopped in his tracks. He stopped for a moment and thought to himself.

He had felt for so long that he wanted to see the world in a greater way than what his life currently had in store. It seemed as though he was realising how this war could indeed impact him. How it could give him the opportunity to travel to a foreign land and conquer it as a British hero.

Archie was picturing himself as the centre of his own book, the hero of his own story which he now had the tools to write himself.

Following a couple of minutes of mindless chatter between the two gentlemen at the front of the shop, Mr Fisher left, and the father and son packed up the shop for the night.

They walked home and went about their evening as normal, Archie's mother had cooked them a meal to arrive to, and Henry had managed to get away from the servant's tea to eat around Archie's house.

The two friends spent the next hours of the night talking and playing cards up the table. All the while, Archie's mind was flashing back to the conversation he had overheard just a few hours ago.

As the moon rose in the sky and the depths of the night drew in, the two boys said their goodnights, Henry returned the short distance back up to the big house and Archie went to bed. He lay there, staring wide-eyed at the ceiling for what felt like forever.

His mind was whirring with the idea of being a hero to his family, and to Henry if he went off to fight for them. All the talk around the town would be about how the war would be over by Christmas, so he felt sure if he went now, and fought bravely for a few months, he'd be home with exciting tales to tell of the adventures he would have overseas. Sometime later, he fell asleep with his mind made up, he was going to sign up to become a soldier.

The following day, Archie's mother had sent him on an errand to go by the local farmer to collect some eggs as she'd run out and wanted to make a pie. He knew that his day was going to consist of more than just collecting eggs from a farmer and eating one of his mother's apple pies. He was going to travel to the nearest recruiting office and enlist in the British army.

As he was walking up the hot, dusty path to the farm, he noticed the farmer on the horizon, handing three large, brown horses over to a man in a uniform. By the time he had arrived, the small group of uniformed men had left with the horses and the farmer stood there on his own in his vast landscape.

He told Archie that they were being taken to help the war effort, the more men they were getting to volunteer, the more they needed horses to aid the cause. For the right price, he had been willing to sell some of his steeds for the nation's great cause.

After a few minutes, Archie was back on his way, he had his eggs with him in a basket and he was determined to start the first chapter of his adventure. It was a long trek to the closest recruiting office and when he arrived, there were a couple of other people waiting outside the doors. There was a small queue, no more than eight or nine people lined up in the hallway of the building.

It was a baking hot summer day; the sun was beating down on the Norfolk streets and Archie looked around at his surroundings. The surroundings of everything he had ever known. He knew nothing of what was to come once he left the building he was about to walk into, but he knew he felt ready for a change.

The sun bounced off the windows of the bakeries and the shops along the street. It kissed the top of cakes that were attracting passers-by to sample them. As Archie looked around, he could relive the memories of his childhood, roaming the streets around here with Henry, racing each other to be the first one to the butchers.

As he stood there waiting to enter the building, he did not think of his parents whom he would be leaving behind, he was too excited about that. But the recurring thought he had spinning around his head was, *what about Henry*?

His whole life for as long as he could think back, they had done everything together, brothers forever as they used to say. The only thing to stop him in his tracks was the constant thought of wondering if he could ever go through with this on his own, without Henry there.

While they both worked different jobs at the big house, they would make time to see each other every day. Even if it was for nothing more than a game of cards, or a conversation in the courtyard, Archie knew he was the person who always looked out for him, the one who was there no matter what.

As he stood there, gazing into the distance Archie heard the call of next. Almost without realising, he had become the next in the queue and it was his turn to go and sign up. In a moment that felt like an eternity, everything he had ever felt about his life, and about wanting adventure crossed through his mind. It was now on his doorstep, yet he felt nervous about it all. He shook off the momentary hesitation and walked in as broadly as he could.

He entered the small office building, which gave the impression that its current purpose had not been so for very long. There was a small desk at the back of the room where the strong-looking recruiting officer was sitting with a pen in his hand and a stack of papers in front of him.

He was immaculately dressed in uniform and had his moustache delicately pointed at the tips of either side of his face. To the left of the desk, there were several chairs stacked up, which clearly held no current place in the building's use and had to succumb to the fact they were no longer needed and had started to gather cobwebs in the corner. The room was dingy and dark.

There were no windows in the building, the only light passing through the door, creating a tunnel of light from the entrance to the desk of the recruiting officer. Behind the officer, there was a door, with a plaque fixed into the middle reading, Doctor.

On the wall above the desk, there was a page of a newspaper ripped out that had been framed and hung up above the officer's head. It was an excerpt from 'The Times', calling soldiers to sign up and fight for their country.

Archie stepped up to the desk and the officer looked up gradually from his papers.

"I want to enlist, Sir," Archie said proudly, with a beam across his face.

"Age?" the officer asked abruptly, not entertaining small talk as he seemed as though he wanted to rattle through as many people as quickly as he possibly could.

Archie hesitated for a moment; he knew he had to be 19 to fight overseas, he was still a year and a half away from that age, and he didn't have the face of a mature man either. He swallowed subtly to compose himself.

"I'm 19, Sir," he replied confidently, in a bid to convince the officer as well as himself that it could be somewhat believable.

The officer paused for a moment, placed his pen down on a bit of paper, and lowered his glasses down his nose so they stopped just before falling off, caught by a small ridge in his rather large nose. He scanned Archie up and down for a moment without a word. Archie could feel a singular bead of sweat begins to form on his forehead.

The officer nodded calmly. Whether suspicious of Archie's age or not, he did not question it.

"Name?" he asked another one-word question, in the same monotonous tone.

"Archie Baxter," this answer Archie had enough practice in giving and did not feel any sweat come on this time around.

The officer noted the name and age on the piece of paper on top of the stack before handing it to Archie.

"Through this door, and the doctor will see, you go through your medical checks."

Archie nodded excitedly before collecting the form and marching through the door to be greeted by an old doctor in white overalls.

His room was slightly more furnished. The walls were adorned with eye charts and medical notices and there was a long bed for Archie to take a seat.

In what seemed no time at all, Archie was shaking the doctor's hand after exemplarily passing his medical tests. He knew that if he was able to pass with a fake age then he would have no struggle medically. He had always been fit and spritely, and his eyesight and vision were about as good as he could hope for.

Archie stood across from the doctor who turned to his side, smiled at Archie, and handed him a piece of paper.

"You start training in two weeks, congratulations, boy," the doctor said, before ushering Archie out of the door.

He walked back through the same dingy recruitment office he had been waiting in only a matter of minutes earlier, yet now, he walked out as a soldier. Someone who could be a hero to his nation. He beamed proudly, struggling to conceal his excitement. He left the building which had contained the key to changing his life.

He walked slowly down the coast. He sat on the promenade wall and looked out to see. Small boats were sailing up and down the waters and he looked out onto the horizon. He could almost smell the foreign air. He'd never left Norfolk, let alone the country, but he couldn't wait.

The realities of the war his father had experienced, that he was bound to encounter, had never crossed his mind. He viewed it as a challenge, as an exciting adventure worthy of a classic Stevenson novel.

He stayed there for a few moments, taking in the calm, tranquil Norfolk surroundings. For the first time in his life, Archie felt he had found what he was looking for. The purpose he had so desperately craved, was the chance to be something bigger than what life had carved out for him.

He had a chance to be a warrior, like King Arthur and the great knights he had read about, and the bravery of Admiral Nelson he had heard about, who originated from the very country Archie had lived his whole life. He finally felt a sense of calm wash over him. There were no nerves attached to going to fight, he knew it was what he was meant to do, his calling.

It was an exciting walk back home for Archie whose imagination was filling with images of his glorification at war. It was only when he approached the road up to his house that the realisation dawned on him. He had to tell his parents. He had to tell Henry. He did not know the best time to tell them as he knew they would all have opposing views to his.

His father despised any talk of war, and his mother feared anywhere he travelled on his own, let alone overseas to fight. As for Henry, he had always felt very bitter towards wars, for they had taken his father away from him.

As Archie approached the front door, he felt it best to conceal the information until he felt the time was right and tucked his slip of paper in his inside breast pocket.

Hours passed and Archie still had not found the right moment to tell his parents of his news. They had just finished their dinner and his mother was collecting the dishes to wash up. It had been a meat casserole, one of Archie's favourite dinners.

His mother's warm homecooked meals were one of the only things he felt he would miss being away. As she was standing at the sink, looking out of the window to the sun setting behind the great oak tree in the back garden, and his father slumped into his chair reading the newspaper, Archie gulped before making his announcement.

"I…I have something to say," Archie stumbled, struggling to know how to get the words out, to convey his news into words, that would create the least emotional reaction possible.

"I've signed up," he continued, his mother placing a plate down on the work surface and his father looking up from the paper.

"You've what?" his father asked seriously.

"I've signed up father. I'm going to fight; it is my duty. For the king and for the country, you know that. I'm going to fight for this family, I know it's the right thing to do." Archie said proudly, as he clutched the slip of paper in his hand.

His mother tutted as she dried her hands, "Huh, you are not, Archie Baxter." she said, sternly looking deep into Archie's eyes.

"Mother I—"

"No, you listen here to me," she cut Archie off before he had a chance to say another word. "You are 17-year-old, you are not going to war. I will go down to that recruiting office at once and tell them they cannot take you away from us," she continued abruptly.

"But mother, they aren't taking me away. This is my decision; I want to do this," Archie pleaded passionately to his mother, willing her to see his perspective.

"I won't listen to it…Robert, haven't you got anything to say?"

His mother was getting frantic and began pacing around the kitchen, the back of her hand fixed tightly to her forehead with her other hand clutching onto her stomach as if to stop her from being sick.

Robert sat there for a moment, motionless. The pain in his eyes was clear to see, with them straining to hold back any sign of emotion.

"I won't ever support you going to war, I've seen what war does to a man…how it…how it corrupts a soul to the very core, how it changes you, and I don't want that for my son." he said, his voice very monotone, not cracking like his wife's. He spoke with an assured calmness that he needed to keep his emotions in check.

"I know, Pa, but it's something I want…something, I need to do. I can't watch good lads around us going, like Mr Fisher's lads, and sit here and do nothing. I have to go, to write my name in the history books Pa. My name can be written down in books for years to come, imagine that."

The passion exuded from his voice as he looked at his father tucked up in his chair, his hands scrunching the corners of the newspaper that he held to suppress his feelings breaking through. As much as he hated the words leaving his son's mouth, he knew he couldn't argue with it.

It would seem almost hypocritical of him. He had found himself in the same position, some 15 years earlier, where the glamour of conquering South Africa had seemed too much of an opportunity for him to miss out on, no matter the cost. He knew the will of a young man wanting to fight for his country, and for himself, and he knew once Archie's mind had been made up, there was no turning back.

"I can't say I'd ever support it, boy, but I can't say I'd stop you," he said softly and quietly, before calmly standing up and tearing himself away to his bedroom where he shut the door, slumped down on the end of his bed, and broke down in tears.

He feared for his son, and he could not hide his emotions once he was on his own. He had seen the horrors of war first-hand, although he knew he couldn't force his son to feel the embarrassment of watching his friends go off and fight while he was kept under lock and key.

Downstairs, Archie and his mother stood, across the room from each other, the room was so silent you could've heard a pin drop. His mother was staring at the ground, solitary tears rolling down her cheeks.

She raised her head up, supported by her hand, and looked at her son, her eyes welling up as she tried, as hard as she could to conceal the tears building up in her eye sockets, like a tidal wave waiting to hit land.

"Ma—" Archie started before his mother abruptly raised her hand up in the air to signal him silence.

He stopped suddenly in his tracks.

His mother waved her finger at him, submitting. "I will not lose you, Archie Baxter," Archie shook his head, as a single tear was fighting its way to the surface in his right eye. "You come home to us," she continued.

Archie nodded firmly, sniffling once, "I will mother." He replied, a smile creeping across his face towards his mother.

"There isn't any other way," his troubled mother said before untying her apron and leaving it neatly folded over the kitchen chair.

She left the room to go up to bed, but as she passed Archie, she stopped, softly put her hand to his cheek, and moved on without another word being said.

Telling his parents had been harder than he had envisaged. For all he knew, there were thousands of other lads signing up like he was, and it was just something to deal with and he had to get on with the task at hand. He had neglected to think of the impact his absence may have on his family.

Archie realised that if telling his parents was hard, telling Henry would be even harder for him to do. He started training in two weeks and would be heading down a day or two early to get his bearings before training began, so he realised he still had time to tell Henry, he just had to search deep within to find what to say. He went to sleep that night tossing and turning, trying to work out and decipher the words he would use.

Three days had come and gone and still Archie had not told his best friend. His parents had begun to come to terms with the decision, more and more of the people they knew in the town were saying goodbye to their children every day and it was something they just had to get used to. Robert had tried to reassure his wife that it was better for Archie to sign up of his own accord rather than be forced into going.

Despite not finding the right time to tell Henry, the two boys had seen each other every day since the signup. Henry had been rushed off his feet for work with a royal visit to the Hall to occupy his mind that Archie had decided it was best to wait and let him work. He had come to the decision, in his own head, that

Henry wouldn't miss him too much as he'd be keeping himself busy at work and that would occupy his mind and his time.

After a couple more evenings of card games and conversations passing the moonlit hours, only a week was left before Archie's departure, and he had decided that this night was the night.

The moon was full and high in the sky, it was surrounded by thousands of sparkling companions dazzling the night and illuminating the ground below. Archie strolled down to the big house, which was no more than a quarter of an hour, but it felt like a quarter of his life, as he knew, he would be telling Henry that he'd be leaving. They tended to talk very little about the war, as Henry had no time to entertain such talk.

As Archie arrived, he asked Henry if he wanted to go outside and look at the stars in the courtyard. The servants' courtyard was a small concrete area at the back of the house. It provided a less prestigious entrance into the house for the workers and deliveries. In one corner of the courtyard was an old bench and the two boys went to sit on the bench and look up to the sky.

"I wonder if when we die, that's where we go," Henry said jokingly, with his trademark beaming smile on his face.

"There'd be worst places to be," Archie chuckled, knowing what he had to say. He shifted his position on the bench and looked at Henry more seriously.

"Listen, I need to tell you something—" Archie opened, before taking a long pause to compose himself.

"Course, what is it?" Henry replied, mirroring his friend's position on the bench.

"Really, I mean, I should've told you a couple of days ago, I mean, I guess, I just didn't quite kn—" Archie found himself falling over his words, his brain unable to scramble the right thing to say.

"What is it, Arch?" Henry pressed him for an answer.

"I've signed up." Somehow, this time the right words fell out of his mouth, somewhat bluntly but nonetheless, they were the much-needed words all the same.

"You what?" Henry asked, a frown forming on his once smiling face.

"I've signed up." Archie couldn't seem to find any more words than that.

"Yeah, I got that bit. Why?"

"I needed something Henry, you're here, you know what you want and you're achieving it and mate believe me I'm very proud of you, really, I am, but this is my chance to do good."

"You do good, you've got the bookshop."

"My father's bookshop."

"Yeah, that one day will be yours," Henry was becoming exasperated.

"When did you sign up?"

"Last week."

"Last week! And you didn't think to tell me."

"I tried—"

"Not very bloody hard, Arch," the atmosphere shifted, the boys had never argued but now tensions were flaring.

Henry tried to cool the situation by applying a calm head.

"I can't come with you, Arch; I can't leave what I've worked so hard to build. Mr White, he's taken a shine to me, if I leave now, I'll be forgotten and won't ever run this house." Henry said, in a way almost pleading for Archie's forgiveness for leaving him on his own for the first time.

"I'd never ask you to give it up."

The pair sat in silence for a moment, the still breeze the only faint noise accompanying the calmness of the summer's night.

"Do something for me," Archie looked directly into Henry's eyes, who nodded for Archie to continue, "look after my parents for me…especially if…especially if—"

"Until you're home, I will." Henry cut Archie off, as he could see the tears forming and pulled his best friend in for a hug. For that moment when the two lifelong brothers held each other in their supporting grasp, time stood still for a moment.

"Best friends stick together like glue, eh?" Henry mumbled into his best friend's ear, Archie chuckled at the words sending him back to his childhood and he laughed and the two broke out into laughter together. A laughter, almost representing all the laughs they had ever shared in their life, up until this moment.

Henry turned to his side and slipped a hand into his pocket pulling out his deck of cards.

"Fancy a game?" he asked and the two shared a smile before spending the next couple of hours laughing and playing in the cool breeze of the August night.

The following days passed by in what felt like the blink of an eye for Archie. Before he knew it, the day was on his doorstep. He had left work with Mr Humphrey who was very supportive of his decision and had spent the last couple of days spending time with Henry, whenever possible.

The two rarely brought up the war as a topic of conversation. They both knew what was on the horizon but neither wished their departure from each other any sooner than time would bring it.

Archie, deep down, was feeling very excited about the prospect. He viewed it as an overseas adventure with a spice of danger, after all, that was what all his favourite books consisted of. He felt the protagonist of his own tale and the closer it got the more he wanted it to happen.

The night before leaving he ate a meal with his family, just like any other day, and they conversed just like any day, talking of things they would do on Archie's return home, as though he was just going to travel the European landscapes and return home.

Thinking of it in this lighter approach helped his mother accept the process of her son going off to war. Following the meal and ensuing tidy-up, Archie made his way to see Henry. Henry had been allowed the evening leave after the family had finished eating and his main duties were done.

The two made their way to the pub where they spent the next hours drinking, laughing, reminiscing, and playing cards with some of the regulars. After several hours of merriment, the time came for the two to say their farewell.

Barely a day had gone past in the last 17 years where they hadn't seen each other, and the truth was, they weren't to know when, or if, they would ever see each other again. Archie may have a day or two after training before being shipped out but beyond that the future was unknown.

Coming the end of the night, there were no words left unspoken and with heavy hearts, Archie took one more walk back to his house, while Henry, took the familiar amble back to the hall. Archie got very little sleep that night, half through fear, half through excitement.

His motionless body lay there in his bed unable to get the sleep it so needed. The light creaking through a slight break in his curtains and the soft sound of the bird's song told him morning was here and the day had arrived.

It was with a tired reluctance that he dragged his weary body from his uncreased sheets, dressed himself, collected the pre-packed case of a few clothes and belongings, and made his way downstairs. His mother had prepared him marmalade on toast with a cup of tea.

The large, dark rings under her eyes indicated she too had slept very little, and the pastry set aside on the worktop showed she had been up for some time too. His father was opening the bookshop late, in order to see his son off on the first train of the day.

After breakfast, he picked up his bags from next to the door, took one look around his home, the only home he had ever known, and with a deep breath left the house, his parents close behind. Walking through his front door felt like he was stepping into a new chapter in his life. He was walking into, what he viewed to be, a time of great enthusiasm and promise.

The walk was a short one and they arrived at the train station a few minutes early. His father always ensured his family was early, his strict military discipline had taught him such. Skills that Archie was soon to learn for himself.

The father and son embraced and looked each other in the eyes, nodded, smiled, and let go of each other's hold. His father was saying very little, a man of few words at best, these circumstances had reduced his vocabulary even further.

His mother pulled him to one side and brushed his hair down on his head.

"Now," she started, the tears already visibly forming in her eyes.

"I want you to have this, to take it with you, keep it safe, and bring it back home," she said, reaching into a bag she was carrying and handing Archie a pocket watch.

His grandfather's pocket watch. He would've recognised the shine of the golden watch from a mile away. He had not laid eyes on it since his grandfather passed away, neither had he known where it was kept, should he have tried to see it.

"Are you sure?" he queried softly.

"I want you to have it and so would your grandfather, as a little reminder of home. Keep it safe, my boy, and by God keep yourself safe."

She was battling to keep the tears back, knowing that once the train rolled away and Archie left, the barriers holding them in would become too weak and let them pour out.

"I will, Ma," he said, shortly before hugging his mother tightly as he could feel her body trembling up against his as he held her.

He then let her go to his father and the two parents stood, arms interlocked, as the train rolled in and the steam puffed high into the sky as the doors flung open and Archie prepared himself to leave. He kissed his mother on the cheek and hugged them both once more before picking up his suitcase and walking to the edge of the platform.

As he was reaching the train doors, he turned back for one last time. As he stood smiling, the great clouds of smoke began slowly dispersing around them. As the white fog rose into the sky, a silhouette began forming next to where his parents stood. The silhouette got taller as the mist cleared and once the figure was in full display Archie realised who it was. Henry.

"Henry?" he exclaimed, surprised. He had not expected him to be here to see him off.

"I didn't expect to see you here, shouldn't you be working?" he asked, with his friend now in full view.

"Not anymore, no." Henry returned, smiling and Archie and his parents stood next to him, whom he softly nodded to.

"What do you mean?" Archie asked, looking at him puzzled.

As he asked the question, he looked down, noticing a case, very similar to the one he was holding himself, firmly in Henry's hand. He looked down at the case and then back up at Henry.

"I thought you'd need someone to play with," he smiled, pulling his customary deck of cards out of his pocket and flashing them at Archie.

The dimples in Archie's cheeks indented as he smiled at the revelation of not embarking on this quest alone. A single tear crowned the corner of his eye, as he stood there, he was unsure the purpose of its arrival.

He could not determine if it was relief, anticipation, or the reality of a change in life. What he could make sense of, however, was that the looming thought that had haunted the back of his mind, of approaching the upcoming challenges without Henry by his side, had been eradicated.

A sense of calmness and a sort of confidence had washed over him by the mere presence of his closest confidant.

4

The train that carried them was grand in scale and complicated in its mechanics. Strange as it seemed to him, Archie had never been on a train before. In his early years, he had often wandered down to the closest station to see the contortion of steel and pistons in all its glory, with tufts of steam rising to fill the air above him. He had always remembered staring at the fireman and stokers shovelling great heaps of black coal into the fire fuelling the mechanical colossus.

This train seemed bigger than any he had previously seen. It consisted of multiple carriages joined together like a conjoined twin fixed at the hip. They were immaculately painted, with the bottom half of the carriages decorated in a blood-red colour with a golden trim above the wheels, curving with the natural movements in the locomotive's design.

The carriages were vast, filled from one end to the other with compartments, comprising two navy-blue benches, both could seat a maximum of three people at a tight squeeze but were rarely filled to their full capacity.

The first-class carriages at the end of the train seemed another world away from the two young men. They were furnished with elaborate chairs, and a home-like comfort to ensure a comfortable journey.

The train was carrying them to a training camp in Suffolk. They were unaware how many other men in the vehicle shared the same fate as them. On the first leg of the journey, they were joined by an old man, he sat with his head drooped and his fedora hat concealed the inevitable balding on the middle of his head, which came as a sign of his ageing.

He was immaculately dressed and held his hands on his walking stick between his legs, as though its purpose was to prop him up and keep him from falling to either side. They engaged in small talk and pleasantries, but the hunchbacked man communicated no more than that.

Sparing the occasional eyebrow raise exchanged between the two, very little communication was made until the elderly gentleman departed a couple of stops after the journey commenced.

To pass the time, Archie tilted his head against the glass window, which offered a welcome cooling sensation to his cheek, making the hairs on the back of his neck stand on end. It was the best relief he would get from the rising temperature in the train, reflecting the summer's morning outside. His hair was ruffled against the glass as he gazed out into the distance.

Below the train, a wide stream was running down into a larger body of water somewhere concealed by the tracks change in direction. The water was deep blue, the occasional small fish could be seen throwing itself out of the water, catching a glimpse of the world above the surface for a matter of moments before returning to its natural habitat.

The stream moved quickly, the ripples brushing through the reeds that protruded from the water's edge. The beating sun-kissed down on the blanket of blue, creating a silver glimmer that bounced up into Archie's eyes as he stared down upon it.

Beyond it, were a series of rolling hills. The carpets of green were intersected by a jagged, grey edge that protruded itself from within, showing the natural development of the land mass. Archie could see distant trees atop the mounds. From where he was, the thin trunks were topped with a ball of green, the leaves indistinguishable from afar.

To Archie, they resembled candy floss on a long white stick he might have enjoyed from the fairground in his youth. The jagged intersections of rock made it appear difficult for animal life to exist, so all Archie could make out were the gliding movements of flocks of birds skimming the leaves of the trees before disappearing into the endless blue of the August sky.

As the line of hills passed them childhood memories flashed before Archie's eyes. He had often been curious about the concept of time, and the creation of memories. His father had once told him that in the end, that was all we had left.

He saw the rolling mounds and saw a real of memories flash past him. His carefree youthful years had escaped him, he was seeing his life escalate to adulthood, to responsibility, to the future he was about to embark on.

Henry's gaze out of the window was more of a passive one. His eyes glazed over the hills rising and falling as the land ebbed and flowed. He was still unsure if he had made the right decision by being seated on the train he was on, but there was a burning fire inside him that he knew would have consumed him had he allowed Archie to go and fight on his own, alone in the great unknown.

"It's funny," Henry started, with a chuckle. "All those trips the family took down to Suffolk and I never went, never stepped foot there. Who'd have thought this would be the reason for my first visit."

"Why'd you do it, Henry?" Archie asked curiously, as the conversation picked up, following the older passenger's departure.

"Couldn't let you do it on your own, I tried," Henry managed a soft laugh, "I just couldn't do it. After all, how can you stick to your best friend like glue if he's down in another country."

Archie laughed and stooped his head low before looking up to meet Henry's gaze.

"Your mum?" Archie asked, his face turning serious.

"Much the same as yours, I'd imagine. She worries about losing me, I don't blame her course with my dad and all. I tried to explain my reasoning and she kind of got it, she was happier that I'm here with you than on my own, gave her a bit of comfort I think." Henry explained, as Archie nodded, knowing his own mother would have felt the same consolation with the two boys being there together.

"What about the big house? Mr White?" Archie asked, concerned for Henry's prospects on their return.

"Was all quite easy, to be honest, I told Mr White a few days ago I'd be signing up and starting training camp on this date and that was it. At first, he seemed a bit disappointed, but you know him, that family above all else, and then the king," Henry broke out into a laugh, almost a hint of mockery towards Mr White in his tone.

"So, he understood and if anything supported it and held me in higher regard for it," Henry continued. "I told the family last night when we served dinner. I thanked them and hoped that my job would be waiting for me on my return."

"And will it be?" Archie interrogated, making sure his friend's future was not put in jeopardy because of his decisions.

"Hard to say," a serious look striking across Henry's face. "The hope is we'll be back by Christmas, and they'll find cover, one of the hall boys or someone who works at his Lordships' cousin's, only about an hour away. I'd like to think when I'm back we'll pick up where we left off."

It was easy to detect the uncertainty in Henry's voice. His words reflected optimism, but they were words to reassure himself he was doing the right thing, rather than believing what he said.

"You nervous?" Archie asked.

"I suppose, you?"

"Nervous. And excited. It's all an adventure at the end of the day isn't it?" Archie said smiling, trying to lighten the mood in the carriage as they neared their destination.

"Right, fancy a game, reckon we can squeeze a round or two in before we get there," Henry said, unleashing the deck of cards from his pocket and sliding the cards effortlessly between his fingertips, he shuffled them and dished them out in a clean sweeping action across the table separating the two.

The train rolled in half an hour later and within an hour they were part of a large group of men walking into the entrance of their training camp. The small luggage they had accompanied them into a long, thin building with a row of metal framed beds on either side. The wall was a dim, pale blue matching the thin sheets that adorned the mattress. At the end, were two curtains that were pulled across concealing a bucket to use as a toilet.

The room housed about 40 people, 20 on each side, and Archie and Henry occupied the two end beds, near the toilet curtain. Archie viewed it as a blessing and a nightmare, he often needed to use the toilet during the night, but the smell that would no doubt rise from the bucket would fill his nose with unpleasant sensations.

The corner of the room they chose to make their own had five beds in close proximity as the room narrowed at the tip. They waited to see who would accompany them in their section of the room, as they had made their way to the end of the room as one of the first to settle down as they were at the front of the pile.

The first neighbour to make their way over to them was a shy-looking man. Archie presumed he exceeded their age, but Henry found it difficult to age people, as they all seemed smaller than him. The man did not say anything at first, rather bowed his head in a soft nod and placed his small briefcase of belongings on the bed.

He was a medium-sized man, in between Archie and Henry in height, and had a very sensible appearance to him. His hair was perfectly brushed over to one side, matted down with copious amounts of oil. His face was perfectly smooth without a hair to be seen, as though he conducted multiple shaves a day.

He had a large mole on his right cheek and a large nose that curved at the tip. He placed his case on the bed, and unclipped it, containing a couple of clothes and on top, a small black and white image, though Archie could not make out what the photo was of in the split second his eyes gazed upon it.

The next neighbour could be heard before he was seen. Both boys thought he was considerably older than they were, which proved to be correct. He strutted in with an assured confidence about him, his hair was already shaved to his head, and he had a brown leather satchel containing personal belongings which he flung onto the bed next to Henry.

"Frank Howells," the brash man reached out his hand to shake Henry's before turning to do the same to Archie and the quiet man who was now sitting on the edge of his bed. Archie and Henry returned the man's pleasantries by exchanging names while their silent compatriot returned with a nod.

The final bed in their cluster was occupied by the man at the back of the queue as they entered the long building. He walked over, a smile adorned his face. He had curly light brown hair that sat above his head, it bobbed up and down as he walked like wool on a sheep.

"All right fellas," he chimed on arrival, his Irish accent distinctly noticeable from the first utterances that left his mouth.

To the naked eye, he looked distinctly similar to the age of Henry and Archie. Henry looked around at the new faces and introduced himself, and his background, doing the talking for Archie as he could see him recluse into his shell at the arrival of so many new men.

The first man who walked in, who was still gingerly perched on the edge of his bed was called Arthur Collier. He was a farm labourer and a very keen fisherman. He would often spend many long summer evenings sitting by the bank of a calming riverbed, waiting to find his latest catch.

He had grown up in Brancaster, with his mother, father, and younger sister. The age gap between himself and his sister was vast, he was 22 and his sister was just nine years old. His parents had struggled to conceive a child after Arthur until the miraculous discovery of the pregnancy with his sister, Florence when they had almost given up trying.

Arthur's father had fallen ill when his sister was just three and died shortly after, leaving a gaping hole in the position of father figure, which was very quickly occupied by, the then 16-year-old boy. His mother suffered terribly following the passing of her husband and became somewhat of a recluse. She could barely muster the strength to lift her head off the pillow let alone raise a toddler.

Therefore, many of the responsibilities fell onto the willing shoulders of her son. He would take his sister to the staithe every evening after finishing work on the farm, but when all the other boys he worked with signed up, he felt compelled to join them.

It was a gut-wrenching decision to leave home and move away from his sister, and he regretted it the second he stepped foot out of the door. He had made her the guarantee that he would keep her photo with him always and that he would write every day.

Just as his word had promised, he sat at the edge of the bed unfolded a small sheet of paper took out some ink and a quill, and penned his first letter to his sister.

Their confident compatriot had barely stopped for breath since arriving. It did not take him long before he was locked in a monologue about the anticipation and rush of excitement, he got at the idea of killing the Germans.

Frank was the largest of the lot, his stomach drooped over his belt which he would constantly readjust to try to contain the bulge that protruded from him. His hair was parted down the middle, with both sides matted down flat to his scalp. His jet-black hair coupled with his black moustache which grew from under his nose and curved round to the crevices in the corners of his mouth.

He was the smartest dressed of anyone in the entire building. He wore a black suit with fine, white lines streaking through the jacket with a red hanky crowning out of his breast pocket. He liked to give the impression of sophistication and class when in truth he worked in a steel factory and came from a poor family who lived in a small house with his aunts and uncles. Frank kept these roots deep underground in any conversation and only referred to his role as a senior employee at the steel company.

The curly-headed man introduced himself as Alan Prior. He was 18 and had moved to Norfolk a couple of years earlier. He had been forced to move out of his small home in Cork after his mother gave birth to her sixth child and there was no more space, so as the eldest, he was forced to live on his own accord.

He felt he wanted a completely new life, and moved across the water to England, making his way east, and discovering a passion for shoemaking. When he settled in Norwich, he found work with a cobbler in the centre of the city, but when the cobbler's son signed up for the war, the day after it was declared, he got swept up in the storm of it all and signed himself up a few days later.

The men came from all different backgrounds and walks of life and found themselves thrown together in an orderly fashion and soon they had no choice but to get along. As far as they knew, the men that lay either side of them every night, would be the only company they would be exposed to for quite some time so why quarrel?

Their days were long and filled with rigorous training exercises. Due to the surge in sign-ups, the army did not have all the weaponry and uniforms to provide to every training soldier.

Therefore, some in the group were forced to make do with a temporary uniform that made them feel, they looked quite like a postman, while others were made to make do with wooden rifles while they waited for real weapons to be provided for them.

Despite the arduous days filled with discipline and drills, in which many men found something to complain about, no one had any issues to raise when it came to the food. For most, the food provided by the army at this stage was far superior to what they were used to at home.

Despite being a portly fellow, Frank was used to gruelling meals that were forced to be spread around an entire extended family, whereas here, he could enjoy plentiful portions all to himself.

The nights provided the men with a short period of relief before they needed to slip into sufficient slumber before the next day's training. Archie, Henry, and the three lads who had, by now, befriended them, spent their evenings talking of their home lives, their families, and their jobs.

They got to know each other in a way one wouldn't normally have the opportunity to do so. Henry wasn't too fond of Frank but got on well with the other two. He detested arrogance and people who were too full of their own self-importance, both categories in Frank took first prize.

With entertainment limited beyond routine conversation and the occasional folk song, Henry had taken it upon himself to experiment with his deck of cards. After a few nights of experimenting and practicing, he had learnt a magic trick. He had always admired sleight of hand but had never given any time to learn it for himself.

However, when there was nothing else to do except chime in with the next verse of 'It's a Long Way to Tipperary', he plugged away, mastering a card trick. He would go around the group and hand them the king of hearts, he would turn his face away and ask them to slip the card anywhere on the deck they fancied.

He would ask them to shuffle the cards before returning them to him where he would then give it another mix-up before making the desired card appear at the top of the deck. He enjoyed the way it made the men laugh and cheer in surprise and he felt a sense of fulfilment being able to give some joy back to the men after tiresome days.

One evening, Frank and Alan were desperately trying to figure out Henry's trick as Archie and Alan sat quietly on their respective beds. Archie peered across to his silent neighbour who was locked in gaze at the photograph he carried around so religiously. Archie pushed himself up onto the bed and made his way to Alan's where he sat gingerly on the edge of the bed, so as to, not to ruffle the bed sheets.

"Who's that?" Archie asked, smiling at the man sitting in front of him.

"Florence, my sister," Arthur replied, his gaze not leaving the photo as he spoke.

"You must be very close to her to carry her photograph around wherever you go," Archie stated, though with an interrogative tone, wanting to find out more of Arthur's life that he hadn't concealed with the group as the shyest member of them.

"Yes, very close," Arthur said looking up. "She just turned nine before I left, sometimes, I sit here and wonder if I did the right thing by signing up." He looked back down at the picture and his bottom lip began quivering as he uttered the words softly.

"Why did you?" Archie was determined to find out as much as he could about his comrade.

"All the other men at work you see, they were all signing up right away. I was one of the last left. I don't know if I wanted to really. At least, I thought, I did, I thought, it was the right thing to do. But you get caught up in it, don't you?"

"The wave of excitement, it, just washes over you. I don't regret my decision, not really. I just wonder about little Florence, on her own with my mother, just want her to be all right."

Archie digested everything that was said and chose to pick out the reference of only Arthur's mother being left at home.

"You've got no father then?" he questioned.

Arthur shook his head. "Died…well must be six years ago now. Blimey. My mother took it hard you know, and a lot of the parenting fell to me. I did my best and loved it. She was like…she was like," a tear began to formulate in the corner of Arthur's eye.

His tear ducts almost pushed for it to tip over the edge, but his astute determination fought it back.

"Well, she was like a mini version of myself, really. I taught her to like the things I like, we'd take walks down by the river, and fish until the moon was overhead. We'd walk back over a bridge in the middle of a little wood, we'd both drop sticks and see who's came out the other side first," he said, a smile coming across his face, as though he felt freedom to speak in an expressive manner when talking about his sister.

Archie sympathised with a smile as Arthur became lost in his words. It was almost as though he was reliving the moments in his mind as he told them, as though he was looking down on the ripples on the water as the sticks collided with the surface. There was a light in his face that Archie had never seen before.

The two men spent the next hour exchanging details of their private lives that they had not shared with the group, and Archie felt himself form a connection with Arthur that night. As though they had bonded in a way that they both understood the way each other was feeling.

They grew tired after a while of talking and Archie retired to his bed next to Henry who had a beaming grin on his face, as despite countless attempts to foil his trick, no one had been able to work out its simple execution.

"They still don't get it," Henry laughed through his words, "go on, give it one more go," he sniggered, before brandishing the deck of cards to Archie lying in the bed next to him.

As expected, Archie could still not fathom the way it was done, and his lack of explanation was the cause of great jubilation from Henry.

"Ha! See, Arch, no one will ever get it, I bet, I could take this trick overseas and still no one would get it. A cask of beer says that by the time we get home, my trick is yet to be figured out?" Henry was clearly proud of himself, as he offered the wager to Archie.

Archie chuckled and nodded accepting the proposal through a handshake before the two men turned over onto their sides and closed their eyes to welcome the world of sleep once more.

As Archie lay there, his brain turned over all the things he had spent the last couple of months learning. He thought about all the people he had grown to know and befriend, especially the group that occupied most of his time.

He had even become rather fond of Frank in his own way when only exposed to him in small doses. He lay there, his eyes closed from the outside world, but his mind was active as if it were the start of a new day.

Thoughts whirred around his head, each one, in turn, filing its way to the forefront of his focus. He thought about how all the men he was training alongside had all descended upon this one place from all reaches of life, he ruminated on how if he was killed at war, the men inside the four walls he was currently residing in right now, would bury him ahead of his own mother and father.

When turning this idea over and over in his head like cotton spinning on a loom, he found rather a sense of contentment about it. It made the bonds he had created with the soldiers he trained with even tighter, he valued what they meant to him, the way he hoped they valued him.

He thought about how, if the worst was to happen, and Henry was not by his side, then there would be worse people in the world than Arthur, Alan, and even Frank to protect his lifeless body.

Archie could feel his train of thought steering its course into a dark abyss, a place he did not wish to be. He quickly regained control of his thoughts boxed them up and locked the key in his mind, allowing his body to sink, to the best of its ability into the thin, hard mattress below him.

5

"Just over a mile to go now lads, let's keep it going. Higgins, keep that pack up." A loud voice filled the air like an echo in a well, the sound reverberating around the French countryside.

The voice came from a tall man heading a pack of soldiers down a dirt road, carving their way through the landscape, boots kicking up clouds of dust as they walked as smuts were shooting up from the trucks that preceded the men.

The man giving the orders was Sergeant Frederick Parker. He was leading his platoon through a series of barren fields; autumn was in full swing and there were little signs of life left as leaves and sprouts of greenery decayed into the harsh surface of the land as it bore the scares of a year of constant war.

The war had not yet reached the path they were taking but they were less than a mile from the front and the distant murmur of shell fire was getting louder with every passing step.

Sergeant Parker was a friendly man by nature and by contrast to his fellow officers. His brother had been killed in action in Marne in the early stages of the war.

It had been this which had softened Parker, he had not yet seen action at the time of his brother's death, and it opened his eyes to the reality of what the war was really like, beyond the triumphant parades in Regent's Park and local pubs in rapturous performances of 'Keep the Home Fires Burning'.

He understood the reality of the men you fought alongside being the last faces you ever see on this planet. He had taken solace in the knowledge that the men his brother fought and died alongside were kind, honourable men.

He viewed his role as a compassionate leader among the men he served on the front lines with. He didn't want to appear as unapproachable, rather he hated the thought of his men not confiding in him if they had a concern or request that he could help them with.

Sergeant Parker was older than many of the men around him, he had turned 38 on the Christmas just gone. He had been married for over half of his life which had resulted in three children, of whom he kept a photograph of each inside the front cover of a small Bible he kept in his breast pocket.

His eldest child was 10 years old and was his only son. The youngest two of six and four respectively could do no wrong, as was often the case with men with daughters—or at least that was what Parker would tell people who would see him faun over his daughters' every request.

He used his innate, soft fathering qualities when dealing with his men. Many were no more than 17 and 18, barely men at all. He understood that he was more loving than even many fathers he knew, but he attributed it to the cold upbringing he had from his own father. After meeting his wife, Maude, he became set on having children of his own and determined to do a more loving and compelling job than his father.

It had made coming to war a tear at his heart for leaving his children behind. He had instructed his son, Stanley, that he was the man of the house in his absence, and he was to look after his mother and sister until he returned home.

Parker carried with him the final image of his children, as he stepped onto the train to leave them, their tear-stricken faces looking up at him, his wife consoling them under her arms as she nodded at him, sending him the signal that it was all right to leave. He had only just got onto the train before the conductor blew the whistle and he rolled out of sight.

Behind Parker, there was a trail of fresh-faced men, cheering and singing as they traversed the bumpy terrain. Among them, were Archie and Henry. They were in full uniform, kits on their back and rifles over their shoulder.

As they walked along, Archie took a moment to look around him, taking in what could be the last peaceful scenery he could see for some time. All of the men had heard stories from the front, but seeing as none of them had experienced anything, there was less reason to be scared and more reason to feel a sense of excitement.

Archie tilted his head up, letting the crisp September breeze hit his face. Despite the chilling temperatures, he was feeling hot under the weight of his pack and uniform. A few blackbirds soared overhead. He wondered what it must be like to be a bird.

Up there in the sky, flying freely and completely unaware of the trials and tribulations of the world on the ground. The clouds in front of him started grey and faded into a bright white as they brushed past him overhead. He thought perhaps the change in colour in the clouds was not due to the weather, but a sign of the flumes of shell smoke getting closer to them.

Archie looked across to his right where Henry was walking, head down, shuffling through his deck of cards to pass the time, his rifle swinging by his side. Behind them, Arthur, Alan and Frank were walking three-a-breast in deep conversation about which brand of cigarette was the best.

The spirits were high as they neared to climax of their journey, after all, this was the moment they had all been building up towards. From the moment of signing up in the small building near the sea and leaving his parents to become a soldier, this was the moment Archie and all the men around him had been waiting for.

Above all else, there was a sense of relief. A relief that, after over a year of waiting they finally were about to serve their purpose. It was as though they had been waiting around for this very moment and now it was in touching distance. It felt as if what lay on the other side when they reached the trenches really didn't matter.

Archie being the more pragmatic one of the groups by nature, wondered how long the excitement that was bouncing from man to man would last by the time they reached the front lines, by the time they heard the crackle of German gunfire heading towards them.

He blocked his mind once more from falling down its dark trap, and after splashing his face with a small handful of water, poured out delicately from his water bottle, to feel the cool liquid run down his sweating cheeks, he chimed in with the circling chorus of 'It's a Long Way to Tipperary', giving him a spring in his step to march the rest of the way in unison with his comrades.

It did not take long for the men to become very well accustomed to trench life. They had spent a period of a few weeks in the reserve trench behind the front-line, with days filled with polishing and cleaning their kits while there were often expeditions to carry supplies down to the front-line trench a few hundred yards away.

One evening as the sun was setting, Sergeant Parker told the men that the morning would bring them their first rotation in the front-line trench. They had all been able to hear the intermittent German shell barrages that they were set to be exposed to, and it instilled an instant deep-rooting fear in Archie's stomach as he struggled to swallow his next spoonful of bully beef.

"You must be prepared, the Fritz will try to scare you, they'll try to drown us out, but we must never give in," Parker rallied his troops as he noticed the worried expressions creep across their faces.

"Wonder if we'll be going over the top," Frank whispered in between both Archie and Henry, who looked at each other with panic in their eyes as the reality of what may be to come was setting in.

Archie sat with Henry and the others in a small corner of the trench as they lashed around their feelings, it was the closest they were to action. When the wind blew just right, Archie could almost taste the gunpowder in the air, its potent particles settling up his nose and, on his tongue, when he would go to breathe or talk.

"I'm ready for it," Frank said, slamming his right hand into his left palm and grinding it together aggressively. "We've been waiting long enough, it's about time we do something."

"How are you feeling, Arthur?" Henry asked, noticing Arthur's gaze had not lifted from his boots.

His eyes had just been glazing up and down the crusts of mud on his toecaps.

Arthur didn't answer, he just nodded. Before Frank had the opportunity to interject with another comment displaying his excitement or arrogance or to make any derogatory claim at Arthur's strong display of fear, Henry got in there first.

"Who knows what we'll face when we get there, time will tell, won't it? But these fellas coming out now didn't do much, did they? We were down there just yesterday dropping off their supplies and most of them were dead bored." Henry tried to encourage his friends, whose minds had started flirting with the notion of fear and death.

"Ay, I'd rather be dead bored than dead," Alan said with a smile, the combination of his upbeat accent and his joke creating a ripple of laughter among the group as they sat waiting for the sun to complete its daily ritual of rising to bring about a new day.

When morning did inevitably arrive, they made their way to the front-line to begin their first taste of front-line action. As they passed the men who had just finished their latest stint on the front, Archie could see a look of relief on their faces. When they exchanged glances, it was as though the relief in their eyes was difficult to conceal, but as though they were also offering a hand of sympathy to the soldiers taking their place. As though they knew something was on the horizon, something they had just escaped.

"You see those men earlier?" Archie asked Henry as they had settled down their kit and taken a seat on a small wooden pallet in a small carved-out area of the trench wall.

"What about them?" Henry replied.

"It was just…just the way they looked at me. Almost as if—" Archie stopped what he was saying, as a stream of soldiers passed in front of them.

"Almost as though they were warning me about something," he whispered to Henry, as the men passed by.

"In what way? How?" Henry asked, confused as to how Archie could have gauged this message from them in their eyelines fleetingly crossing paths.

"I don't know," Archie said, taking a deep breath. "I just gotta bad feeling about what's to come," he continued as night started to fall and the afternoon's occasional shower of shells had come to its natural close.

Most of the jobs they conducted in the trench took place at night-time, while they were under the blanket of darkness and hidden from German snipers. When they were in the reserve trench, a man had been carried through on a stretcher after a bullet passed clean through his helmet and straight through his skull after a sniper had picked him off for just stepping up on a pallet, his head above the parapet, while trying to make his walk down the trench for more entertaining.

The first night, Archie and Henry were tasked with pumping out a flooded section in front of the officer's dugout. The dugout was a small room built into the side of the trench, the walls reinforced with sandbags, with a desk in the middle illuminated by a single lamp.

As they were pumping, Archie could hear a conversation ongoing between Sergeant Parker and his commanding officer. He held his hand out over Henry's to get him to stop pumping, so that he could make out fragments of conversation.

Every time they would hear a break in speech, they would work frantically to avoid giving the officers on the inside of the dugout any impression as to their true intentions.

Through the broken sentences they managed to hear, they were able to work out Parker's commanding officer telling him, the soldiers were to be braced for an attack in three days' time.

"Nothing is to be said to them for the time being, do you understand me, Parker? Our artillery boys will hit the Germans from dawn until dusk for the next couple of days, nothing out of the ordinary, nothing that would arouse suspicion."

"Then the evening before the attack you will inform them of the plan. We are to push the Germans back, and start reclaiming the land. Do you understand Parker?" the unknown voice said. behind the walls of mud and sandbags.

"Sir," Parker replied, nodding at his superior.

The officer giving the instructions then saluted to Sergeant Parker before making his way out of the dugout, turning his head to see Archie and Henry working on reducing the levels of flooding, as though they had been there for hours, and then walked off into the distance of the night.

The two finished their work in silence before making their way back around to try and get a couple of hours of shuteye as Arthur and Alan were on sentry duty for the night.

"Don't tell them," Henry said to Archie, grabbing his arm before they reached the others. "It's better they don't know, not until they have to."

Archie nodded and the two of them found an unoccupied stretch of dirt cut into the wall. Henry took out his rifle and pushed a rat out of the cavity, clearing space for them to curl up next to each other for a brief escape from the world.

Archie felt lucky to have Henry with him. He knew it was best not to tell the others. He knew Frank would become insufferable until going over the top and he knew that it would cause Arthur to live in heightened fear until the time of the attack. It was better for them to continue the daily jobs they were given and keep themselves safe from the flying debris of German artillery raids.

The next couple of days brought the promised artillery bombardment from the British heavy guns. The constant berating of the enemy lines lifted morale among the troops in the trench. Frank would throw his arms in the air and wave his fists in the direction of the German trench every time an explosion was heard.

As the afternoon grew on the first day of shelling, Archie noticed Arthur sat in a corner of the trench, his head in his hands, his kneels curled up creating a hard resting place to perch his chin on as he rocked back and forth, the barrage of noise chilling him to the core.

Up and down the line, there were men trying to get moments of solitude to close their eyes, as there was only so much that could be achieved while waiting under the constant wailing of shells flying through the sky. Naturally, most attempts of sleep were greeted to no avail.

Not long after the bombardment began, the Germans started up their attempts of retaliation. Archie had neglected to think of this potential scenario, and when the first eruption happened just in front of the barbed wire protecting the trench, he was knocked back against the wall.

His legs gave way and he found himself slipping down until his bottom became submerged under a thin layer of mud and grime. He looked straight for Henry who had just returned from carrying a message to the reserve trench. Henry made his way running back through the swaths of men to find Archie and hauled him up to his feet.

"Come on, Arch," he shouted, to try and elevate his voice above the volume of explosions all around them.

He grabbed him to his feet, and they began moving to one end of the trench where the explosions appeared less frequent. They had grabbed Arthur on their way down who had started letting out a soft, high-pitched whimpering noise as his feet shuffled through the mud to keep up.

Alan and Frank were already taking cover, with Frank's nonsensical chatter proving to be quite the Godsend in this situation. It allowed them all to focus on something other than the onslaught of flying shards of metal and matter whose origin had been obliterated beyond the point of recognition.

Hours passed and the battle of superiority showed no sign of stopping. Archie thought it had become a game of tit-for-tat with the enemies determined to meet each other with equal ferocity, forming a never-ending cycle of trying to outdo each other.

As they stood, backs pressed up against the wet facade of the trench, beads of congealed, muddy water slipping down their backs into their boots, Archie heard a shrill, piercing scream. The earth beneath their feet began to rumble, there could be no denying the shells were getting closer to them and there was nowhere to run.

They huddled together, hoping, and praying. The hair-raising scream had come from a few hundred feet down from where they were attempting to seek refuge. The explosion had occurred so close to the parapet that the force of the blast had torn a man's arm clean off from the shoulder.

The scream had come as his flesh was ravaged away from the rest of his body, his lost limb flying down the line, landing somewhere near Arthur's feet but was quickly buried by more flurries of dirt washing over them, filling the air with the smell of gunpowder and deteriorating flesh. The explosions in no man's land was regurgitating once-buried corpses from battles long ago and resettling them in newly formed craters.

Archie thought back to the tranquil, untouched countryside they had been walking through just a couple of weeks before. Where the birds were flying high in the sky, their wings open wide, soaring through unchartered skies.

He looked up from where he stood, the blackening sky made it appear as though they had become trapped in a land where all the happiness and life were being sucked out of the world, and all the darkness and anger were concentrated into this small stretch of the French countryside.

There was little let-up for the rest of the first and the second day. The shelling would come to a civil cease as the moon replaced the sun. It made Archie think, if they could both agree to stop shelling each other in the thick of night, why could they just not agree to never start shelling each other in the first place?

As the bombardment stopped on the second night, Sergeant Parker called all the men to group together.

"Tomorrow, men, there will be an attack. Our objective is to take the German trench, pushing them back to the next village, to start driving them out of France once and for all," Sergeant Parker tried to keep his voice steady and calm, as he could see the expressions on the men's faces change.

He could sense their realisation of why there had been such heavy shelling for the last couple of days.

"At 7:00 a.m., we will go over the top, push the Germans back and celebrate a triumphant victory by lunchtime," he said with a triumphant tone at the end, to help raise a cheer among the men.

The reaction was split, there was a raucous applause following the announcement, as for many, this was it. All the waiting around was only preventing them from getting in the way of what they were really here to do.

Kill Germans. For a lot of the men around Archie and Henry, this seemed to be all that clouded their minds, a feeling of resentment fuelled determination above all else.

Sergeant Parker left the troops to spend what could be their last hours on Earth to be spent, however, they so desired. A cluster of men stood in a circle, smoking as many cigarettes as one could manage until they had ploughed their way through three boxes.

Alan and Frank were talking softly, they had no cigarettes or alcohol to indoctrinate their mind, they let the peaceful autumnal evening descend on them and calm their bodies.

They spoke about their home lives, revealing truths to each other that, in the comfortable knowledge of survival they had kept to themselves, but when facing an unknown future, they felt a desire to share.

"How are you feeling, Arch?" Henry asked, placing a hand on his knee, the two sat on a small pile of sandbags.

"I'm scared," Archie said, making no attempt to hide his feelings.

Henry nodded at him, then turned to look out to the sky above no man's land where a few stars were breaking through the thick carpet of smoke still yet to have fully dissipated from the day's artillery attacks.

"Yeah. Me too," he replied, a quiver in his voice as he answered.

"If anything happens to me, write to—" Archie started before Henry raised his hand to stop him, shaking his head with a soft smile.

"Not now," Henry said, a small gathering of tears visible in his eyes, which when Archie caught sight of as the emerging light of the moon bounced off Henry's face, his own tears started to take shape.

A few paces down from where they were sat, Arthur was leaning up against a protruding wooden step with two pieces of paper next to each other, the photograph of his sister in between them. He reached into his pocket and pulled out a small, blunt pencil. He took out his knife from his kit bag and sharpened it to a point before arching his body over the paper to begin writing on the first piece of paper.

My dearest Florence,

I'm sorry, I have not written to you for almost a week now, I have been working very hard, and have not had much time. I am sure that is a poor excuse from your silly old brother!

Are you looking after our mother for me? And most importantly yourself?

Oh Florence, I do miss you a great deal. I miss our walks down the staithe, it was always so beautiful this time of year, with the crisp leaves on the ground and the clumps of conkers. How about we see it in autumn next year?

What a jolly plan that will be.

Do not worry about your big brother, I will take care of myself as you must do also. My darling little sister, I hope with all my heart to see you very soon.

I love you dearly, make sure you never forget that no matter what.

Your loving brother,
Arthur

He folded the letter in half and slid it into a small envelope, a small tear rolling down his cold cheek as he placed the packaged letter to one side and began to work on the second:

Dear Mama,

I do hope you are keeping well and not worrying too much about me. How are you? Is Florence still doing well at school? I do so often find myself worrying about how she is without me. Although I'm sure, you are doing a wonderful job on your own.

I apologise for writing to Florence more than I do to you. I also apologise if I left you with any hard feelings towards me for signing up. The truth is Ma, my real reason for writing is we are to see our first action tomorrow. I'm not too nervous, I've made some great pals and that helps.

I just thought I'd write to say, in case anything happens tomorrow, thanks for everything Ma. And do me a favour, never let little Florence forget about me.

Your loving son,
Arthur

The second letter seemed to have finished Arthur off, as he was almost audibly crying by the time he had sealed the second letter and placed his photograph back inside his pocket. He sat, staring into the wall of the trench for a moment as his eyes regained their control and his tears stopped rolling down his face.

"Are you going to write a letter home? You know, before tomorrow," Archie asked Henry, as his eyes were still looking across at Arthur.

"I penned one yesterday when I had spare five minutes when you went to collect the rations. Told them what was coming and said I'd write if I made it through," Henry replied, taking a sip of his water.

"Guess I should say something," Archie replied, a hesitant note in his voice. "I just don't want them to worry, or think, you know, if anything does happen, then I was alone and scared," he continued, sniffing slightly as he concluded to conceal any emotion.

"Then don't tell them, tell them you're alright, you're not alone and you hope to write soon," Henry said smiling, brandishing a pencil and sheet of paper for Archie to use, knowing he'd regret writing while he still had the chance to.

"I'll give you a minute," Henry said, patting Archie on the back before making his way over to join the conversation between Frank and Alan.

Archie sat there for a moment, pondering the words to say, struggling to translate what he meant from his brain through his arm to the pencil loosely gripped between his fingertips. He hovered it over the paper for a couple of minutes before settling on what he wanted to say.

Hello Mum, Hello Pa,

I'm sorry I haven't written for so long, time just gets away from you here, and it's really rather enjoyable spending so much time with all the lads.

Some of the scenery here in France is lovely, the fields and countryside, Pa, you'd love it, straight out of a novel the setting out here. Even in Autumn, it looks more beautiful than anywhere I've seen before.

Word has it, we may see our first proper action tomorrow, Henry says there's nothing to worry about, and he's usually always right in these scenarios!

Well, I'm running out of paper, Henry only had a small piece to give me! I'll write to you tomorrow to tell you about our latest adventure.

Love always,
Your son,
Archie

He folded the letter up, sealed it neatly in the envelope, and made his way to the rest of the group, of which by now Arthur had re-joined.

The hours ticked by, slowly and rather tormentingly as they stared up at the sky watching the different shades of black and navy-blue intertwine themselves above as night drew into the early hours of the morning.

Alan reached inside his breast pocket to his small watch to check the time. It had been a strange sensation where time seemed to last forever but go by in a flash. They wanted the night to never end but naturally, it was going to, yet the process of waiting had become torturous.

The time read 4:52 a.m. and in eight minutes Sergeant Parker would be making his way around, making all the men stand to make sure they were ready and prepared before the rum ration.

None of them had really had any sleep, Henry had nodded off leaning against a step but woke up no more than an hour later with a cramp in his neck from how he was sitting. Frank's incessant drivel had started earlier than normal today and, in a manner, more aggravating than usual.

He would barely stop for breath before delving into another mind-numbing topic that was of no interest to anyone else, meaning Frank would be the only one to contribute to the one-sided conversation.

The minutes ticked by slowly but surely and Sergeant Parker rounded all the men up, made sure they were properly presented, and made his way down the line smiling deliberately at each man as he went passed.

Then it was time for the rum ration to be handed out, it was the only part of the morning's endeavour that garnered any enthusiasm. Despite his talk of confidence and his brash persona, Frank was the first in line for his rum to settle his growing nerves.

Archie turned to Arthur who was standing to his left, he could feel the ground by his left foot shaking slightly as Arthur was visibly trembling.

"You'll be alright, you know," Archie smiled, placing his hand on Arthur's body, feeling the vibrations through his body calm at his touch.

"You think?" Arthur asked back, his voice cracking halfway through his question.

Archie looked down and saw Arthur was clenching his fists tight, his fingernails digging into the palms of his hand, and tightly concealed in his right hand was the photograph of Florence.

"Yeah. Yeah, I know so. Some people, you just know are gonna live it and make it home. And you're one of them," Archie knew there could be no certainty in the words he said to Arthur, but he believed it was what his friend needed to hear.

Arthur nodded several times, almost as a way of plucking up his own courage before taking a swig of rum as it came to be his turn.

The men stood there waiting, the rum swimming in their system was not enough to completely extinguish the impending sense of doom they were all feeling. Alan looked at his watch once more, 6:42 a.m. The big hand on his watch was wrestling its way around the face but it seemed to be met with heavy resistance every second it tried to pass through.

The noise was subsiding, it had started to form more of a low murmur. Even Frank was just mumbling to himself, his words were indistinguishable, and even when Henry tried to focus on paying attention, he could not make out what Frank was saying despite the occasional reference to his mother.

Sergeant Parker walked up and down the line. 6:56 a.m.

"Fix bayonets," he called out, as all the troops completed the order in unison, standing ready, just steps away from the ladders, leading them up over the parapet into the unknown.

Archie took a deep breath. 6:58 a.m. He looked up and down the trench, the men he had trained with and spent the last few months with day and night had fallen silent for the first time since he had known them.

He turned to his left, Arthur was staring straight ahead, his eyes fixated on the gateway to no man's land he would soon be clambering over. He turned to his right, Henry was there, he didn't know how, but Henry looked so calm and confident, as though he knew nothing would happen to them.

Henry returned the gaze, winked subtly at Archie, and smiled, punching his arm in a teasing manner.

"We're gonna be alright," he whispered to Archie, any soft murmurings of sound could be heard above the first true silence they had known since coming into the trench.

"Just stick with me," Henry added, as the time had ticked into the final minute.

There were just over 30 seconds left. Archie looked over his shoulder where Sergeant Parker was transfixed on his watch, martialling every move the second hand made around the clock.

He lifted his whistle slowly up to his dry lips, placing it delicately in between them, a pale glow had washed over his face as he dabbed a bead of sweat that was escaping down his forehead, waiting for the last few seconds of torment to release them from its cruel grasp.

10 seconds to go, he walked to his position, his right hand gripping onto a middle step on the ladder next to Henry, as he waited to give the signal, his men had been waiting, all night to hear.

"God be with you, men," he called out, taking one final glance up and down the trench of young, innocent faces. The with a short, sharp blow of his whistle, the men let out an animalistic shout as they rushed up the ladders and hauled themselves over the parapet of the trench and into the vast expanse of no man's land.

Archie was one of the first lines of men over the top. Henry was tight by his right-hand side, Frank and Alan on the other side of him, with Arthur marching to Archie's left. They walked slowly, watching as the men around them picked up speed into a fast walk, which transformed into a meaningful jog.

Archie looked around them, they had not gone more than four or five steps before the Germans had opened fire upon them. The sound of footsteps trampling on the ground beneath them was soon drowned out by bullet fire. The Germans had opened fire with their machine guns, bullets rattling through the skies, spraying over the men like a hosepipe over flowers.

Archie heard screams, wailing men falling down, crumbling to the floor like a sack of potatoes emptied out onto the ground. Their legs giving way beneath them. Men falling as though it was the most natural motion of their body to allow gravity to take control. He looked to his side, they were all still together, marching with more intent toward the onslaught of German fire.

With more lines of men coming over the top to provide a greater force of attack, the Germans began attacking no man's land with shells.

There was no care for precision or accuracy. There was no direct target. No man's land was the target. No matter where the shell fell it would inflict death upon unsuspecting British troops. It would separate their flesh from their body as though it had only ever been loosely bound together with string.

The arrival of the bombardment had caused havoc for the troops navigating their way across no man's land. Men broke out of formation, picking up into a run trying to pre-empt where the next explosion would land, trying to outsmart the predetermined position.

The intensity and frequency of the shelling picked up and Archie looked to both his sides and amidst the flying clouds of dirt and metal shrapnel, he could only still see Henry next to him.

There was no time to think of what may have happened to the others. A shell had exploded just in front of them, and Henry hauled Archie by the arm dragging him down into the shell hole for cover.

"We're being slaughtered," Henry shouted, an anger across his face that Archie was not used to seeing.

The force at which they hit the crater had filled Archie's mouth with dirt and he nodded as he spluttered out.

"The others…where are the others?" Archie choked, as he lay tightly against Henry with their backs against the crater wall, looking back out across the distance they'd travelled from their trench to here.

Henry shook his head, "I didn't see them, I just knew I had to get us down somewhere, we're being slaughtered out there. Bloody slaughtered," Henry kept repeating himself, his head shaking furiously as he spoke.

Both men's faces were covered in dirt and small pieces of earth that had settled on their sweating cheeks.

The German bombardment was relentless, it appeared to Archie as if they were trying to bomb their way to the centre of the earth and they weren't going to stop until they got there.

"We can't go on, not yet," Henry added, as the two found their arms gripping onto each other, their fear overcoming them as a tear slid down Henry's cheek as he fought to stay strong in the Godforsaken pit they were trapped in.

Archie nodded. He knew it would be suicide to do as much as poke his head above the surface of the crater. The sounds coming from all around them were chilling.

They could see back in the direction they came, and no more men were coming, they had to hope for victory from the numbers that were out in the open for the Germans to pick off as they so desired, or accept defeat and retreat back to the trench, which would prove equally as dangerous.

Archie and Henry stayed fixed together in the shell hole. They could hear men crying for their mothers in neighbouring craters and could see the blood spilling into the dirt all around them.

Archie lay wondering what had happened to the other three. He was praying they had done the same thing and pulled themselves into the relative breathing space of a fellow shell hole.

They waited for what felt like an eternity but seeing as Archie had left his grandfather's pocket watch which his mother gave him before departing in the safety of his kit bag, they had no knowledge of how long they had been stranded there.

The thought of his grandfather's watch transported him home for a moment. The thought of the summer mornings alongside Mr Humphrey, sowing the seeds of the new flowers which would adorn the vast swathes of the green garden of Huckerby Hall.

His thoughts of home were quickly interrupted by a shell falling just a few metres away from them, shrapnel interspersed in a billow of dirt falling all around them. The dry particles of soil landing on Archie's mouth were making him unbearably thirsty but he had finished all his water before they came over the top. When he was nervous, he found drinking his water was something to pass a few seconds of the time.

"Henry—" Archie coughed, "Henry, I need water," he was struggling to speak, the dirt was drying out his mouth and soaking up the moisture on his tongue.

Henry reached to his side for his water bottle, but it appeared in the melee of trying to reach the shell hole, it looked like it had become dislodged from his belt.

"I've got none, Arch, my water bottle, it's not there," he shouted in Archie's ear, to make sure he could hear the disappointing revelation over the whirring of the guns.

They looked up, there was a young man running in their direction, it was clear he was looking to plunge himself into the shell hole out of the way of immediate enemy fire. They did not recognise the man's face, but they recognised the terrified expression on his face.

The man got within one step of collapsing into the crater. As his right foot was about to launch him into the pit, a flying German bullet collided with his helmet, making a clicking noise as the metal bullet passed through the metal helmet and straight through the poor man's skull.

His right foot continued straight over where his brain had intended on planting it down and his whole body collapsed into the hole, rolling down the side until his small frame lay outstretched in front of Archie and Henry, still and motionless.

Without thinking or hesitation, Archie launched himself at the man, grappled at his belt, removed his water bottle, which to his relief was nearly full, and guzzled the water down his welcoming throat, cleansing his tongue of the grime that had inhabited it.

A little longer passed, and there had been little let-up in the guns and shell fire. Archie and Henry wondered how long this could possibly keep going on. They had seen no new men leave the trench for some time; the Germans could only be trying to purge any sign of life in the vast plain between the two opposing trenches.

"Bloody, Fritz!" Henry screamed out angrily, as he had begun to worry about their missing friends.

They had heard and seen bodies being dismantled piece by piece by shrapnel and feared the worst for their lost comrades.

The faint glimmer from the sun high above the dark grey cover encasing them in this cesspit was rising slowly higher in the sky showing them the hours of the day were beginning to pass. Soon after watching the sun rise to its highest point, the guns began to silence, spare the occasional sniper bullet that would pick off desperate attempts to retreat.

Archie and Henry knew they lay pinned. There was only one way back to the trench and if they attempted to do that in broad daylight their chances of survival were very slim to none.

"Getting hungry now," Henry joked, rubbing his hand slowly over his stomach as they lay, still very motionless, so as to not attract attention to their whereabouts as the noise from the gun and shell fire ceased.

Archie chuckled and they lay there waiting for the sun to finish its daily rounds as they prayed for the night to bring about a starless sky, limiting the light on the ground to a minimum to allow their safe passage back to the trench. The temperature began dropping rapidly as the day progressed into its twilight hours.

The air was filled with the sounds of crying men, a sound which to Archie's harrowing astonishment, he had become accustomed to and the effects of it had seemed to ward off him and he began blocking out the incessant calls for help, and pleas for their mothers.

They were deep enough into no man's land to hear the chilling cheers of German soldiers when they indulged in the killing of a fear-stricken Englishman making his attempt at safety. It filled Henry with rage, he gripped the dirt beneath his hands as the occasional crackle of the German rifles was always proceeded with an erupting of laughter from the enemy trench.

The laughter faded off into the night as the moon began its ascent to the top of the sky, and Archie's prayers were answered, with a thick fog of cloud shrouding the night sky.

Henry had slipped into a light sleep, his body sinking into the dirt beneath him. Archie nudged him repeatedly when he felt the time was right to make their daring return back to the trench. They scuttled on their front to the edge of the crater. Archie had been reacting to every sound and twitch in the air since darkness fell and he had not heard a single bullet fired for some time now.

They struggled to get a grasp on the parapet of the hole as the dirt beneath their fingers dissipated at their touch. After several attempts of trying, they managed to force the weight of their bodies to slide cautiously out into the battered wasteland separating the two trenches.

They slithered along the mud, their uniforms collecting layers of sludge as they neared their trench. They could see very little, but as they were getting closer, they saw the flickering of several lamps, indicating their distance from safety.

Henry's stomach groaned as it caressed the shell-battered earth on the arduous retreat. Archie was slightly ahead of Henry, he had been desperate to make it back for some time, and soon he began to hear the rumble of British voices. The comforting familiarity of the English language, calm, and locked in carefree conversation.

"English, we're English, help us in," Archie whispered, the closer they got, he was still far too cautious to risk speaking any louder than a barely audible level, he was not going to have come this far to be on the receiving end of a German sniper.

As they reached the parapet, two men rushed to their aid, a small ginger man and a small blond man grabbed Archie and Henry, respectively by the cuffs of their uniforms, and heaved them into the confines of their home trench.

Archie felt his exhausted frame slump against the cold wooden flooring boards and felt tears overcome him. He had not believed he would make it back alive, and his weary body became overcome with emotion at the realisation of survival.

He clutched hold of Henry and embraced him for a moment before both their thoughts turned to finding the others. They walked up and down the trench praying to hear Franks vexatious nattering or Alan's calming Irish accent.

They walked the tunnels of the trench, turning round a corner following a sign hammered into the trench wall reading, Petticoat Lane, and no sooner than their bodies had altered direction, Henry started hearing a voice louder than the regular hubbub of evening prattle in the front-line.

"Frank?" he called out inquisitively, hoping to be greeted with the familiar faces they had sought out.

Emerging from a cluster of bloodied troops, a weary-looking Frank and Alan stumbled out to meet them.

"Henry, Archie, we didn't think you'd made it," Alan said, closing the gap between them, placing his hand on the back of Archie's neck and pulling him in for a moment's embrace.

"Likewise," Archie replied, shaking Frank's hand as Alan pulled Henry in, in the same manner.

"Anyone seen, Arthur?" Henry asked looking around.

The moment's elation was cut short, as Archie had been too distracted by the delight of knowing his friends had not succumbed to the barbaric assault to realise Arthur's absence. He stopped suddenly when he realised Arthur was not among their number.

"We haven't seen him, figured he might have been with you guys when we got separated out there," Frank said, a concerned look forming across all their faces.

"Come on, let's go back and wait at the front, if he's made it and he's waiting to come back, he'll come back the same way we did," Archie said, thinking as rationally as he could.

"And by God, let's hope he made it," he added quietly, as he led the group back to the front to wait in hope of Arthur's arrival.

As they navigated their way back to the same place they had tumbled back into the trench, Archie couldn't help but think of the petrified look in Arthur's eyes as they were waiting to go over the top. About the letters he had written to his family, and the letters that would be sent back to him.

They stood there waiting for some time. The occasional survivor was hauled in from the darkness, most with gashes and injuries leaving a trail of blood like a snail's trail back to the trench.

As they were engaging in small talk to distract their minds from exploring the worst-case outcome, they noticed a couple of stretcher-bearers returning from no man's land.

They were sneaking out trying to bring back as many of the wounded as they could, as well as those, whose bodies could be brought back in one piece. They heard some of the men groaning in agony as they pressed themselves against the wall to allow the bearers to pass through unobstructed.

They lingered with bated breath every time a stretcher approached but felt a sense of relief as each one came and passed without Arthur occupying the canvas.

The casualties from the battlefield started coming back in their numbers, and none were Arthur. Archie was starting to grow optimistic that he was out there somewhere just waiting for the right time to make his way back, or better yet, he was already in the trench and just had not yet re-joined his friends.

Just as Archie's mind was beginning to reach positive conclusions, he saw another stretcher beginning to make its way through the huddles of survivors. He saw the face lying there coming towards him. The man's hair was perfectly matted down to one side and his face, though dirty, was immaculately clean-shaven.

He recognised it at once and his stomach began tying itself in knots. As the weary-looking stretcher-bearers got closer Archie nudged Henry's side and nodded at the oncoming casualty. Archie knew it was Arthur.

He stepped out in front of the first medic carrying the front of the stretcher and put his hand on Arthur's boot looking at him hoping to see Arthur's eyes light up to see him, hoping to just see a small injury to an arm or leg that could be easily fixed with a few days in the medical tent. But his eyes were not alit with Archie's arrival. In fact, his eyes were neatly shut, as though in the perfect, peaceful sleep.

"He's gone, I'm afraid," the sullen-looking man at the front said, as Archie felt the oncoming tears mustering in his eyes.

He scanned Arthur's body up and down, there were two small red rings where he had been hit by small flying bullets. One had passed clean through his heart and the other through his stomach.

"He was holding this when we got to him," the stretcher bearer said, reaching into his left-leg pocket pulling out a small, crumpled piece of paper, and handing it to Archie.

Archie unfurled it and saw it to be the photograph of Florence. He smiled down at the picture. He thought how even at his very end, Arthur had not neglected his little sister and carried it with him through to his final moment.

"It would have been quick pal," the man finished his final sentence, and a small queue had started forming behind them and he began to move on past the group whose eyes all followed Arthur's lifeless body round the corner and out of sight, the photograph still in Archie's grasp.

"He was a good man," Alan said, as the emotion was written across all of their faces.

They all nodded in unison and Archie and Henry exchanged a glance, though only quick, it gave Archie a great feeling of comfort and gratitude deep inside him to know he still had Henry with him, as they all slumped down into the mud below them and sat silently for a moment.

Several hours later, the night was in its darkest hour and a silence had fallen over the trench. Partly through the extreme levels of tiredness and exhaustion throughout the day, and partly through reflection on the grand loss of life. Their number had become visibly depleted and when Archie looked up and down the line, he thought of all the faces he had seen the night before.

All the small groups of friends that one rotation of the Earth ago were sipping tea and locked in laughter, now the spaces they once occupied were barren. The life that once filled the narrow cavities of the trench had evaporated and left behind a cold and empty space.

Archie had been surprised at the ease with which life had resumed. The men around him who had escaped the clutches of death in the same torturous way he had, were drinking and joking with strangers they had only just met, and at the time, Archie could not fathom how they could act as though they had not just witnessed friends and comrades mowed down.

For several hours, Archie, Henry, Alan and Frank sat locked together on a narrow bench built into the wall. They exchanged very few words but took sanctuary in the company of their friends.

Once the moon had passed over the trench and light were but a couple of hours away, Frank broke away from the group to lay his head on an unoccupied sandbag opposite them to try and rescue some quiet hours of sleep before the next day arrived. Alan followed quickly behind him, taking the other side of the bag, their backs pressed against each other's.

"Want me to stay with you?" Henry asked, stifling a yawn as he rested his hand on Archie's shoulder.

"It's fine, get some sleep. I'm going to write a letter home anyway," Archie replied, stretching out his arms and legs in the narrow space he had available.

"I said, I would, if everything went well today, and I don't want them to worry. You know what Ma's like," the two chuckled and Henry slumped back and tilted his helmet over his eyes trapping himself in his own world away from the distant starlit sky, secluding him in the safety of his subconscious.

When Archie heard muffled snores echo out of Henry's helmet, he found a loose pencil and sheet of paper that some poor soul had clearly intended on using on his return to the trench, but the cackling German machine gun had meant this would not be a possibility. So, Archie claimed it for himself, stooping down onto his knees and putting pencil to paper.

Good evening to you both,

Well, it might not be evening for you now, but it is here, it's quite a starry night too. There's a chill in the air though so everyone's huddled against each other to keep warm. It reminds me of that night, Pa, when we tried to sleep out in the garden, but I got too cold and ran into my bed. That seems a lifetime ago now, I must say.

How is the weather at home? I know how you hate the cold so, Ma.

I lost a good friend today. It's a rather unpleasant business really. We had our first battle, as I said, we would. It's nothing like fighting in books, I can tell you.

Me and Henry made it back together, so I must feel grateful. But oh, it is a rather terrible, terrible business to lose one's friend. Arthur was his name, a lovely lad. From Brancaster he was, isn't that where your brother lives, Pa?

Anyway, we are unsure what the future will bring. I think today gave everyone a right good shake-up. We will wait for further instructions, and until then I look forward to your next letter.

Be safe, love to you both,
Archie

Archie folded the letter neatly and wiped a solitary tear that was cascading down his cheek. He then wrapped his coat around his chilling body and nestled against Henry's shoulder before closing his eyes to the world, leaving the sentries to watch over him as he succumbed to a couple of hours of peace.

6

Archie wiped the sweat from his brow, the uncharacteristically warm October morning showed on his face from the permeating beads of sweat breaking out of his skin. He ruffled his wet hair in his hands and leaned his shovel up against the wall of the reserve trench.

They had been relieved from the front-line a couple of days after the attack and by the time October had hit its climax, they were back on the reserve lines, carrying out regular duties and improving the trench conditions. Their mornings were intense and packed full of jobs and duties that needed undertaking before any afternoon pleasantries could be enjoyed.

On this particular day, Archie and Henry were reinforcing the reserve trench walls. The tasks were mundane and repetitive, but their afternoon football matches against rival units proved to be enough of an incentive to get the work done.

"It's a hot one today," Henry sighed, as he brushed the cuff of his sleeve over his forehead.

Archie nodded, too exhausted to formulate words.

"Fancy trying out a local café from the village instead of the match today?" Henry asked.

As a matter of fact, Archie had been thinking the same thing. He could feel the inside of his uniform begin to swell with sweat and he didn't want to spend the rest of the day uncomfortably wet from running around. Besides, he rarely got much time on his own with Henry for them to mull over their thoughts in the comforts of their own private space, so this option was far more favourable option to him.

"Good idea," Archie said smiling, his dry mouth struggling to complete the words he spoke.

The sun rose higher in the sky and the day grew older. The soldiers had been allowed the afternoon to enjoy a game of football where the ground was not too waterlogged from the previous weeks' downpour or enjoy a drink in the local village.

Alan and Frank were first on the scene for the football match. Their team had been unbeaten since they moved down to the reserve trench and Alan was their star player they refused to miss a game and risk losing their streak. The rabble of soldier turned footballers descended upon a vast expanse of field some distance behind the reserve trench and Archie and Henry separated from the group and followed the dirt path up into the village.

The further they trailed up the track the village ahead of them began to open up. Archie was taken aback; he had never seen such beauty in architecture. Though the outskirts were carrying wounds from the war showing it had not escaped completely unscathed from the skirmishes of the previous weeks.

However, once the heart of the village opened up in front of them, the mosaic display of colour instantly pulled Archie further inside. He was taken aback by the patchwork landscape of buildings of bright, sunlit yellow, blue, and orange. Each building is adorned with a trail of dark wooden beams winding and crossing themselves across the facade of the structures.

The paved streets marked out designated walkways down the middle of the square, veering off in directions where more secluded alleys were waiting to be discovered.

There was a small white building with a black painted lattice pattern on its wall, with a veranda sheltering only a few of the outdoor tables from the heat of the October sun, with the rest of the tables left exposed to the autumn heat. It had a sign protruding from the top of the wall which contained the café's name and a small picture of a lion.

Henry noticed a few men in a recognisable uniform sitting at one of the outdoor tables sipping from large mugs.

"How about a drink?" Henry said, nodding in the direction of the quaint café.

He led the way and Archie trailed closely behind him as they took their place at a table unprotected from the beating sun. They took their hats off and rested them down on the table, Henry running his large hand through his sweaty, ragged hair.

After a couple of minutes of waiting and taking in the surrounding beauty, a small, portly French woman came outside with a small apron around her waist from which she brandished a small notebook and pencil. She was a stern-looking woman with her charcoal grey hair tightly slicked back to her head with what appeared to be a knitting needle piercing the tight bunch of hair behind her head.

She was wearing a small pair of circular spectacles and rested them on a convenient wart on the end of her nose so she could look down on the customers she served.

With very little knowledge of the French language in their relatively short time spent in the country, Henry looked at the woman with a smile before keeping his request short.

"One coffee please," he asked politely.

"One for me too, please," Archie mirrored Henry's order with a nod of his head, as the small lady scribbled the order down on her notebook before turning abruptly and walking inside to prepare the drinks.

"She was friendly," Henry quipped, as the two shared a discreet laugh.

The village was quiet, and though not untouched by the neighbouring war a few miles away, the local civilians were trying to resume with their daily mundane chores of life, to retain all the normality they could. As Archie looked around, however, he could feel there was something not normal about the small hustle and bustle outside the market stalls further down the courtyard.

It then dawned on him suddenly. There were very few men in sight. All those he could see were clearly of retirement age and were sitting on ornate benches along the side of the main track. It was the most noticeable effect of the war he could see.

Henry could see the thoughts that had begun to formulate in Archie's brain as he too had taken note of the absence of young men when they first entered the village.

"You wonder how many of them will ever come back," Henry said, their eyes wandering around all corners of the square.

"You reckon it's like this at home?" Archie asked his gaze now firmly on Henry.

"Maybe," Henry replied swiftly, "maybe if you were down by the sea there'd be no fishing boats out or great bellowing voices from the fisherman," the two paused for a moment, thinking about how life at home may have changed.

It was the first realisation they had. Archie wondered whether all the boys they had once shared their schooling years with, in the innocence of youth, had now left all that they knew behind also, and whether they were scattered around the continent like they were.

Before too long, two large mugs containing a steaming, black liquid were placed down on the table in front of them.

The tables were much like the benches in the village. They were metal but painted a warming white colour, they were ornately designed with spiralling lines and floral designs built in. The coldness of the metal was of light relief from the warm weather trapping the heat inside their uniforms when they rested their hands down on the surface of the table.

The second the mugs of boiling liquid were placed down, they quickly picked them back up again, gulping down the dark brown nectar. The extreme heat of the drink did not faze them, they both felt as though they had never tasted anything with such a strong flavour, and they nestled back in their chairs with pleasure.

"So, do you miss home?" Henry asked as it was really the first time the two had managed to have some time to themselves since arriving in France.

"At times," Archie replied with a sullen tone in his voice.

"Do you?" he asked looking at Henry, who was sitting with his bowl-like mug in his hands.

"I do," he nodded, "I miss work sometimes, I miss us just being able to go out on an evening and not worry about being blown up by a shell," the two of them broke out in a laugh.

"I even miss, Mr White, sometimes," Henry admitted, before laughing again and smiling, as though the images of his former life were rushing back to him.

"I understand," Archie said sympathetically, "I miss Mr Humphrey, sometimes, I miss the way we used to just watch the world go by and plant seeds day after day. It might've got boring, but it wasn't life-threatening, that's for sure," once more, they both exchanged a reminiscing chuckle, and big smiles drew across their faces as flashbacks of memories were being recalled by their brain.

"You know, what I don't miss," said Henry, his face turning slightly more serious.

Archie nodded for him to go on as his face was half buried inside the large mug as he swallowed more of the rich liquid.

"When I'm here, it's just me, I'm in control. We get orders from Sergeant Parker and what have you, but that's it. The only responsibility is to look after myself and look out for you and the other guys fighting alongside me."

"At home, I feel a responsibility to look after Mum and my sister, and sometimes, it's too much. It's like Mum expects so much from me. But when I'm here, it's just me," Henry's words were soft and tender, he looked out into the distance as he spoke, and Archie could feel the emotion present in his words.

"The thing is," Archie started, slightly unsure how to respond to Henry's comments.

"The thing is, when you're not there, they have to cope without you, they can't rely on you. So, they'll have to get by, and they will get by. Then when we're done here and we get home, there won't be as much pressure on you," Archie smiled, as he spoke, reassuring Henry of his love and support.

Henry did not answer but just rested his hand on Archie's shoulder and smiled affectionately at him.

All the talk of home, for however, long it had been, made Archie feel the closest to home he had felt since leaving. All the talk of work and living at home, the talk of the seaside, it took him back to the sandy shores of Cromer beach, just for a few minutes. His mind had returned to home so much that he could almost smell the boats unloading the daily catch of fresh Cromer crab.

His eyes lit up and his face changed, a happier expression fell upon him as he thought back to his life at home and the thoughts of his old life replaced the thoughts of war for a moment and he felt peaceful and calm.

The two of them sat exchanging pleasantries and stories of years gone by for some time before Henry nudged Archie suddenly and he stopped in his tracks.

"I've never seen anything more beautiful in my whole life," Henry said slowly, each word prolonging its journey out of his mouth as he stared ahead of him wide-eyed.

Archie looked up, following Henry's eye line, and let out a small laugh as he took another gulp of his drink, the level of the liquid was nearing the bottom of the mug.

"I mean it, the most beautiful thing ever," Henry slurred his words, as his eyes began stinging from a prolonged period of staring and he blinked rapidly a few times, before returning his gaze straight ahead of him.

A few tables away from them, opposite from where they were sat, a young woman was sitting out in the sun reading a book. She was dressed all in white, holding a small white umbrella, balancing up against her hip and the armrest on the chair to shield her from the sun. She had a flowing white dress on with a lace trimming around the cuffs and the neck.

The dress was intrinsically detailed with small flowers embroidered into the material. Breaking her white theme was a cream beret perched delicately on her head. The hat concealed her rich, dark brown hair. Each individual strand spiralled down from her scalp to just below her shoulders. Each hair delicately curled and wrapped around its neighbour creating a wave of soft, brown hair.

It was clear from her skin that she had enjoyed many warm days like this one in her youth, leaving her skin permanently tinted a sun-kissed brown. Her white dress flowed down to just below her ankles, the bottom of the dress swinging and blowing around her legs from the delicate breeze swirling around the tight streets.

"Go and talk to her," Archie laughed mockingly at his friend, whose gaze could not be deterred from focusing forward.

"Not likely," Henry replied quickly, enjoying the beauty of the girl from afar, not wanting the risk of engaging in conversation.

"Why not? Look at me," Archie said grabbing Henry by the shoulder and turning his body, so their eyes met.

"We've seen what life can be like out there," he said motioning his head behind them, as to reference the fighting in the trenches.

"For all we know, you might not get another chance to do so. Just go over, introduce yourself, and have a chat, I've never seen you struggle to do that before," Archie chuckled, as Henry sat there silently contemplating what he'd heard.

He gulped audibly, shaking his head, as though his brain did not agree with the movement coming from his body, as he pushed himself up from his chair and stood looking at Archie and then back to the girl across from them.

"Go on," Archie said, flicking his head forwards and giving Henry a pat on the back for a head start, as though he was a horse bolting out of the blocks.

Henry found his feet moving forward, walking further away from the safety of his table into the unknown. He turned back to Archie and reached a hand inside a pocket, pulling out his deck of cards and winking at Archie as he had found some new source of adrenaline-fuelled confidence.

He arrived at the table where the girl was sitting, enjoying the tranquillity of being lost in the pages of her book.

Henry coughed to clear his throat.

"Good afternoon," he said, maintaining surety in his voice as he spoke, holding his hat close to his chest, and sweeping his hand through his hair.

The girl looked up at him and Henry looked deep into her eyes for the first time. He looked down and lost himself momentarily in her big, deep brown eyes. Her eyelashes fluttered up at him as she looked, the reflection of the sunlight reflecting in her eyes. He saw a comforting warmth in them that showed pure kindness about her before even speaking.

"Good afternoon," she said in perfect English, her soft, delicate French accent giving Henry a new, unnerving sensation in his stomach.

"Pleasure to meet you, my name is Henry Baxter, may I take a seat?" He asked politely, as he felt a sudden rush of nerves wash over him as he waited anticipatively for her reply.

At first, she said nothing, she just kept looking up at Henry's tall frame and smiled elegantly.

"Nice to meet you, Henry Baxter, I am Annie Bravoure," her gentle voice filling Henry's ears with all other surrounding noise fading away to nothing.

She then reached out a soft hand and pointed down to the seat next to her to welcome Henry to her table. He smiled surprisingly before swiftly pulling the chair out and slumping down into it.

Archie sat watching them and gave a subtle pump of his fist as he saw Henry make the first step of being able to have a conversation at the same table.

"Let me show you something," Henry dived straight for the conversational comfort blanket of his card trick, shuffling the deck out in front of Annie, instructing her to hide the king of hearts anywhere she so desired, promising he would make it appear at the top of the pile.

Archie, following the events from afar, could not help letting out a stifled laugh, checking his pocket watch to note it had only taken Henry one minute and 10 seconds before turning to his trusty card trick to try and make a good impression. Archie watched as he saw the girl's face illuminate as Henry unveiled the top card to indeed be the king of hearts.

To Archie, it was the perfect card for Henry to use. To him, anyone who met Henry instantly took to him, he was a naturally likeable man who carried himself exceptionally and had a good sense of humour that appealed to everyone he met.

Archie saw him as quite the embodiment of a king of hearts. He had a way that Archie himself could never quite put his finger on, which meant everyone would look up to Henry as a figurehead, he had a way of seeing into and connecting with people's hearts that always fascinated Archie.

He watched as the two began to grow flirtatious in their actions with flailing hands resting on one another's arms.

"So how is it that you speak such good English," Henry asked, his confidence growing with every exchange.

"My father. My father was the teacher at the village school, and a very clever man. Before I was born, he studied in London, learning the language and teaching it to me and my little brother when we were old enough," Annie answered, finely sipping a cup of tea she'd be nursing for almost half an hour.

"Was a teacher?" Henry asked inquisitively.

"Like most of the men around here, he left to join the army. We have not seen him since, but he writes every now and then to let us know, he's okay," she said.

Henry noted a sombreness to the tone in her voice which pricked him, and he felt a strong sense of sympathy.

"So, it's just you, your mother and brother?" Henry continued asking questions, keen to find out as much as he could.

"Exactly. But most days I come out on my own, escape to read or sit by the river, somewhere where it feels peaceful like it used to," she continued, a wistful expression cast over her face.

Henry rested a soft hand on hers, he felt the softness of her skin pressed against his hand. He felt her fingers twitch at his touch as she looked up to him and he noted their eyes lock on each other's.

"It'll all be back to normal soon," he started. "We're trying our best and we'll get them out of here, before too long," his voice was reassuring and calm, a quality he had always possessed to try and make light of a dark situation.

"What's it like? On the front?" Annie asked, the sadness in her voice was prominent.

Henry was contemplating whether or not to tell her the truth. Not because he doubted her strength of mind and character to hear it, but because he knew she would hear the reality and think of her father.

"Well," despite Henry's attempt at concealment, his eyes were giving the truth away.

"It's very hard, very hard. We go at them they come at us; we do our best. I've lost friends," Henry's head began to droop, as he spoke before realising he may be upsetting Annie.

"But I still have my best friend, sitting just there," he said, as they both looked up at Archie smiling at him, as he was gazing into the distance.

"I'm sure your father is holding in there," his composure returned, and he shared a soft, loving glance as their hands touched once more.

"Anyway," he started, the tone in his voice picking up. "I very much would like to see the views that you cherish so," his warm, endearing voice had softened Annie and made her feel comfortable in his presence.

While the two were sitting there exchanging stories of their past, Archie was glaring up into the bright sky, feeling the light reflect off his face. He then looked down at the table and noticed a small olive pip balancing on the edge. He picked it up, rolling it in his fingers and examining it.

In its own way, it reminded him of the war. He thought of how this pip was once the skeleton of a colourful, vibrant olive, full of flavour and life. It made him think of the poor men he had shared the trenches with whose bodies had been pulled from their core, their outside skin torn apart.

He thought about the greed of man. He thought about how a hungry man would have ravished the flesh off from this olive, leaving nothing but the inner structure behind, the same way the blood lust of the German soldiers ravished the flesh off from his friends and comrades leaving behind just a lifeless, colourless skeleton.

Just as Archie began thinking deeply about the intrinsic details of why he was out here killing his fellow men, he heard footsteps approaching him. He glanced up, wrapping his fingers around the olive pip and sliding it into his pocket.

Henry was walking back to him with a buoyant spring in his step. Archie stood up instinctively and Henry pulled his collar in towards him, Archie lurching forward.

"Annie's just going to show me around her hometown and the lake, and you know, wherever else," Henry could not conceal the beaming grin on his face as he raised his eyebrows with glee.

"Annie—" Archie asked, hoping for more details of their conversations.

"Her name is Annie Bravoure, her father's a teacher turned soldier and if I spend any more time talking to you, she'll forget about me," he said slapping Archie's arm multiple times with excitement.

"If I'm not back in the line tonight, cover for me and I'll meet you here this time tomorrow," Henry ruffled Archie's hair and before there was any time for a reply he had bounded back off to Annie, taken her arm in his and they had strolled off down the courtyard and round into a side street.

That night, Archie waited and waited and there was no sign of Henry, the moon was high in the sky before Alan and Frank meandered back to where Archie was sitting, stretching his legs out in the cramped trench.

"Where's Henry?" Alan asked, spotting his notable absence.

Archie raised a single eyebrow and smirked, the two young men latching on to what Archie was insinuating and they broke out into a laugh and a cheer.

"Shhh, quiet. We have to cover for him, if anyone asks, he's not feeling too well and just went to be checked out and hopes to be back tomorrow, but no one mention anything," Archie exclaimed sternly in a strong whisper, so as to attract as little attention as possible, following the raucous noise a few moments before.

"So, is she pretty?" Alan asked sniggering.

"Yeah, I guess so, didn't really get a good look at her. Henry was on her like a leech," the three chuckled in chorus, keeping their heads down and allowing the night to pass them by, getting as much rest as mother nature would allow.

The early afternoon hours soon arrived, and Archie quietly made his way down into the village. As he arrived, he marvelled once more at the quaint details of the buildings. The weather was not quite as hot as the day before, but the sun still lit the sky and the streets below.

He made his way to the same café and took a seat at the same table, which was thankfully unoccupied, and after placing the same order to the same waitress he sat and waited. He was patiently watching the world go by when he saw Henry emerge round the corner, he'd turned almost 24 hours earlier, with Annie round his arm the same way she was the day before.

Henry had a beaming grin on his face as he kept turning to kiss Annie on the cheek. He would press his lips against her round, soft cheeks and feel the subtle shiver run through her body as the hairs on the back of her neck stood up.

When they got within Archie's eyeline, they paused and Henry pulled her into him wrapping his arms tightly around her, holding her close to him, cherishing every moment they shared together.

He broke the hug, taking her by the shoulders and holding her in front of him, he could see the mustering of a couple of tears form in her dark, pure eyes.

"When will I see you again?" Annie asked, knowing the answer was ambiguous as there could be no certainty they ever would see each other again.

"Soon," Henry started brushing a tear away from her delicate face. "But until that day, I will always write to you and keep you in my dreams," his voice began crackling as he spoke.

It was the first time he had wished to not go back to where Archie was, where he wanted to run away from it all.

"Keep this," Annie slid her hand into a small pocket in her dress and handed Henry a small photograph of herself.

"My mother got one done of me and my brother for my father to come home to, but I want you to have it, so you don't forget me," Annie's voice was shaking with every syllable that left her mouth.

She had felt an immense connection to Henry, in a way which only war could bring about. The future's uncertainty made them want to hold onto the present even more.

"I won't ever forget about you. I could never," Henry said, before placing one hand on her cheek, sliding his fingertips down the side of her face and through her hair, feeling each soft strand run across his skin.

He then pulled her into him and placed a delicate kiss on her lips. He felt her soft, pink lips latch onto his and neither of them wanted to pull away. For a moment, time stood still, all that mattered was the tender kiss they were sharing and as Henry began to move his body away, he felt her lips unlock from his and he felt a solitary tear crowning in the corner of his eye before wiping his face with his hand removing any trace of the tear.

"I will see you soon," Henry said with a strong note of hope in his voice, as he picked up her hand and kissed it before sliding his hand through hers as they parted ways, and he made his way towards Archie unable to turn back to face her.

Archie greeted him and put his arm around his shoulder, and Henry turned back before they left the courtyard seeing Annie standing there mustering a smile as she raised her hand slowly to wave him goodbye. Henry nodded at her and blew a kiss in her direction which she appeared to catch the imaginary peck as he and Henry turned the corner out of sight.

"So then, how was it?" Archie asked, as they embarked on the short journey back to the reserve trench.

"Oh wow," Henry scoffed, "I've never met anyone like her. She's extraordinary. We spent the day walking around the village, around some of the hills, and the lakes. We just talked and walked, it felt like life was normal," Henry detailed his day, the joyous memories still written across his face as he spoke.

"And the night?" Archie asked, smirking and raising his eyebrows at Henry who let out a small chortle.

"It was the best night of my life. We spent that together too. We found an old barn in the field and laid out watching the stars overhead, and then, well we just spent the night together," Henry's voice was soft and delicate, trying to convey the sensitive nature of his night with Annie.

"What was she going to tell her mother, about why she never came home?" Archie asked, pragmatical as ever thinking of ways to help Henry stay out of trouble.

"Her oldest friend lives on the outskirts of the village. She was going to say they were out and lost track of time, so she let her sleep around," Henry explained, it had clearly been something they had given a lot of thought to.

"Well for your sake, I hope, she buys it. Will you see her again?" Archie enquired.

"My God, I want to," Henry said longingly, "I will try and see her occasionally for as long as we're here, but we know, we won't stay here forever, so, I have told her I will write to her, and that's what I intend to do," Henry said with surety in his voice, that showed just how serious he was.

Archie smiled at his best friend; he had never seen this kind of light in his eyes before. He put his arm around Henry and locked him tight into him, dishevelling his hair with his other hand as they rumbled with each other the rest of the way down to the trench.

7

My Dear Annie,

I'm sorry, it has been some days since my last letter. And I'm even sorrier it has been so long since I have last had the time to come and see you.

As you are aware the last few months have been overwhelmingly busy. We have been working very hard to push the Germans back and not just keep them at bay. It appears as though we may have been successful, and the army seems very happy with our efforts.

We have been informed that we will be moving down to near the River Somme, the French need some help and we are being sent as one of the units to offer support. Do you know much about that area?

We will be moving in just a couple of days so it is with a heavy heart that I must inform you I will not be able to see you before I go. You must remember dear Annie, that no matter where I go you will always be in my heart. I will continue to write to you every chance I get, and my mind is made up, when I get some leave I will come to visit you, and for more than just a day. What a wonderful thought that is.

Until that day I send you all my love,
May God be with you, Annie,
Henry

The June sun was high in the sky and the trenches were riddled with flies and lice. The flies were preying on the decaying corpses of the deceased and the lice were punishing those fortunate to have survived the harsh winter months. Archie was sitting sweltering in a corner of the trench, ruffling his wet hair with his hand, swatting the masses of flies away that were descending around him.

Frank and Alan were locked in an argument about who had drawn the best portrait of a blackbird sitting on a tree behind the front-line. The heat and extensive time in each other's company had frayed the relationships between the men. It did not take long for arguments to form over unnecessary squabbles, and Archie was growing exhausted with the constant battle with the elements as well as the enemy.

They had done very little moving besides the regular rotations between the front and reserve lines since landing in France, and nearly all the men were hoping for a new challenge to come their way. Nearly all except Henry that was.

Being stationed in the same place meant, at any available time Henry would have to spend time in the village, he would go and see Annie. The two would spend as much time together as Henry could manage and they had grown very close, the impending departure had made it all the harder for Henry to come to terms with.

Archie had been impartial for the last eight months. They had seen horrors and experienced things, he wished they had not, but he had grown comfortable where they were. He knew the surroundings and knew the areas and, though they had moved backwards and forwards several miles in numerous attempts to push the Germans back, they were still close enough to the comforts of the first base they had occupied on French soil.

He had almost found a sense of comfort where they were, although they had faced the Germans in several fraught encounters, he had become accustomed to the lifestyle they had lived the last months.

He had grown battle-hardened, and the task of sleeping during a day of the heavy bombardment was no longer an impossibility. His hair was longer than it was, when he first arrived, and he felt more rugged and dishevelled, but he did not oppose his new, tougher look.

There was a buoyant mood in the trench, as they had received the news from Sergeant Parker, a couple of days prior that they would be moving on. They had a sizeable journey ahead of them, but the way Archie viewed it, was that they would have some time out of the firing line, and he could have a chance to enjoy some more of his surroundings.

The only information they had been told was that they would be relieving the French in an attack near the River Somme. Archie knew nothing more than that, but he had an idea in his head of what the river would look like. He was picturing their destination to give him something to hold onto. He pictured reams of green fields, budding with new summer flowers, and a wide expanse of clear blue water, silently streaming alongside a tall riverbank.

In his mind, he saw great trees, trees that had stories centuries old engraved into the very trunks they grew from. The image his brain had painted made him excited to move on, excited to discover more concealed beauty, like the village he was such an admirer of. He thought of how he would write home to tell his father of more of the scenery he was discovering on his travels.

Their months of front-line experience made them good candidates for the army to send down to their important new offensive. Their selection felt like an honour to many of the men and they relished the idea of a new challenge.

The two days waiting to move slugged by, and Archie watched as his comrades grew tired of more waiting. It seemed like most of trench life was waiting and after the initial buzz of exhilaration ahead of them, the tedious delay had put the high spirits on hold.

The morning, they were due to start moving Henry received a letter and scurried off to a corner, on his own away from Archie and the others to tear open the envelope and hurriedly free the letter from its grasp.

Dear Henry,

It saddens me to hear, I will be unable to see you until who knows when. But you must stay safe and well until the next time we see each other. It will be dangerous, but you must keep safe.

Yesterday we received the frightening news that my father is currently missing, and I cannot live without you both, so make sure you come back to me.

May God go with you and protect you,
Annie

Henry folded the letter slowly, staring straight ahead of him. A wash of emotion fell over him as he read the letter, he felt helpless. The time Annie would need to see him, he could not be there. He had very little time to process his emotions, as the soldiers were swiftly rounded up to begin their journey which was met with a jubilant eruption of applause as the trails of soldiers took their place behind trucks and horses carrying supplies on the journey with them.

Archie came alongside Henry, grabbing him by the shoulder and bringing him into formation by his side.

"Everything alright?" Archie asked, glazing over Henry's glum expression.

Henry nodded, concealed the letter into his pocket and slung his equipment onto his back and the two of them made their way with the rest of the men to begin the voyage.

"You both drew great blackbirds," Archie called out, trying to settle the ongoing debate behind him where Alan was trying to convince Frank that he had given greater attention to detail the bird's feathers.

The miles stretched out in front of them, the French landscaping extending her fingertips as far as the eye could see. It pulled the path over the horizon and deep into the distance, as the sight of fields and blue skies extended endlessly.

Several hours into the excursion, the energy among the group subsided as the heat of the midday sun was pounding upon them. Archie's legs were quivering below him, as his empty stomach and heavy kit bag felt as though they had succumbed to the force of gravity and tried to weigh him down to the ground. As his legs buckled beneath him, struggling to keep him on his feet, he knew he had to distract himself from crumbling under his own body weight.

"So, what was in that letter," he asked Henry quietly, so the question could stay within the confines of the space they were walking in, free from the nosy ears of Frank who was just a few paces behind them.

"What do you mean?" Henry replied in question, trying to play the naivety card over the person who knew him better than any other.

"Don't lie to me, I could see it on your face when I grabbed you," Archie continued with a concerned touch to his voice.

"Annie's father's gone missing," Henry said, looking to the ground as Archie had been caught off guard by the response unsure of what to say.

"It brings it home, really, doesn't it," Archie said sympathetically, unsure of what he was really meant to say.

He knew very little about Annie, Henry would tell him less and less, the more the letters would arrive.

"It's not just that," Henry started before taking a pause and a deep breath.

"It makes me feel bad like I should be there for her but, instead, I'm moving further away," Henry continued, the desperation and despair evident as he spoke.

"But you have a duty to do here, you can't allow that to interfere with this Henry," Archie tried reasoning with him, unsure if he would succeed.

"But you don't understand," Henry snapped. "I think, I'm in love with her and there's nothing I can do about that because this Godforsaken war means, I have to go out and kill Germans, who quite frankly, to a man, I have nothing against them," Henry had spiralled as he was laying his cards out to the one person, he knew he could.

"Nothing against them? Nothing against them? They killed Arthur and would kill you given half the chance, they'd kill us all," Archie was growing incessant by what he was hearing.

"I know, but the sooner we stop killing them, the sooner this whole thing will end," Henry's voice cracked as the emotion overwhelmed and broke through his normally calm demeanour.

Archie agreed with him, though not for the same reasons as Henry. He had no lady he wanted to run off to, he had no future he wanted to build. He just didn't want to lose anyone else close to him.

"It will not last forever; I have no doubt before too long it will be over. I'm sure we'll do what we have to do here and hopefully, we'll get some home leave soon, that'll cheer you up," Archie said, trying to bury the fact that Henry's greatest concern was for Annie and not returning home.

"I have already given my word to Annie. The next time we get leave, I will be going to see her," Henry answered solemnly.

Archie felt a knot turning in the pit of his stomach. It was not jealousy and it was not a fear of being replaced. He knew his brotherhood with Henry ran too deep for him to be simply discarded for another. It was a fear that if they both were to survive the war, life may not return to the way it was before they left.

He felt as though, all the times he felt discontented with his position in life, he had neglected the true value of what was important in his life. If he had prioritised that, they may never have been in France, they may both have stayed at home and continued to work in the big house, where they were safe, comfortable, but safe.

He did not want to argue, he knew his emotions may be being contorted with the heightened emotions of being tired, exhausted, and hungry. The thought of his waning legs was more favourable than a journey arguing with Henry.

"Well then, we best get you back to her," he said with a soft smile, his kindness oozing out of his words through the thick fog of confused emotions.

Henry slung his arm around Archie, looking into his eyes, and grinned. He could see the kindness that had always existed there, the love that they had for each other stored deep within their eyes that had seen and experienced so much together.

"It's a long way to Tipperary," Frank began to bellow behind them in an attempt to raise the deflated spirits of the exhausted troops as they waded through the never-ending flat, French fields.

"It's a long way to go," Henry chimed, singing in unison with the rest of his comrades, his arm still around Archie, encouraging him to join him.

"It's a long way to Tipperary, to the sweetest girl I know," Archie sang, looking around him at all the wide-mouthed, merry soldiers sharing a moment of entertainment, cut off from the world.

Archie looked diagonally ahead of him to see Sergeant Parker's lips flickering as he was silently carolling with the rest of his men. Archie calmed, he knew the future was unknown, and he also knew it was uncertain how many more moments he would be able to share like this, peaceful and free, with Henry and Alan and Frank, so he did not intend on wasting it wallowing in his own sadness. He beamed, puffing out his chest and belting out the rest of the song, his arm now mirroring Henry's around his neck, the two joined together, the way they had always been.

Dearest Annie,

My thoughts are with you and your family, and I do hope to hear the good news about your father, soon.

We have arrived at the reserve trench; we moved past the river and it did so remind me of the river we used to sit by.

We shall see how the next days go; I always look forward to your letters and hope your next one will bring better news.

I shall inform you of our next move, when I know more.

Sending love,
Henry

Henry trailed his tongue along the seal of the envelope and tucked it in his pocket to send off later. Archie was sat up against a small pile of sandbags, covering his ears, seeking refuge from the onslaught of German shells.

The month of June was growing old, and they were being prepared to move to the front-line, with the support line trench rotating back to take the space they were currently occupying.

The racket they were subjected to in the reserve trench was spine-tingling enough, that the thought of moving to the line of fire did not fill the men with enthusiasm. They had only been there for four days, but each day brought the same as the last, ceaseless bombardments trying to destroy the German blockades and spirit.

The change in location, however, had not brought about a change in routine. Their days were still long and filled with the same monotonous tasks that had plagued their days for the last few months, but Sergeant Parker had just given the order for the men to get themselves ready to make their way to the front-line.

"You, reckon something's on its way?" Alan asked wading through the masses of men over to Archie and Henry who were ensuring their kit bags were ready to move down.

"Could be," Henry replied, with an assured confidence in his voice. "If it is, I'm sure it'll be after we've served our stint in the front," he nodded reassuringly at Alan who smiled and walked off to gather his kit.

"Really?" Archie asked Henry, when Alan was clearly out of earshot.

"There must be some reason there's a lot of us down here, but his guess is as good as mine," Henry slung his bag onto his back, and they joined the line in formation with the rest of the men, making their way down to within touching distance of the harrowed ground of no man's land.

"It's funny, I don't really hear the noise anymore," Archie said to Henry as they strolled.

"I mean naturally I hear it and know it's going on, but I don't really hear it anymore. I know that doesn't make much sense but—"

"It makes perfect sense," Henry intersected. "You've just become so used to the noise that, it just doesn't register with you anymore," Henry looked across at Archie, sweat beads rolling down his cheek.

It was better this way, Archie thought, *to be numb to the shelling.* It proved to him just how long he had been away and fighting but it made each day easier. He learnt to block it out, he learnt to live with it, stop it eating away at him. They all had, they'd had to learn to live with it or they would not be able to live at all.

As they made their way through the maze of underground passageways he thought of Arthur. He thought of the way the assault the days before his death had shaken him to the core. The way his eyes called out for his mother as the fear ran deep through him.

Archie almost felt relieved that he had been put out of his misery so early into their fighting lives. He knew that the amount of pelting they had been exposed to in the months since Arthur's passing, would have driven him to death in one way or another, had he survived in no man's land.

They passed some men making their way from the front back to the support line. They looked tired and weary. Their eyes told Archie they had experienced no sleep for some days, and the way they looked at him, he had only seen once before—the first ever time they entered the front lines.

It was the same longing look of sympathy and despair. A look of warning, one of prayer. Archie had not felt this deep-rooted, ingrained level of trepidation since the first time he went over the top.

All the times that had followed, there had been a buoyant mood among the men, the men they passed in the trenches, would stop and exchange biscuits or cigarettes, this time however, it was the same despondent stare he had seen just that one previous time.

He gripped on tighter to his rifle, channelling his feeling of unease into the tight clench of his fists.

Henry,

How I do so wish, we could relive the days by the river, the fresh baguette and cheese we would eat on the old blanket, under the tree. I do hope those days will return.

Unfortunately, we have no news on my father, mother fears the more the days go on, without words of his safety.

Are you keeping safe? It worries me so, you are so far away. The village does not feel the same since you all left. The new soldiers who visit are not like you or your friends, they are not as kind.

My days are often filled with praying, I pray for the safe return of my father and the safe return of you. May God protect you, until we meet again.

My love and prayers,
Annie

Henry slipped the note into his right trouser pocket and took a seat next to Archie who was sipping a cup of tea Sergeant Parker had just given him.

"Can I have a sip?" Henry asked, as the two of them looked up to the sky, the usual, warm blue blanket of summer had been replaced by a cold, dark grey curtain blocking out any attempts of light.

The smoke from the explosions rose up, filling the air with devastation and potent fumes. It lingered in the air until it reached the clear innocence of the summer sky, corrupting it and trapping the soldiers under its cruel grasp on their corner of the world.

Archie handed Henry, the cup, he stared down at the familiar, homely liquid and took a large, comforting gulp.

"Doesn't get much better than, that does it," Henry chimed, clicking his tongue against his teeth as he savoured the taste in his mouth.

"How long can they keep going on for?" Archie asked, their pleasant afternoon tea was being overshadowed by a barrage of bombs overhead.

"God knows. Hopefully, we'll find out soon, it's not normally this constant for so long," Henry replied, the pair of them transfixed on the swirling plumes of smoke and dirt flying up in the distance.

"Hey," Henry started, a bright light entering his eyes as he spoke.

"Imagine a nice cup of tea like that on the table with some fresh bass straight from the summer seas," he exclaimed, painting a picture in both their heads.

"A fresh fish and chips would hit the spot now," Archie answered, the two gazing longingly into the distance, hoping for a miracle package to arrive with the delights of a homecooked meal.

"I wonder when we'll next be having one?" Archie asked as the talk of home dominated more and more of the conversations the longer, they were away.

"Ah, you'll be having one soon enough. Legs swinging in the high tide, sitting on the promenade, fish and chips," Henry smiled, nudging Archie as he spoke. "Soon. Very soon," he said, the pair's mood-lifting from the mere mention of home comforts.

"Right, fellas, listen up," Sergeant Parker's voice was loud and strong as he made his way over to the rabble of soldiers containing Henry, Archie and the others.

"I'm sure many of you have wondered why there has been such heavy bombarding recently. Well, tomorrow, we launch an attack on the Germans. We are to relieve the French and blow the Germans so far back the war will be over before you know it."

"One mission and you'll be home before you know it," Sergeant Parker spoke with an enchanting spirit in his voice. He had the men encapsulated in his every word.

"We have a lot of units supporting each other, and the artillery bombardment will have crushed the German trenches, that any men left standing, will soon follow suit and fall to the superiority of the British army," his speech turned to a rallying cry towards the end as he tried to sew the seed of confidence in his men.

"Baxter, Longley, Prior, sentry duty tonight. The rest of you, get sleep where you can," Sergeant Parker looked around at the men, with a subtle, assured smile.

He then stepped down from the fire step in which he had delivered his speech and made his way back down the line and out of sight.

Archie, Henry and Alan all looked at each other.

"Sentry duty and over the top all in one go, aren't we lucky," Alan chippered, breaking the ice and settling the mood among the three of them.

It was a familiar feeling for Archie, he'd known the constant barrage must have been for something big. An attempt to push the Germans back to win the war. It wasn't exactly what he was expecting. However, the way Sergeant Parker phrased it, they could not lose.

The incessant delivery of shells into the German lines was bound to have destroyed all their barbed wire, all their communication lines, and no doubt countless lives at that.

He thought, *Surely when they got over the top, it would be easy pickings to take out any surviving Fritz and by the end of the following day, with any luck, they would be sending the enemy back to their homeland.*

The darkness rose above them, covering the multitude of sins happening below, hiding them under the night sky.

"It's peaceful out there isn't it," Alan said to Archie, as the two of them were keeping a close eye on night-time activity from the Germans, while Henry rested for a couple of hours before his shift. He had tried to sleep, but his body had betrayed him and instead, he turned to writing another letter.

"It is. It's unbelievable, really to think what tomorrow will bring," Archie replied, neither of them looking at each other with their eyes fixed ahead of them.

"Do you ever get scared?" Alan asked, his tone changing.

"Of course. I wouldn't be human, if not," Archie replied.

"I'm terrified," Alan started, his voice quivering.

"I don't know how much longer I can keep riding my luck, keep surviving," his words tumbled out of his mouth quickly, Archie struggling to hear every muffled word he uttered.

"It's all in God's hands now," Archie said looking up to the sky. "It's up to him," He looked across at Alan next to him and punched his arm.

"Go on, get some rest, Henry will be along in a minute for his shift, I'll cover it for now," Archie said sympathetically, as Alan smiled delicately and made his way next to Frank who was peacefully in a faraway world, in his dreams slumped in thick mud.

Darling Annie,

Tomorrow is the day we attack. We received the information this afternoon and I am writing to you now, at the earliest time I have had to do so. I am scared naturally, but it is not death that scares me the most, it is not seeing you again.

I pray for your father's safe return, and if God wills me to survive, I hope to hear good news from you soon.

Be safe and may God watch over and protect you.

All my love,
Henry

"My turn?" Henry called over to Archie, as he left his letter down on the post behind him.

"Over here," Archie whispered back, patting down a piece of dirt next to him, making a clear space for Henry to occupy.

"Here we are again," Henry muttered, "another big attack, there's a lot of men in here aren't there," he continued.

"I heard Parker say something about a third army and a fifth army," Archie replied shrugging.

"It's weird, it's peaceful tonight, but tomorrow…all hell's gonna break loose," Henry became transfixed by the stillness of no man's land.

The calm before the storm lay ahead of him, unknowing of the future that would befall it.

"I know, I don't need to say it now, I say it every time, but if anything does happen this time," Archie began to proceed into his regular speech before Henry cut him short.

"I've got it," he said, shooting Archie a reassuring smile. "On that though," he continued looking down at the dirt below him.

"If I don't make it, or something happens, can you let Annie know, I've written her address over there on the letter I just wrote to her. Take it, and if anything happens, you let her know. Tell her—" Henry stopped for a moment, he looked at Archie, then down at the ground again.

"Tell her, I love her," the words seemed difficult for him to say, but he pushed them out of his mouth and sighed afterward.

"You have my word," Archie said comfortingly, firmly placing his hand on Henry's shoulder, as the pair of them looked out into the lifeless landscape ahead.

"You have written home, like normal," Henry asked, knowing Archie made it a ritual any time before they engaged in a battle to write a letter home to his parents.

This time, however, Archie shook his head slowly.

"They know, I love them," his words were soft and true.

He did not want to send his parents another letter informing them of impending danger. He knew it would only leave them anxious for a follow-up letter to arrive, a few days later. He thought it is best, that if anything happened to him, they found out naturally, and not riddled with fear.

The midnight hours arrived and quickly left again making way for the morning twilight sky to come out of the mist. The men had all been long awake before the order to stand to was delivered. They were all patiently waiting for the rum ration to settle the rising nerves inside them.

Frank's belligerent chatter had started from the moment he opened his eyes. His pre-battle routine consisted mainly of mindless nattering and as much rum as he could guzzle down. He stood next to Alan, the morning's alcohol had just reached him, and it barely brushed the sides of his mouth as it filled up his stomach, breeding his newfound Dutch confidence. His drivel turned into talk of how he was determined to kill every German in sight, that no German bullet would touch him.

The only silence arrived when Alan threatened to kill him himself if he made one more sound.

Sergeant Parker gathered the men up, informing them they would make up the second wave of attack. This gave them more torturous waiting. Their only mental salvation was the thought that comes at the time they came to go over the top, there would be little to no resistance, standing in their way.

There should be no reason to fear, as long as they stayed alert, they should be able to follow behind the first wave and clear up any mess left behind and that would be that.

Archie stayed close by Henry's side who handed him a small, hard, rectangular-shaped biscuit that seemed determined to break his teeth as he tried to bite it. Archie struggled but ate his biscuit, lining his stomach with a resilience to settle, to the rising nerves inside him.

It was time to take their position. The commanders of the first wave had their whistles in their mouths, ready to blast their men over the top. Archie felt a wave of relief that they were in the second wave.

He felt the first wave was more of an experiment. They were being sent out to test the success of the week's onslaught. He felt more comfortable in his role of aiding those who went before him. They looked around at the blank faces staring at the ladders ahead of them.

The sight was dominated by clusters of men locked in prayer, audibly calling for their God to protect them. Many men were praying for their safe return, and if, that was not possible, they were praying for a swift entrance to heaven.

Henry couldn't help but feel a sense of guilt at the men, going over the top, before him. It was not a situation he had been used to and he felt it wrong that they should not all encounter their fate together.

While Archie and Henry were locked deep in thought, the shrill, piercing siren of the whistles sounded, and with a great cry and a chorus of bagpipes from within the trenches, the first wave embarked into no man's land. No sooner had they launched their bodies over the parapet, had the sound of their rallying cries been lost to the overhead support of the British artillery guns.

The loud barrage of shells was providing a wall of cover ahead of the troops, distracting the Germans from the masses of men descending upon them. The barrage met with great cheers from the second wave in the trenches as confidence filled the air.

Several minutes before the attack was launched, a colossal mine exploded, down near the German line. Archie felt a change inside him, he could see no way out for the Germans. He thought if the week's battering had only wounded them, the mine would have finished them off.

Sergeant Parker's face remained unchanged, he stood leaning against a ladder, his whistle in his mouth ready to wait a few minutes before giving his own orders of attack to his men. His eyes were transfixed on the small watch hanging loose around his wrist.

The magnitude of noise in no man's land had elevated to new heights. The distinct sounds of gunfire and explosions had become indistinguishable, merging together into a constant pandemonium, the sound of which, drilling its way further into the brains of those, who stood waiting.

The minutes ticked by, and the time was upon them. Sergeant Parker removed the whistle from the edge of his lips.

"Godspeed, men," he said, his words softly travelling around the men.

"Ready," he called out, his voice booming and echoing against the walls of the trench as he placed the whistle in a firm grip between his lips and blew hard, the high-pitched sound filling the space around them as the farewell tunes of the bagpipes fired up once more, and Archie and Henry locked together, clambered up the ladder and over the parapet.

The sight that greeted Archie as he reached ground level made his legs buckle and his eyes sting. There was barely a British soldier in sight. All he could make out amidst the shoots of smoke forming around shell holes, were the small flying bullets of German machine guns, rattling through the air, beating down anything that got in its path.

His legs moved involuntarily from his brain; he was shocked, amazed. He could not grasp how this could be happening. The days of rampant explosions, the earth-shattering mine that only a short while ago he had witnessed tear the ground apart from below. Yet after all of that, he had never seen such strength in numbers from the enemy.

He looked across at Henry, his eyes were wide and his expression vacant. He turned to his right where Alan and Frank were scuttling alongside him, Frank's penetrating screams cutting through the sound of explosions. He saw them launch themselves into a large crater a few metres in front of his current position.

As he looked forward, he could make out the contortions of bodies that had made it, as far as the German barbed wire, only to be picked apart like a toy, body parts laying strewn out in front of them, as they lay stuck in thick layers of wiring, not yet dead.

He saw that the bravest of men who had navigated the treacherous depths of no man's land, were being made to wait for the welcome grasp of death to take them, from their torture.

The once, strong line of men only a couple of minutes ago, were now heavily depleted in their numbers. Small gaps in the lines turned into gaping holes where 20 strong men once walked side by side, now laid face down, motionless in a pool of army's blood.

"Over there, Alan, Frank, we need to get to cover," Archie formed the closest thing to a sentence he could, as he grabbed Henry pulling him in the direction of the shell hole.

In reality, the distance could have been no more than 12 feet, but every step they took seemed to move them further away from their target.

As they got closer, Archie could see the beckoning arm of Alan waving them into the hollow pit in the ground. Henry rushed a few steps ahead as he saw Frank's arm reach out to grab them in, saving them a step or two of walking, as they could collapse their bodies down to safety.

Archie watched as Henry picked up speed and latched his hand into Frank's firm grip, who thrust him over the lip of the shell hole as Alan stopped the momentum of Henry's flying body with his own. The pair of them then turned to help Frank in reaching out for Archie, who was but a couple of steps away from them.

As he began to lean forward, his fingertips clutching at thin air, as he tried to lure Henry's hand, further out to grab him, he felt a sudden, dull sensation hit him in the shoulder. He thought nothing of it, there was debris flying all around them, mounds of dirt and clumps of rock thrown up from the explosions.

However, as he went to place his right leg down in front of the other, as he closed in on the crater, he found himself falling backward. His body collapsed back, his helmet clouting against the ground, his body lurching as it made contact with the dirt beneath him.

Henry and Alan instinctively launched themselves at his feet and dragged his body down into the pit.

"Arch! Arch!" Henry called out, his face almost pressing against the skin of Archie's cheeks.

"I'm fine, I'm fine," Archie uttered, brushing the hands of Henry and Alan off his body, as they perched his back against the wall of the crater.

"You're hit, Arch you're hit," Henry said, his words softer and his voice shaking more the second time he repeated himself, as the realisation began to sink in.

Archie had obviously known something had hit him and found Henry's words nonsensical and unnecessary. Did Henry not think he would realise if something had knocked into him? He ruffled the flailing hands away from him and sat up against the wall of the hole.

He raised his hand to hit the inside of his shoulder, where he had felt the cluster of debris fly into him. It was wet. His uniform all down his left-hand side, was wet. He lifted his hand away from his shoulder and up towards his face.

It was red. His hand was drenched in his own blood, his breath started to pick up pace as he realised what had happened.

"Henry," he said slowly, the word spoken tentatively and with a child-like terror in his voice.

"It's alright, Arch, you'll be alright," Henry said, as he lifted Archie's helmet from his head, placing his hand on the back of his neck. He felt blood running down his hand. Archie had clearly cut the back of his head from his hard fall.

He slid down the crater, his hand back up to his shoulder. It had not been a stone or large clump of earth; it was a German heavy bullet. He could feel the gaping wound in his body and Alan pressed down onto it, encasing the blood inside him.

Archie's eyes began rolling, they glazed over the conversations and cries happening around him. A silence fell about his ears as he could no longer make out the whir of machine gun fire or the thundering of shells.

He looked directly up above him; Alan was frantically busying about the crater in search of a loose bandage or clean dressing to address the wound with. His eyes then settled on the looming figure of Henry above him. He was holding Archie's head in his hands, and his lips were moving, letting out words Archie could not make out.

"It's alright, Arch, it's alright," Henry repeated, as he stared down into the fading eyes of his best friend.

He knew they needed to get him medical help. *He would be fine if they could just get him the assistance he needed,* he thought. His eyes darted in circles around him, looking for a sign of a red cross armband anywhere in sight. He could not find one, he knew they had to stop the bleeding until they got him to safety.

Archie was still lying, his body not moving and his eyes watching the frantic movements of Henry. He looked down at his shoulder once more, watching the blood run from his wound like water from a tap.

He then rolled his eyes back up to Henry, seeing his gaze meet his own before his eyes began to close. The world around him began to fade away, until all that was left was the figure of Henry looming over him, until that too disappeared, and his eyes closed, and his breathing cooled.

8

"Sir, can you hear me? Excuse me, Sir, can you hear me?" a soft voice echoed around, the words reverberating with a signal of intent.

Archie felt his senses return to his body, he felt a sharp tingling sensation in his fingertips as he stretched them out, extending them at the joint, curling his aching fingers, scrunching a creased sheet in his fist.

He licked his dry lips, feeding them moisture which it felt they had been starved off, for some time, as he felt the cracks and cuts on his lips as he ran his tongue along them.

His eyelashes fluttered, it took some time for them to open, but gradually, he began blinking, taking in what at first was just a bright white light but soon, he began making out shapes and objects around him.

"Sir, can you hear me?" the same voice echoed again, this time his ears could descramble the words and formulate the question being asked to him. He want to speak but choked and only a cough escaped.

"Yes, yes, I can hear you," he finally mustered the words out of his mouth, looking his body up and down as he became confused and restless.

"You're alright, Sir," the voice belonged to a short round woman, who to Archie had a very typical cockney accent.

He thought this bizarre, he had not seen many English women out in France in nearly a year.

"Sir, please relax, you're alright, you're safe, you're in England," the words rang around Archie's ears, spinning circles around his brain.

It cannot be, he thought. How could he have ended up in England, when the last thing he remembered was being out on the battlefield with Henry. If he was in England, where was Henry? His mind began escalating ideas to the forefront of his brain, he began jolting in his bed as reality set in.

"Sir, try to stay calm. You are alright, we have seen your wounds, the infection is on its way out and you should be too soon. You can thank the man next to you, he told us everything we needed to know," she smiled at Archie.

She could see the distress the whole situation was causing him and spoke in a soft comforting tone.

Archie looked puzzled and turned to his right. Laying upright in the bed next to him, his leg upright in plaster and an eyepatch over his left eye, was Sergeant Parker.

His weary face turned to greet Archie's; it was the last sight Archie was expecting to see.

"Sir?" Archie asked, still needing verbal confirmation from Sergeant Parker that it was in fact him.

"Baxter," Parker replied in a monotone voice, his calm demeanour unwavering.

"What's going on here, Sir?" Archie asked, still perplexed by his surroundings.

"You were wounded, I was wounded, we got sent here. That's the long and the short of it," he replied with a slight chuckle, choking right after he did so.

"I figured, Sir. But I mean, what exactly happened, you know, out there? I don't remember what happened to me," Archie's voice was growing impatient, he had awoken, out of what felt like a fever dream, in England.

He did not know where, or how he got there. The ambiguity of the situation was rattling him.

"It did not go the way, we expected," Sergeant Parker started, hanging his head low.

"The bombardment, the mine, for some reason didn't kill them. When we went over the top, it felt like there were more of them than there were of us. We lost most of our men."

"When I returned back to the trench at nightfall with a handful of survivors, we rationalised a plan to head back out, and bring as many of you in as possible," the pain of the event was clear in his voice, and his eyes were not focusing on the room around him, they saw through it, his mind was back on the battlefield, his eyes seeing it, reliving it.

Archie watched him, unmoved, he said nothing at first, just listened, hoping for a moment of recollection to remember what had happened to him.

"I remember going over the top, seeing everyone mown down, but that's it," Archie intersected.

Parker looked at him briefly, before returning his gaze out of the window opposite him and locking himself back in his mind's eye.

"When we went back over the top to save as many as we could, you were lying in a crater, unconscious, close to death, I must say. Longley was with you, and Prior and Howells. We slid you onto a stretcher and dragged you the distance back to safety where you were carted out of the front-line."

"We knew there were still more out there, so, I returned with Longley and Prior to see who else we could rescue. I found Higgins, he was whimpering and had a bullet through the shin."

"We carried him out of no man's land and as we got close to our trench, I was hit twice," Parker animate recalling of events stopped, as he pointed down to his right thigh and a small bandage, Archie had not spotted at the bottom of his stomach.

"The bullets passed clean through me," he stopped for a moment, "Longley saved my life," he turned to look at Archie, his voice solemn.

"Prior dragged Higgins to safety and Longley noticed I'd been hit. We had no time to wait once Fritz had spotted, so he flung me over his shoulder and carried me to safety," a painful expression cast over his face, the memory of it almost too hard to recall.

"Was he hit? Henry. Did he make it back?" Archie asked, his concerns in only one place.

"We all made it back; I was taken off to the medical tent, where I saw you. Your shoulder soon became infected, and we could not be treated there and were sent home. That was quite some time ago now," Sergeant Parker said softly, he could tell from the puzzled look on Archie's face that he was trying to piece together all the parts of the story.

"And your eye?" Archie asked, trying to fill in the blanks.

"When I was hit, I fell forward, the scum from the ground got lodged inside my eye, it became infected, but they treated it. I just have to wear this fashion piece for the next few weeks," Parker joked as he grimaced and winced in pain, as he adjusted his right leg.

"Your son would love that look on you, Sir, you look just like a pirate in uniform," the two shared a soft ripple of laughter.

"Sir," Archie started, an earnest tone in his voice now. "You said we've been here for some time, how long exactly?" He asked the question tentatively, almost fearful of the reply.

"Almost a month, Baxter," Sergeant Parker replied with a sigh.

Archie's eyes widened, and he felt a rush of urgency, a force trying to push him out of bed, to prove he was well enough to return to the front, he had been away now for too long, he felt.

"A month?" he exclaimed, almost an anger in his voice. "When do we go back?" Archie asked.

"It's too early to say. We should both be ready for discharge soon, they will send us to a convalescent home to recover and find our feet again, quite literally in my case. It could take months, but we will return eventually," Sergeant Parker spoke reassuringly.

"Months, I can't wait months, Sir, what about Henry and the others?" Archie asked frantically, panic setting into his voice.

"As far as I know, they are all fine. Any casualty lists to have reached me, have not contained their names," Archie felt comforted by his sergeant's words.

He looked around, he recognised a few of the faces in the hospital, many he imagined that had arrived with him had already left within the month. Each face sat around him however, all carried its own unique scar from the war.

"You care for him a lot, Longley?" Sergeant Parker asked quizzically.

"He's like my brother, Sir, we grew up together. He signed up because I did, he came to look out for me, and he wouldn't let me go alone. He's more than just my best friend," Archie's mind wandered back to Henry, out in France somewhere alone, without him.

"You spoke his name," Sergeant Parker replied calmly.

"What?" Archie asked, confused.

"The last few nights, when you've been coming back round, when you slept you spoke his name. You spoke about you and him and your life at home," Sergeant Parker turned to Archie who had a tear forming in the corner of his eye.

He woke up just a few minutes ago to a world he had left behind almost a year ago, to find it was no longer his world anymore. His mind and his thoughts were back in France.

It was strange, he thought, when at war he would think of nothing but home. Now he was stuck in a hospital bed in England, and he wanted to be reunited with the shells and gunfire.

"Can I get you anything, Sir?" the rotund nurse had returned to Archie's bedside.

"Yes, could I please have a couple of sheets of paper and a pen?" Archie asked, the woman slightly confused by his request.

"Of course, I'll get that now for you, Sir," she smiled and walked off to retrieve Archie's summons.

"Your family has already been informed of the situation, they have said they will visit you, as soon as they can," Sergeant Parker said, relaying the message to Archie.

"It's not for them, Sir," Archie replied as the nurse returned with two sheets of white paper and a navy-blue fountain pen.

Archie tried to steady the paper on his legs to create a stable writing surface.

Dear Henry,

I write bringing you the news of my good health—at least recovering health that is. I woke up this morning, for the first time, since I left you all, that time ago. They say the wound became severely infected and it knocked me out for some time. Now, I can finally write to give you the news, I'm sure you've been waiting for that. I am on the road to recovery and hope to return to be by your side soon.

Sergeant Parker is next to me in the hospital, can you believe it. He said, you saved his life. No more heroics until I'm back, please, I can't be having you killed a martyr!

Sergeant says, I used to talk about our old life in my sleep, the last few nights. It's weird, being back in England, it doesn't feel the same as it did before. I don't feel right being here, and you being there.

How are the others, Alan, and Frank? I hope you are keeping each other company until my return. And Annie, any news on her father?

I do not know what comes next, the whole thing has been a bit of a blur, sergeant says, we'll be moved to a convalescent home soon to recover, but he doesn't know how long that will take.

Stay alive until I return, and God protect you, my friend.
Archie

"Longley?" Sergeant Parker asked, as Archie waved the sheets of paper in the air with his good arm to dry the ink quicker.

"Yes, Sir, I need to know how they all are," Archie replied, his mind wandering to the distant French shores, the fields they walked through, and nights spent under the starlit skies.

***

"Jesus Christ, get down or they'll blow your bloody head off," a fiery Irish accent called out as German shells rained over the trench.

"Henry, letter for you," the burley, gruff tones of Frank breaking through a crowd of hungry, tired men.

"Who's that from?" Alan asked nosily, as he stuck himself to Henry's side, rearing his head over Henry's shoulder to see the handwriting.

"I don't know," Henry answered, confused as he did not recognise the chirography on the envelope.

He unsealed the envelope with great haste, tearing the letter out from within, and his eyes scanning over both the concealed pages.

"It's Archie," he exclaimed, beaming. "It's from Archie," the jubilation strewn across his long face.

"Let me see that, how he says he's doing?" Alan asked, his regional vernacular still difficult for Henry to follow sometimes.

Henry paused for a moment, giving himself enough time to skim over the whole letter to get an understanding of what Archie had said to him.

"He only woke up today, he's been out cold since the day he was hit. Sergeant is with him in hospital, they'll be moved elsewhere soon, but they don't know when they'll be back. But he says they will be back at some point," the three men looked at each other with excitement.

Judging from their sapped faces, it was a welcome piece of good news.

"The sergeant? They're together?" Frank said, snatching the letter from Henry's grasp.

"That's what it says. Ha ha! I knew he was alright; I knew it!" Henry exclaimed, his voice cracking slightly as he spoke.

He had begun to give up hope, he thought surely, if Archie was alright, he'd have heard from him by now. The feeling of elation stemmed more from an immense weight of relief lifted from his shoulders. He found a new determination, a resolute strength, a need to stay alive until Archie returned.

"It doesn't say when they'll be back," Frank asked, reading the letter over to himself.

"But they will return, that's what we do know," Henry said, opting to dwell on the positive aspects of the letter.

He took it back into his own possession, keeping it firmly within his grasp, sheltering it under his curled fingers. He walked over to a small fire step up against the wall of the trench and slumped down onto it, his eyes examining every letter of Archie's delicate handwriting.

"He's alright, I told you, he'd be alright," Alan uttered tenderly, placing his hand on Henry's shoulder briefly before passing through the trench on his way to use the makeshift toilet.

Henry sat there a while longer on his own, taking in every word, his eyes hovering over Archie's talk of being back in England. About the way he felt being there. It was difficult for Henry to imagine, the difficulties of returning home to safety.

When he thought of home, he could only picture the summer setting of the crowded beach at Cromer, children with ice cream, spilling down their chins onto their clothes, the unmistakeable smell of fish and chips rising from the fryer. He closed his eyes and allowed his senses to be overcome by the feelings and memories of his past, of the innocent folly of youth, of a peaceful time.

***

"Alright, fella's this way, please. Those of you that can walk follow me, the rest of you, assistance is on its way," a loud, domineering call came from a large old man with a clipboard placed under his nose.

He had white tufts of hair sprouted randomly all over his head and a pair of half-moon spectacles bouncing on his large chest, suspended by a thin chain around the back of his neck.

Archie joined the back of a relatively long queue of able-bodied men and men on crutches. Sergeant Parker had spent the last week in hospital getting used to a wooden crutch under his arm to aid his walking.

He had a resolute determination to be back on the front-line, as soon as possible and had adamantly refused the use of a wheelchair for their final week under hospital protection.

The sun was high in the sky on a warm August afternoon, the smell of the hot air and the leaves rattling around the trees in the gentle breeze comforted Archie. It smelt like home. The simplicity of a subtle smell soothed him as he let the summer's zephyr cool his face and rustle the hair on his head.

Sergeant Parker followed a couple of men behind Archie, they trailed their way into the grand entrance of the convalescent home. It was like nothing Archie had ever seen before. Its scale was grander than Huckerby Hall and he felt almost an intruder as he stepped foot into the great entrance.

There were colossal white pillars surrounding the front doors, as though something out of a Greek mythology story. There was ivy spiralling its way around every facet of the walls, skimming along windowsills and climbing up over the guttering. There was a tall flagpole rising from the roof with a patriotic flag swinging in the subtle wind.

Inside, Archie and the line of men were directed into a room that had clearly been repurposed to house them. Archie was taken aback, there were more books adorning the walls of the room than they had in the entire bookshop at home. His eyes flittered up and down, scanning the vast array of titles on offer.

All of a sudden, this period of convalescing might not have been such a terrible thing after all. All the men were each assigned to a small, metal framed bed, with around 30 beds tightly packed into one room to maximise the space available. Archie was put in the far corner of the room, and to his welcome surprise, Sergeant Parker took residence in the bed next to his.

The same man with his clipboard still firmly in his grasp strutted into the great room, his glasses jumping against his body, as he did so. He turned the page on his clipboard and bellowed out a list of instructions, detailing the times they would eat and the availability of the grounds to use for exercise and pleasure as well as rehabilitation and recuperation.

Archie knew not who the man was but, could tell he was enjoying his moment of power and authority. Once his task of unloading information was complete, he turned with a sharp swivel and exited the room, leaving the men to settle in and become accustomed to their new surroundings.

"It's an upgrade on my family home," Sergeant Parker muttered to Archie, as he marvelled at the splendour of the décor.

The tall ceilings, each corner of which was delicately and ornately decorated with carvings of small animals, with a grand chandelier illuminating the room below. The bookshelves rose from floor to ceiling with a small ladder in one corner of the room to reach the books that were too tall for human reach.

"Do you miss it? Your home?" Archie asked, perched on the end of his bed looking across at his superior.

"I do. But naturally, it's what's inside the house, I miss more," he replied, staring out of the window behind Archie, looking out onto the boundless grounds, lined with rows of red and purple as the summer flowers twinkled in the sunlight.

"Your family?" Archie asked softly.

"Yes," his gaze now met the dusty wooden floorboards beneath them.

"I received a letter not long before we went over the top that day, saying my son has been taken ill," his voice cracked as he finished his sentence, the wall of emotion he had become so accustomed to building up was beginning to crack.

"I'm sorry to hear that, Sir. Will you have time to see them before we return?" Archie asked, also hoping for an answer that would indicate whether he could see his own family.

"Yes, I should think so, when we are released from here, we will know more, but I would imagine there will be time, yes," he continued, Archie's mind wandering to the cobbled path that leads to his cottage, and the crunch of the small stones beneath his shoes.

"Have you got other children, Sir?" Archie asked, despite serving alongside each other for almost a year, the intrinsic details of their private lives were never discussed.

"Yes, two others. Stanley, my boy, and then my two girls, Margaret and June," a smile crept across Sergeant Parker's face as he spoke, thinking about his small family.

"How old are they, Sir?" Archie asked, making sure he kept his formalities about him.

"Stanley is 10, Margaret 6, and little June only 4," his voice was far softer than Archie had ever heard him speak, a vulnerability about him appeared when talking about his children.

"What about you, Baxter, any siblings?" he coughed, recomposing himself.

"No, Sir, only me. Well except Henry, he's not really my brother, but I see him as one," Archie said.

"I see, and it's Cromer you're from, isn't it?" Sergeant Parker asked intently, showing an interest in Archie's life which surprised him.

"Yes, Sir, yes, it is, it's a lovely place really, especially this time of year," Archie's face lit up as visions of his hometown flooded his imagination.

"I have been," Sergeant Parker said coolly, "my girls, they love the beach, and they do the most excellent crab," the two locked in a conversation that showed no barriers of rank, just two men trapped in a moment in time.

"We're famous for it," Archie replied, as the two broke out into a laugh.

"Here," Sergeant Parker started, before diving his hand into one of his pockets.

"They gave me this, it was in your pocket. I was certain, I'd seen it before, then it dawned on me, I'm sure, I used to see Collier with it all the time before he was killed. I'm not sure why you took it but here," Sergeant Parker explained, handing Archie a small-crumpled photograph; Florence's photograph.

"Arthur," he mumbled quietly to himself.

"I was right then," Sergeant Parker started. "Why did you take it?" he asked curiously.

"It just seemed wrong to let it be discarded, or lost. It was the one thing Arthur valued the most, it just seemed wrong," Archie said,, as his eyes stared down at the innocent girl in the photograph.

"You're a good man, Baxter. The two of you, you were close?" He asked, trying to unearth as much as he could.

"He was one of us, Sir. He became part of our little group, I'm not too sure, how it happened, I think it was from training, Sir. We all just latched onto each other, the five of us and that was it," Archie explained, recalling the details from almost exactly a year ago.

"You, Longley, Collier, Prior and Howells?" Sergeant Parker asked, evidently having noticed them spend most of their time clustered together.

"Yes, Sir, that's it," Archie answered, feeling slightly interrogated.

"Well, I'm sure, we'll be back out there soon, and you'll all be reunited once more. For now, we must stick to the old man's routines and focus on getting back to full fitness," he patted Archie on the shoulder before standing up to bend down towards his toes, stretching his legs before taking a stroll around, checking up on some of the other men.

Archie laid back on his bed, his head resting against the thin pillow that was nestled delicately on top of a small mattress. He let his eyes shut from the hubbub around him and allowed his breathing to take over. He focused on the rise and fall of his breath as he drifted off into a deep and peaceful sleep.

"Excellent progress, Sir, one more week and you'll surely be ready to be released," a small nurse was walking along a narrow stretch of freshly cut grass, guiding Sergeant Parker unsupported on his own two feet.

It had taken him three months of recuperation to get to a point of walking on his own, after suffering a small relapse in his recovery, when he began to lose the muscle mass in his leg.

It had taken him weeks and months of working with a nurse to improve his strength and get him to a position, where he would be ready for war once more.

Archie's wound was nearly healed. The nurse had been scheduled to remove his bandaging after aiding Sergeant Parker with his walking exercises. Archie's wound became infected again not long after they arrived at the convalescent home after he took a fever and fell over on ground.

Dear Henry,

How are you? Your last letter brought me much happiness hearing you all our safe and well. I was upset to hear about Annie, you are in my thoughts as always, my brother.

I bring good news with my letter. We are to be released from the convalescent home, within the week. Then it will be a brief visit home before we return to reunite with you, back in France.

Has there been much movement recently, or are you still in the same place?

My shoulder has now made a full recovery, and I will be back to keep you safe again soon!

Take care and God bless
Archie

Archie enclosed the letter into the envelope and left it on a small unit next to his bed where the nurse would collect it to be posted.

As he placed the pen and paper back down by his side, he let out a heavy sigh and turned his head to look out of the window. He watched as the November wind was ripping through the trees, bringing the brittle, brown leaves tumbling to the ground.

The grass was wet where the week's rain had settled and made a home for itself in amongst the blades of the deep green grass. He looked up to the sky, there was a storm brewing. It was filled with patchwork shades of grey, taking Archie back to the gunpowder-filled skies of France.

His eyes began focusing in on the rolling clouds, as his mind began to contort them with the rising plumes of smoke from exploded shells. His ears began hearing the shrill, ear-splitting siren of German bombs, flying through the air. His eyes began to close as he became immersed in his imagination, and immersed in the thought of the world, he left behind.

"I got the post here, Alan, two for you and, Henry, one for you," Frank had nominated himself as postman among the group, collecting letters on behalf of them all to pass around the three of them in Archie's absence.

Henry stood holding the letter in his hand, almost not wanting to look at where it came from.

"You reckon, it's from her? Is it her handwriting?" Alan asked, incessantly bridging the gap between him and Henry, looking up into his eyes and questioning him.

"I don't know," Henry replied sullenly, as he inspected the writing on the front of the envelope. "Looks like Archie," he said, letting out a sigh, a look of disappointment on his face, as though he was holding out for someone else.

He opened the letter and read it with little enthusiasm.

"So, what did he say?" Frank asked, his blank expression displaying his lack of empathy or ability to read a situation, as Alan looked sorrowfully at Henry.

"They should be back soon," Henry replied nodding, before turning and walking away from the group, finding a solitary sandbag for a chair and using it to his advantage.

He sat resting his head on his hands. He rubbed his eyes vigorously with the soles of his palms and sniffed several times.

Henry carried the letter tightly in his grasp and went to sit on a small firestep at one end of the trench. Alan noticed him sitting there and made his way over toward him.

"This seat is taken," he asked, pointing down to a space next to Henry's leg.

Henry shuffled closer to the edge leaving ample room for Alan to sit next to him.

"Still not heard from her then?" Alan asked, the tone in his voice surprisingly mellow.

Henry shook his head, his head still hanging low as to conceal his emotion. "Nothing, nothing for three months," he said, his voice wavering.

"What was the last you heard? Have you still got the letter?" Alan asked, consoling Henry with his arm around his shoulder.

Henry reached inside his chest pocket and pulled out the folded letter, sat close to his heart.

"This one," he started, brandishing it between two fingers. "The last I heard was in August. They'd just found out her father had in fact been killed, but that was it, I replied, the day I got it and I've had nothing since," Henry's voice quickened as he spoke, he was not succeeding in keeping his emotions in check.

"Well then, I'm sure you'll hear from her soon. No one's been left untouched by the war, now she and her family, they're victims of this war Henry. She's lost her dad."

"Her family, they're out on their own, it's difficult after the man of the house dies, it won't be easy for them," Alan said comforting Henry, as he spoke to him, he could see the distress in his eyes.

Henry had not thought about it that way before. He had only viewed it that it must have been something he had said or done, or she must have met someone new. He knew better than anyone what losing the man in the house could do to a family.

He was forced to take on that role, sooner than he would have liked, in his own life. Maybe Alan was right, maybe he should not worry himself so, maybe someday soon he would receive a letter from her.

Though, try as he might to believe Alan, he couldn't. He had known Annie, he had known the feelings they shared for each other, she wouldn't have just run off and left without saying a word to him unless there was something else. Unless she had met somebody else.

But even then, Henry thought, *she wrote to him telling him of her distaste for all the new soldiers who had arrived at the village.* But what if it wasn't a soldier?

Henry had tormented his mind over and over about all the possible reasons why he had not heard from Annie, for the past three months. He had exhausted his brain. He threw his head back against the wall, wanting to shout out.

"Listen, Archie will be back soon, think about that. He'll need you when he gets back here eh. Come on, I'll go get you some tea," Alan had grown to become very protective over the men he served with.

Since leaving his family in Ireland, he had no one. No family and very few friends. Since arriving at war, he had found that in Archie, Henry and Frank. Though Frank often drove him to new levels of resentment and made him often feel more angry than he ever felt towards the Germans, he loved them all like brothers.

He had comforted Henry in Annie's absence when Archie wasn't there, he filled a hole that Henry needed filling and wished for Archie's swift return, so they could finish the war the way they started it, together.

Henry's head nestled into the wet, muddy trench wall. There were rats roaming around his feet as he swatted the shaft of his rifle around them to make them clear off. His eyes followed the flight of a couple of small blackbirds roaming overhead.

He watched them enviously, they were undeterred by what was going on below, and they were oblivious to the dangers. He thought of the birds that would sit on the trees outside the servants' courtyard, the way they would boldly flutter their wings down to the bench to accept small scraps of bread from the kitchen.

As he sat there daydreaming, he began shuffling his deck of cards, feeling the thin card brush through his fingertips, the same way it did when he would deal the cards across the table to Archie, when they would pass the long summer evenings playing games, under the watchful gaze of the full moon. He closed his weary eyes and dreamt of Mr White, polishing silver and waiting tables of noblemen.

***

The nurses made their way around the library making sure each soldier had what they needed, before being released. Archie was sitting on the edge of his bed, the bedding neatly folded into a small square next to his pillow as he sit, his uniform pristinely clean, his buttons polished.

"So, off home then for a few days, Baxter?" Sergeant Parker asked, now with the renewed ability to walk properly on his own once more.

"Yes, Sir, I will be, although there's something I have to do first. I hope your son is alright, Sir," Archie said with compassion.

He had seen Sergeant Parker receive a few letters about his son's declining health over the past few months.

"Thank you, Baxter. Now, make the most of your time here, as you have seen, it is difficult to know if and when we will return," there was a sincere tone in Sergeant Parker's voice, as the two stood up and made their way to the entrance of the grand building.

Winter was on its way in and there was a great sense of change in the air. The leaves were settled in the ground, decomposing into the dirt, leaving behind a barren, crippled spine. The early morning frost was still leaving its remanence on the grass, the short shoots of green-capped off with frosty particles clinging on in the bitter air.

Archie took a deep breath and the air that escaped his lungs formed a visible plume in front of his face. He was ready to welcome the comforting heat of the fire in the living room when he arrived home, but as he had told Sergeant Parker, there was something he had to do first.

As he made his way out into the open streets, he saw the small rush of cars propel past him, it was a welcome sight. He flagged down a taxi that was trundling down a road, and when seeing it was unoccupied by a passenger, he made his way round to sit in the back of the car.

"Brancaster please, Sir," Archie said politely.

The taxi driver bowed his head and did as Archie requested, taking him to his desired destination. When Archie arrived, he did not know where he was, he knew where he wanted to end up, but he'd wanted to walk there, he wanted to know, what the area was like, he wanted to know, if it really was as easy to fall in love with, as he had been told.

He knew where he was going, 52 Mayfield Road. He had found the address easy to remember as his father was 52 and he used to love walking the fields at home in the month of May.

He asked an old man who he thought must be a local for directions, he was carrying a small carrier bag having just left the local greengrocers and was heading north down the main road. He'd run after him and asked him if he could point him in the direction of his desired address.

To his relief, the man was, in fact, a local, and lived only a few streets away from Mayfield Road. He used a series of hand signals and gestures to instruct Archie on the turns he needed to take, to end up where he was wanting to go. Archie then marched on ahead of the man and to his pleasant surprise realised it had only taken him about 20 minutes to reach the address.

He stood across the road from the house, looking up at it. It was a small, terraced house; the brick was dark and old. It appeared a Victorian house to Archie's fairly uneducated eye and there were a few children running up and down the road beating a hoop with a stick to keep it rolling.

Archie crossed over the road and stood in front of the door. He raised his fist to knock before pausing momentarily, he questioned whether it was the right thing to be doing. He battered away the seedling of doubt in his mind and gulped down any doubt before knocking several times on the door.

A fatigued-looking woman answered the door, an apron tied around her middle and her hands covered in flour. She rested the back of her hand on her forehead, catching falling beads of sweat. She looked at Archie, confused when she saw his uniform.

"Can I help you?" she asked perplexed.

"Good morning, I'm sorry to disturb you, Miss, I served with your son in the war, is your daughter home with you by chance?" Archie asked calmly, as the woman's knees slightly buckled when Archie gave the revelation of fighting with her son.

"Why?" she asked, her voice harsher this time.

Behind her, Archie noticed a small girl, no older than 10, cowering behind her mother's apron, hiding up against her side, peering one eye around the corner at Archie. Archie noticed her and knelt down on the concrete doorstep.

"Hello there," Archie uttered softly as to coax the child away from the shelter of her mother's pinafore. Archie looked down into the palm of his hand where a small, innocent face was looking up at him. He then looked back up into the eyes of the little girl who stood in the doorway, brushing herself past her mother to be in Archie's eyeline.

"You must be, Florence?" Archie asked with a welcoming smile. The little girl nodded in reply and a wash of calm fell upon Archie.

"I was a very good friend of your brother," Archie started, Florence's face lighting up with mention of her older brother.

"You know, he was the bravest man I've ever known, and he loved you very much," Archie said, feeling the emotion brewing in his stomach as he rested a hand on the little girl's shoulder.

"He wanted you to have this, he carried it with him every day, wherever we went. He was always telling stories about you, you were his favourite person in the whole world," Archie said smiling, as he saw Florence's eyes light up and her small dimples appear in her round cheeks as she beamed.

"Here, take this," Archie said, handing her the little photograph of herself which she grasped with both hands, holding it close to her heart, and swaying her body as she hugged it.

She ran inside with her photograph and Archie stood to his feet.

"What's your name?" The lady asked him, the tears still streaming down her cheeks.

"Archie, Miss," he replied, bowing his head and tipping his hat.

"Well, Archie, thank you very much for bringing that home to us. I cannot quite express it in words," she began sniffling again, trying to get through her sentence.

"Your son was a very brave man," Archie said, as his mind redrew images from the very first battle, he fought.

"It brings me comfort knowing my Arthur fought alongside such good men like yourself," she said, her voice full of gratitude. "Won't you come in for some tea?" she asked wiping the tears from her eyes.

"I won't, thank you; I have other places to be. But it was a pleasure to meet you," Archie nodded and fixed his hat back on his head.

"The pleasure is mine Archie," Arthur's mother stepped outside the doorstep to watch, as Archie made his way out of the small walkway, and down onto the pavement before he made his way along the road.

Archie felt a great sense of contentment as he marched proudly down the road. He felt he had done what Arthur would have wanted him to do, no matter how long it had taken him, he had found the purpose of why he took that photo from the stretcher bearer that night.

As he walked down that road, he felt ready to go back. He wanted to finish what he had started; he was ready to rejoin his friends and face whatever the world and the Germans would throw at them.

***

"Silent night, holy night, all—"

"Shut up Frank! It's not even December," Alan called out frustratedly.

120

"Yeah, I know that, but it nearly is. Besides, we only just survived all that, who knows, if I'll make it to Christmas, so, I'm starting early," Frank replied briskly.

Alan shook his head and made his way over to Henry who was leaning, back up against the trench wall, laughing at the conversation as it had unfolded.

The men had only just made their way back to the reserve line after a series of bloody, harrowing bouts with the Germans. They had pushed each other to the final round for the past four months and Henry, Frank and Alan spent every night questioning how they had survived.

The truth was, however, that they had. And for every day that they stared death in the face they had not succumbed to its willing grasp.

Henry was particularly buoyant since moving back to the reserve line as they had been expecting Archie's return any day now.

"Can you believe him? He does my head in," Alan muttered to Henry, as he walked past shaking his head ferociously, as Henry continued to be amused by the whole thing.

"No carolling in November, Howells," a deep voice descended on them from a crowd, the men were not too deterred by the calls and barely looked up to see whose voice it belonged to.

"Or at least wait for all the choir to be present," Archie's familiar tones broke through, as he emerged through a small crowd of men, to be face to face with the friends he had left behind, all those months ago.

The three men looked up, their eyes illuminating at the sight of Archie walking towards them, Alan letting out a triumphant cheer.

"Arch!" Henry exclaimed loudly running over to him and clawing him in for a hug, his hand repeatedly patting the back of Archie's neck as the two beamed at each other.

"We didn't know when you'd be back," Henry said, the distance between them close.

"We've been travelling back for a few days, Sergeant's been itching to get here ever since we got on the boat," Archie told him, as they embraced each other once more before breaking to allow Archie to share a tender welcoming moment with Alan and Frank.

"So, how's the shoulder then," Henry asked, as they sat in a circle around a table behind the reserve line.

Archie pulled the corner of his uniform down, just stretching it far enough to reveal a painful-looking scar, where his mangled flesh had been hastily reattached to his body.

"Proper scar that is," Frank said, his hands resting on his belly as he spoke.

"What was it like then? Being home, I mean," Alan asked, crossing his arms and leaning on the table looking at Archie intently.

"It was strange, it wasn't how I remembered it. It was quieter, it was like, like I got back there, and it felt like, I didn't belong. No one you passed in the streets knew what was going on."

"You spend your whole time out here longing to go home, and when I was, I spent the whole time waiting to get back out here," Archie said, as he watched the expressions on his friends' faces cool, and the atmosphere had changed.

"But I did see your mother," Archie said turning to Henry, "she told me to give you this," he continued standing up to give Henry a big, playful kiss on the cheek, which swiftly brought the merriment back to the afternoon.

"So, then, how's it been out here?" Archie asked as the men's faces changed once more, this time the scars and horror emerged from their faces.

"It's been tough," Alan started, Frank's gaze glued to the ground. "Four months, we've been at it, they told us the other day we'd won it, but hardly feels like a win when everyone you know gets mown down by the damn Germans," the anger grew in his voice the more he spoke, with his fist slamming against the table as he finished.

Henry reached out a consoling arm and Alan settled back down.

"There's been very little let-up. I never thought we'd make it out, we pushed them they pushed us, and by the end, no one had any energy left to push," Henry said, their battle-hardened faces smeared with speckles of dirt and mud that they had become too weary to remove.

There was a brief moment of silence, as all the men hung their heads low. Archie had witnessed horrors; he had lived what they had all lived to starve the last few months. He had seen how it had changed them.

When he had been around, no matter what they did and what they saw, they always made time for a joke or a game, and they would come back to the trenches to light up the mood and none of them knew whether the next day carried a German bullet with their name on it.

However, that seemed to have dissipated. As Archie sat looking around each of them, they barely had the strength to hold their heads up. He felt as though the things that had happened since he had left, had made them wish they had been killed, rather than be forced to live with the images of what they experienced haunting them forever.

"Right, so to celebrate my safe, albeit late return, should we go down to the local village, and have a drink?" Archie asked, noting a short time away from the sights and smells of the trenches could provide his friends with some well-needed relief.

Frank's eyebrows raised when he heard the word drink. "I'm in," he chimed as Alan nodded in agreement.

A lot of men had been out in the local villages the last few days to blur their memories of what had happened. There were many soldiers returning to the reserve lines at all hours of the day with a quiver in their legs as they tried to walk.

"I need to use the toilet, then we'll go," Henry said, as he made his way to the far end of the trench, where the latrines were located.

Archie followed him, telling the others he also needed to go.

"It's good to have you back," Henry said, holding Archie uncharacteristically tight around his shoulder, his hand clutching on, unwilling to let him go.

Archie could tell Henry had been waiting for something good to happen, as it felt like his world was crumbling, but his return had turned the tide of Henry's emotions.

"It's good to be back," Archie smiled. "So, still nothing?" He asked softly.

Henry shook his head, a resigned look on his face. "Nothing," he said bluntly.

"As I've said in my letters, I keep writing to her but nothing, I haven't heard anything since August. Before that, our letters were as regular as clockwork. Now, nothing," he said getting exasperated.

"Something will turn up, mate, it always does," Archie tried to give the only consoling words he knew how. Henry had given up hope on hearing from Annie by this point, but in his long absence, Archie still felt it right to offer his words of sympathy and support.

"It's fine, it's forgotten about, I've got to move on, I haven't got a choice. Let's go and have a drink, it's been a long time," he punched Archie's arm, laughing and cheering as he hopped onto the latrine chuckling.

They followed behind a large cluster of excitable men making their way into the nearest local village. They were cheering and chanting and talking about how they wanted to hurry if they wanted to make it before it opened. Archie didn't know what they were referring to.

He hadn't spent any time in the local villages when he was last there, as he'd been injured before he had the chance, and Henry and the others had received very little respite, and what they did receive they often felt too exhausted to march down into a foreign town.

As they made their way into the quaint village, the gas lamps were already lit, illuminating the paving below. It was no later than 04:30 p.m., but the sun had already begun its descent, and some of the taller buildings were already reducing the sun's pathway into the village. There were a few pubs and cafés scattered around, with a handful of soldiers drinking and dining in each.

The most populated area, however, was at the end of the main square. There was a tall narrow building, there was no sunlight shining down in front of it, it was set in a dark backdrop as the evening twilight sky created a navy-blue halo over the head of the building. The building had a few wide windows, each with thin, silk-looking curtains draped down, sheltering the activities of the rooms from the outside world.

They decided to get a closer look at what was going on, there was a line of about 20 men waiting impatiently outside the front door. As they approached, they saw an older woman standing outside. She seemed fierce and was shouting in French.

Whoever she was, Archie thought, *she clearly owned that building.* She was dressed in a long flowing dress, Archie thought it looked rather scruffy, but the woman seemed very proud of it, thinking it flaunted some kind of wealth that clearly the uneducated eye of Archie could not see.

"What are you all waiting for?" Alan asked one of the men in the queue, rubbing his hands together to stay warm.

"Waiting for it to open course," the man looked down at his watch. "Only five more minutes by my watch. Apparently, there's a new girl, only been here a few days and word have it, all the men want a go with her, but they say she's hard to get, only saved for the best, if you know what I mean," the man joked crudely nudging Alan's side.

He did not know what he meant, none of them really did.

However, they had become worldly enough to work out they were standing in line for a brothel. They had no desire or interest in staying where they were, and Frank had begun complaining about his stomach feeling so empty that he was on the verge of collapsing. The wafting smells of pork chops were drawing Frank in the opposite direction, and Alan and Archie began following him.

As they began to turn away a roar erupted from the men in the queue as the woman opened the door and a series of women walked out of the door to stand alongside the older lady. Their ages varied, some were young, and some were old, but they were all dressed in minimal clothing, especially given the cold months, and they all looked exhausted from just walking a few short steps.

"Now for our latest, most valuable new girl," the woman in charge, Madame Rusé called out, waving her hands around flamboyantly, as a timid younger woman made her way out of the building, her head hung low, her brown curly hair covering her eyes.

Archie and the others had their heads reared over to see what all the commotion was about as they made their way to get some food when Henry stopped dead in his tracks. His eyes widened and his mouth dropped. Archie noticed why Henry had stopped and a look of shock broke out on his face too.

"Is that—"

"Annie," Henry mumbled at the end of Archie's question, as he could not quite believe his eyes.

Henry found his legs turn direction and made his way through the rabble of desperate men.

"Henry, wait," Archie called out, but he'd already lost himself in the crowd, trying to break his way through.

"Oi mate, there's a queue here, wait your turn," Henry was met with a chorus of anger-filled shouts as he pushed his way past the tongue-wagging men, and all of a sudden, he found himself at the front of the queue.

"Annie?" this time the word left his mouth a bit louder than it did the first time.

He made his way towards the line of women before their leader stepped out in front of him and raised her hand to his face.

"Oh, we have an eager one," Madame Rusé shouted, a ferocity in her voice, as Henry tried to push past her.

"Money," she shouted, grabbing his arm and swinging him back in front of her.

Her eyes met Henry's with a fire inside them, her thin eyebrows sharply pointing down at him.

He clutched at the small amount of money he had and forced it into the woman's hand before walking past her and making his way closer to the girl he was after.

"It'll be more for her," she called out her latest demand with a sly smile on her face.

"That's all I've got!" Henry snapped at her, his fists closing in frustration.

Just then, there was a clambering of metal hitting the cold stone ground. Henry and the woman turned to see what it was. Archie was throwing down all the coins he had to make up the extra money Henry would need to be able to see and speak to Annie if it was indeed her.

Archie looked indignantly at Madame Rusé as she stood speechless as the money arrived at her feet. Henry's stare met Archie's and he nodded at him, Archie replicating it, giving him the nod of reassurance, that it was alright.

"Annie," Henry repeated for a third time, this time, in front of the girl's face, shaking her shoulders.

She stood her head hung low. She lifted her head slowly, and her eyes looked vacant at first. As though she had blocked out all that was going on, as though she was so consumed within herself, that she did not pay attention to the hordes of men swarming around her.

As she met Henry's frantic gaze, her eyes widened. She could not believe what she was seeing. Her eyes welled up with tears, they sat looming on the edge of her eyelids, mustering all the strength she could to fight them back.

"H-Henry," she stuttered, the commotion occurring was overwhelming her.

"Come with me," Henry said, leading her by the arm inside, finding a spare unoccupied room, which he thrust her inside, before turning to lock the door behind him.

He turned back to her, and for a split second, they stood staring at each other, reassuring themselves that it was real life and not a fantastical dream. Henry closed the gap towards her, reaching down for her hands and interlocking his fingers in hers.

"Annie," the words dropped quietly from his mouth, he seemed unable to say anything else but the two fell into each other's arms, holding each other and the pair of them shedding tears that trailed down their cheeks.

"What are you doing here?" he asked turning a curly strand of hair behind her ear.

The jubilant expression on Annie's face quickly turned to one of fear and trepidation. Henry could read from her face she was concealing something from him, something she was afraid to say.

"Henry, I must show you something," she uttered, her voice quaking as she spoke. Henry nodded nervously, not knowing what was in store for him to see.

Annie clutched onto the corners of her long, flowing satin dress. She pulled it just above her knees before pausing and taking a deep breath.

Her breathing stuttered as she inhaled before she continued to raise the dress over her waist, stopping just below her chest. As she did so, Henry noticed a round bulge in her stomach. He stared at it, then he looked up into her eyes and back down to her stomach.

"Are you…?" he started; the words exhaled out rather than spoken.

"I'm pregnant," she spoke, this said with a relative calmness.

Henry stepped back, grabbing onto the edge of a conveniently placed chest of draws by the door, to stop him from falling over.

"W-when?" he asked, stumbling over his words as he had done his feet just moments earlier.

"June," she answered swiftly.

Henry processed the information slowly, taking his time to cast his mind back over the preceding months. *June,* he thought to himself, *they were seeing each other in June. Had she been seeing someone else? Was this other person the reason she disappeared and stopped sending him letters?*

The look on his face turned to one of anger, he had resigned himself to the idea, that she had been seeing someone else at the same time, that the feelings they spoke of, that they wrote about, she had fabricated all of them. His eyes narrowed as he looked at her.

"How did this happen? Who? How?" he asked desperately, unable to fathom this new information.

"Henry," she started slowly. "It's yours," her words cut through the silent room.

Henry stumbled back once more, grateful for the presence of the chest of draws. His jaw dropped and his hand clutching his chin was the only thing stopping it from falling to the floor. He started panting, his eyes swirling around him, and his head spinning.

"How? How? Why didn't you tell me? June?" he felt as though he had stepped into an alternate universe where he had slipped into the place of another man's life.

He could not comprehend the information he had just been told. Only a few minutes ago he was outside, his lungs filled with the cold November air, on his way to watch Frank fill his face with pork.

"It happened in June; I did not find out for a couple of weeks, but I did not want to tell you until I knew for certain. And even then, I did not know if I should tell you, what if you were killed?" Annie spoke hurriedly as though unloading information she had concealed for a long time.

"So, you didn't think to tell me? You thought you'd just leave instead, and never speak to me again?" Henry was still frustrated, the second he saw Annie, he wanted to make sure she was alright.

Then he wanted to find out why she left. He had already found out far more than he had bargained for and still didn't have the answer to his original question.

"I didn't just leave you, it wasn't like that, it was not my choice," Annie answered, a desperation in her voice.

"Well, who's choice was it then?" Henry replied hastily, an anger in his.

"My father was killed!" she yelled, silencing Henry and bringing a tear to her eye.

"My father was killed. We found out at the beginning of August. The letter came, he had been discovered by a group of soldiers in a forest. He was killed alongside everyone he fought with. When we found out it shattered my mother, it shattered us all."

"I tried to comfort her, but I could not, she could not afford to look after us both on her own, and by that point, it became clear that I was pregnant. When she found out, she cast me out of my own home, saying she could not look after me and I would have to fend for myself."

"I had nowhere to go, I was alone. So, I did the only thing I could think of. I tried to find you. I only knew you were near the River Somme, so I made my way, doing any job I could do on the way. It took me a long time and I'm not proud of a lot of what I've had to do to get here."

"But when I arrived here, a lot of British soldiers started coming by. I heard some of the terrible stories and had lost nearly all hope you had survived, until tonight," Annie's eyes were full of tears.

"Why did you never write?" Henry asked, his voice had softened.

"I had no means of writing to you; I was constantly on the move. I thought it was quicker and easier for me to get to where I thought you were, as fast as possible, and pray to God, I found you."

"The closer I got to the Somme, the worse the stories got, then, I suppose, I feared you must be dead, so, I wanted to save myself the heartbreak of sending a letter for you to just not reply and for me to know, you had been killed."

"In not writing to you, I could always keep a little bit of hope alive," by now the tears had begun rolling down her cheeks as she spoke, Henry's eyes reciprocating the action as he listened.

He wanted to be upset with her for not trying to write to him, but he could not find it within him. He had seen the horrors; he did not need to know the stories of them. He understood why she did, what she did, and he more than anyone wanted to bury the memories of what he had seen and the way he had fought.

He had no words to say, for months, he had longed for the opportunity to see her face once more and there she was sitting on the edge of the bed in front of him, bearing his child. He said nothing, but, walked slowly over to her and sunk to his knees. He picked up her soft, delicate hands and kissed them firmly before hugging her tightly. He hugged her, as though he would never hug again, reluctant to let her go, even to breathe.

"We're having a baby," he mumbled his eyes meeting hers.

Her big, dark eyes shone in the flicker of the candlelit room as the light reflected off the tears in her eyes. She smiled, and then they both broke out into a small laugh. The reality of what was happening only became apparent to both of them as they spoke it to each other.

"I wonder, what they're doing," Arthur joked as the three of them sat round a small, crowded table, Frank delving into a thick pork chop.

Frank raised his eyebrows promiscuously a couple of times, forcing a childish laugh out of Alan, and even Archie succumbed to a little chuckle.

"I wonder when they'll be out," Alan asked seriously, looking down at his watch to check how long they'd been sitting around the table.

Archie remained silent; his eyes fixed firmly on the door of the brothel, waiting for Henry to make his way out. He was not imagining what was going on within the walls of the building, but he imagined it must have been Annie standing there, otherwise, he was sure Henry would have turned right back around.

The evening was growing old, and the temperature was dropping. The middle of the street running through the square was dark, the illumination of the gas lamps on the edge of the pavement had not reached the middle of the road. The area where they were seated outside was well-lit, and Archie could see a flurry of stars overhead as he looked out into the calmness of the night.

He knew they would have to be making their way back before it was too late. The wind was picking up with a bitter bite, he pulled the cuffs of his sleeves over his hands to allow the blood flow to return to his freezing fingers.

Their hot mugs of coffee did not take long to be defeated by the elements and were not hot for very long. Archie had already ordered two and very little of the dark liquid had entered his system, at the temperature it was intended to be.

As he gazed around him, watching the world roll by, it surprised him how much his life had changed at war. *When he left over two years ago,* he had thought, *he was embarking on an adventure, one that may encounter some rogue pirate-like obstacles, but nothing too dangerous.* He was hoping it would open up new pathways for him in life.

Sitting there that night, however, he thought the only path in life he saw while being at war was, the path to the end of life. He had seen more men in the trenches than he'd ever seen in his life before joining the war, and nearly all of whom he only saw once. He thought about how war had changed him. When he had been sent home, he did not feel at home, he felt no one there could understand what he had seen.

His parents were delighted to see him of course, and concerned for his safety, but they never asked how he was or what he had seen or done. Archie had left home a boy, whose head was too full of dreams for his own good. He had not only become a man, but he had become so accustomed to death in a way that no man or human could ever comprehend.

He had faced such levels of murder and extermination it could only conceivably have been the work of monsters. *What he had witnessed had been no level of humanity, there had been no regard for life, if there was a God,* Archie thought, *then no man on these battlefields would be going to heaven.* It made him think, *If the acts committed by all men had shown them to be bestial in their nature, did that make him more beast than man?*

If he could kill with no remorse, if he could become immune to the cries of his fellow countrymen, what kind of man was he? How could he show his face in Mr Humphrey's garden again? How could he hope to have civilised conversations with civilised gentlemen after the war, knowing he had partaken in the killings and slaughter of a nation, even if, some lords and noblemen did perceive them to be an enemy of the country?

Archie shifted his focus back to the large oak door smeared in red paint as he anticipated Henry's return. The sound of Frank's loud chewing, as his teeth crunched through the tough fat around the pork chop drilled deep into Alan's brain as he became impatient of the mind-numbing wait for Henry's return.

"Listen, you will not work here anymore. I'll get you out of this place," Henry told Annie looking deep into her eyes.

"How?" she asked, nervousness in her voice as she thought about the treatment of Madame Rusé.

Henry looked around, hoping for inspiration from the minimalistic-designed room.

"The café. Across the road. Me and my friends were about to eat there. I'll speak to the owner there try and get you a job, put you up somewhere here for a short time, just until the end of the war. Somewhere, I can come back to visit you until we can be together, properly," Henry said softly with a smile.

Annie's eyes began welling up, not more than an hour ago, had she believed Henry to be dead. She had resigned herself to the fate of the nightmare she was currently living. Now, Henry had returned, filling her heart with hope.

"Listen, you leave it with me. I'll sort something out and I'll be back tomorrow. For now, say, you're too unwell to be seen," Henry spoke softly, in the charming way he had done the first time they met all those months ago.

He placed a soft kiss on her plump cheek before leaving the room, gently closing the door behind him and making his way out of the building, tugging at his uniform to make him appear dishevelled. He gave Madame Rusé a scolding stare as he passed her at the entrance to the brothel before being hit by the cool air of the night on his face.

"There," Archie said sharply, seeing Henry emerge from the darkness of the dingy doorway.

Archie and Alan made their way swiftly over to him, Frank still indulging in the few straggling chips on his plate.

"Was it her?" Alan asked before they'd even reached Henry and before Archie had time to draw breath.

Henry nodded as he joined in stride with his two friends, breaking them apart and walking in the middle. Archie looked at him silently, the simplicity of their exchanged glance reassured him, that, it had all gone well. They made their way over to the table where Frank was yet to look up and Alan went to pull over a seat for Henry.

"I need to tell you something, later," Henry whispered to Archie for the brief moment they were out of everyone's earshot.

Archie nodded and patted Henry on the back before they sat down, eager to find out what had happened.

"So, tell us everything," Alan said with a broad grin on his face as he slumped back into his chair, folding his arms.

"Well," Henry started slowly. "It is her. Her father did die, he was killed, his whole unit wiped out," the faces of the rest of the men had darkened, and the original excitement in their eyes fizzled out as the realities of war could not even escape any romantic story.

"Her mother couldn't cope with her, and her brother on her own, so as the oldest, she was forced out of her home, to fend for herself. She didn't know what to do and so she knew I, we, were here around the River Somme, so she just made her way down until she got here," Henry explained, not lying to them, just eliminating important parts of the story.

"Why did she not write to you?" Archie asked sympathetically thinking of his best friend.

"She was afraid, I wouldn't reply. She began hearing all the horror stories coming out of where we were and she wanted to save herself the upset of me, not writing back," he explained as all the men hung their heads in reflection.

"How did she end up working there?" Alan asked, unlike most of the men he served with, he detested the idea of such a place.

"Only place offering work she had to take, what she could get," Henry explained, as Frank licked the plate clean of any mustard and sauces left behind.

"You gonna go back and see her again?" Alan asked quickly, his accent sometimes making it hard to follow, what he says when he talks so fast.

"Any time we get while we're here for a few days, I'll make sure she can write to me, wherever we go," Henry nodded as he spoke, his eyes then darting to Frank showing he had finished talking about it.

"If you're done, we should be heading back, don't want you all getting into trouble," Henry added, as he pushed himself up from his chair.

The other three mirrored his actions and followed. They all made their way round to the front of the café.

"I just need to pop in to use their toilet, Arch, you wait up for me, and you two make your way back before the Sarge finds out you've been gone for too long," Henry called out, as Alan and Frank nodded and set off, Frank's hands above his head to allow his airways to open up through his fattening body.

Archie pulled up a chair and waited for Henry who disappeared inside.

"Excuse me, Madam," Henry started, getting the attention of the lady in charge behind the counter.

"Do you speak English?" he asked.

"I do, how may I help you?" she replied with a delicate, gentle smile and rested her hands on the counter.

She must have been easily in her 50s; she was a slight woman with a kind face as she looked at Henry.

"My friend, well my girlfriend, sort of, you see, she's just started working across the road at the…at the brothel," Henry tried to speak swiftly, so as to, not allow the café owner to dwell on the mention of the brothel.

"She told me today she is almost six months pregnant. I'm on the front-line and, so, I can't look after her. But then Madame, as I'm sure you can understand, I cannot have her stay there."

"I suppose, what I'm asking is, if there is any possibility, she could come and work here for you. Wait tables, pour drinks, anything small, she won't take much money, I can give you what I have," as Henry spoke his words became more pleading in their nature.

He watched as the woman's expression softened further, her eyes showed compassion and tenderness.

"My daughter died, but a few months ago," the woman started catching Henry, slightly off guard. "She was taken ill, the man she loved died at the war, heartbreak it was, I think, that killed her. I can see you are a good man Monsieur—" she said waiting.

"Longley, Henry Longley," he replied on cue.

"You seem a good man, Henry Longley. I live in the rooms above the café. My daughter's room is available. If your friend or girlfriend," she said with a coy, sarcastic wink at Henry which made him chuckle.

"If she needs a place to stay, she is welcome there. However, I do not make much money, if she works hard for me, she can have the room, she will pay no rent, and have her meals cooked for her. But she will receive no wages, just a roof, and care," she explained her terms to Henry, but they were far more than, he was hoping for.

"Thank you, Madame—" Henry, this time hoping to learn the name of his new acquaintance.

"Soignant. Madame Soignant,"

"Well, Madame Soignant, that is quite amazing thank you. Tomorrow afternoon, I shall return, fetch her, and bring her to you. May I hug you?" Henry found himself asking the intimate question and only realised the words that had left his mouth when it was too late.

The lady smiled, she could read the purity of Henry's heart and embraced him before they said their farewells and Henry returned outside to the patiently waiting Archie.

"You, take your time," Archie said as he heard Henry's footsteps approaching him.

"Long story," Henry replied shortly as the two of them got up to walk away.

"So, what is it, you wanted to talk about?" Archie asked, intrigued.

"Where do I start?" Henry asked himself audibly. "Well, everything I told you and the guys is true," Henry added covering his tracks.

"But—" Archie said, anticipating a twist in the tale.

"You see the thing is, when I found her and we sat down, she told me…she said, she's pregnant," Henry uttered, his words quieter at the end.

"What!" Archie exclaimed loudly, turning his head back to the brothel, as they walked further away.

"Pregnant, how? Are you alright?" Archie asked with a note of anger in his voice, presuming it had been some new lover.

"Well, that's the thing," Henry started, as the penny finally dropped in Archie's head and his eyes turned to fix on Henry.

"She's pregnant with my baby," Henry announced.

For a moment, Archie was speechless, he knew not what to say and couldn't even muster a grunt or gesture in response. He stopped still, speechless.

"This is the part where you say congratu—"

"Congratulations," Archie mumbled, as he pulled Henry in tightly for a hug. He still could not quite come to terms with the discovery.

"Are you ready for that?" Archie asked, the fog of shock clearing to a sky of realisation.

"What do you mean?" Henry asked perplexed.

"Well, you're 19 years old, you're at war, not to mention when this is all done, you live in different countries," Archie said, his words coming from a caring place, but they did not reach Henry's ears in a caring manner.

"This wasn't my choice, Arch, I had no say in this. I didn't want that to be the way things are, but it is the way things are. I've got to man up and deal with it and what happens later we'll deal with it when we get to it," Henry replied defensively.

"Well, aren't you scared?" Archie asked him sincerely.

"I dunno, I haven't really thought of it like that. We're out there, she's back here. I'm not really gonna be a father, not while there's a war still going on," Henry answered.

His words made sense. Though they showed his youthful naivety to the situation, it could not be argued there was truth behind what he said. He could not stay with Annie while she had a baby, that was not an option. He could barely let his mind run away with the idea when all that was ahead of him appeared to be endless fighting.

"What about Annie?" Archie asked, their attentions shifting. "Surely she can't raise a child in a brothel?"

"That's where the toilet trip comes in. I've arranged a room and a job for her with the owner of the café. It'll be a poor way of life, but it still is a way of life, not like she'll get in there," Henry responded, Archie could tell his care for the girl.

The way he had gone to all this trouble, he could tell she was far more than a way to pass the time at war.

"Will you tell the others?"

"Not yet."

"Why not?"

"I don't want them to know until everything's alright, you know settled, the baby is here and everything. Until then, who knows, what could happen," Henry said, clearly calculating the situation in his head.

"Well, listen," Archie started. "You're my best mate, you always will be. And I'm happy for you, I really am. Just remember, you're not on your own alright," Archie smiled as he spoke, comforting Henry with his unwavering presence and support.

Henry said nothing, he just slung his arm around Archie's shoulder and matched his stride with his own.

"Come on, let's get you back," Archie said leading them back down the path to the trench and the hubbub of the life he had just returned to.

As sure as he had given his word, Henry returned the following afternoon, while the rest of the men had a few free hours to themselves after the morning's rituals were conducted. He arrived at the café first, making sure everything was still in place with Madame Soignant.

When she gave him her green light of assurance, he made his way to the brothel where he knocked on the door several times. At first, his attempts were to no avail. However, after a few more tries, the blundering, angry face of Madame Rusé appeared at the door. She insisted Henry must leave, but he stood his ground firmly, unwilling to move without Annie.

Madame Rusé grew impatient and the volume of her voice rose, drawing attention from the girls on the other side of the doors in the brothel. Annie heard the commotion and made her way out to the front of the building where Madame Rusé was berating Henry.

Annie instructed Madame Rusé, that whether she approved or not she was refusing to work for her anymore. The revelation came as a scolding shock to her boss, who latched onto her arm, not willing to let Annie pass. Henry pushed Rusé away and swiftly swooped in, scooping Annie's body away from the sprawling grasp of the cruel owner.

They escaped across the open plains of the courtyard and made their way to the café.

"Listen," Henry started, taking Annie's hand in his. "I have spoken to the owner of this café, and she is willing to give you a spare room above," Henry said motioning with his head to the open windows, above the café.

"She gave me her word, you would be well looked after, a shelter and food provided for you at no extra cost. There will be no wages, but that is because everything you need, she will provide."

"This way you have somewhere to live, somewhere safe, and somewhere you can write to me," Henry uttered calmly, as Annie was still shaking from their escapade with Madame Rusé.

She planted a soft kiss on his lips and pressed her small fingers against his rough cheek.

"Thank you, Henry," she whispered, a tear or two crowning in the corner of her eye. "You must promise you will come back to me, even if you move on you must come back," she held his hands tight in hers, until he gave her as much assurance as he could.

With that, he led her into the café introduced her to Madame Soignant, and settled her into a small, cosy bedroom on the floor above, where you could hear the whir of the oven below.

After an hour or two spent together, Henry kissed Annie delicately and made his way back through the now familiar track, out of the village back, to the trenches. Winter was creeping in on them and the new year was not far away. Henry knew it would bring about a year of great change in his personal life, and he had only one goal going into it: to stay alive.

***

December soon fell upon them and with it, they descended on a new corner of the scorched battlefield. The men had been moved once more to provide aid in the depths of wintery fighting, meaning Henry was once again reliant on letters from Annie to update him on the latest news, regarding her new life and the developing pregnancy.

The harshness of the winter months showed itself on the faces and in the characters of the soldiers. The chilling temperatures restricted their bodies to very little sleep, as the depths of the night were often filled with small huddles of men grouping together, hoping their collective breath would provide some warm release to the whipping winds.

Not long after they arrived, Archie saw a man peeling off his boot and sock, revealing a harrowing, black deformity where his foot had once been. From the discoloured details that he could make out, the poor man had already succumbed multiple toes to the stinging weather conditions.

Since that day, he had witnessed more and more people taking the lighter decision of removing their own fingers and toes. One evening, he was on sentry duty, when he heard a man whimpering behind him. He was shaking his hand vigorously, supporting it with his other, tears streaming down his cheeks, but the noise of his crying was drowned out by the incessant shivering whimper.

Archie turned around to see what was going on, and to his horror, the man was removing two of his own fingers which had turned somewhat a navy-blue colour, no doubt on their way to the deathly black he had also seen. He watched the man slice through his own fingers, as though, he was chopping carrots for a stew.

To Archie's surprise, the whimpering subsided when the fingers were lying motionless in the thick layers of mud and grime below their feet, the pain of them still being attached to the man's hand was clearly considerably worse than the pain of their absence.

Warm meals, such as stews and soups were hard to come by, and Archie often found that, if a small metal dish of food was intended to reach him hot, by the time the fork entered his mouth, the food had too fallen victim to the cruel climate.

"I'm so cold, I could cry," Frank uttered, one night as they all sat in a small huddle talking through the shuddering of their lips.

"I'd take the shells and bombs any day over this," Alan chimed, punching the wall next to him, that now, instead of having the consistency of dirt and earth, was more that of a brick wall.

It was Christmas Eve, and as far as high spirits in the trenches go, they were approaching the time when spirits would often be as high as possible. A man had come round earlier that evening handing out parcels from home for all the troops lucky enough to receive home comforts.

Archie had received a small box but tucked it inside his kit bag for the following day, and Henry had done the same. In the same vein, as the previous year, Alan had not received anything from his family, given the fact, that he left home before the war and had only written to his mother at best twice across the months they had been there.

Last year, Frank had received a parcel from his family, containing a little bag of nuts with a little box of candied fruits. Laying neatly on top of the parcel was a folded knitted scarf. He prided himself on telling the rest of the group, how he had received the same Christmas presents from his family for all the years he could remember, and he made very clear the joy he felt, that they had continued the tradition while he was away fighting.

This year, however, no parcel arrived. When Archie and Henry received theirs, he could not hide the disappointment that covered his face when the delivery man bypassed him completely. He had thought it odd for some time, how the once frequent letters from his family had started to dry up the longer, he was away. He felt as though they had become acceptant of the fate, that befell many of his comrades, and they had already begun blotching him out of their lives.

Archie could see the hurt in Frank's eyes and quickly concealed his parcel to ensure conversation could remain undeterred by the deliveries. Archie could guess the contents of the parcel from his parents.

He expected it to be the same as last year, partly as there were only so many items they could send out to the front-line, but also because his mother had heavily hinted at what would be arriving for him. His Christmas delivery last year consisted of a couple of bars of soap, a striped handkerchief, and a neatly decorated box of marzipan fruits.

"Hey, look at that, five minutes until Christmas," Alan said, as he brandished his watch to show everyone the slowly ticking time.

It appeared, that even the second hand was becoming frozen in its tracks, as it struggled to do its usual circuit around the face of the clock.

"All I want is a bit of warmth," Henry said, his head bowed low, his hands frantically rubbing the top of his head hoping to generate some heat from the friction.

"You, spoken to Annie? Is she doing anything tomorrow?" Alan asked, trying to steer the conversation away from the weather.

"Just dinner with the woman who owns the café I think, she hasn't heard from her mum since all this happened anyway, so, she's certainly not going back there," Henry answered, as his voice became smoother and less stuttered when speaking about Annie.

"Nothing from her mum on Christmas?" Alan poked Frank, looking away knowing he too had heard nothing from his mother.

"Why would she? She doesn't know where Annie is, she hasn't told her. It'll just be a quiet meal, but at least they'll be in the warm," Henry said, as all their minds wandered to the thought of an open fire, crackling and flirting with them as its flames danced around.

"Well, Happy Christmas, lads!" Alan exclaimed, looking down at his watch to see the time tick past midnight. All the men cheered softly and embraced each other, mainly to try and heat their bodies against one another.

"Happy bloody Christmas," Frank said shuddering, his lips turning a vicious shade of purple. "I just wish, I could escape this bloody wind," his voice turning into more of a shout as the frustration broke through.

"The sandbag toilet area," Archie started, "round the corner, there's a couple of sandbag cubicles, if Alan goes with you, you can have a chat, the sandbags block out the wind, it's warmer than it is here," Archie said, subtly raising his eyebrows at Alan he took the hint and slowly rose to his feet, his legs numb below him as he dragged Frank round the corner, his body still doubled over, his joints almost frozen in place.

"I've got a little something for, you," Archie said, turning his back to Henry to retrieve his kitbag.

"Now it's only something small, but I found it in a small shop, one day when I came to the village with you, when you went to see Annie," Archie continued, reaching his hand inside the bag, pulling out a small, delicate baby's rattle.

It had a small, light, wooden circle to hold, with an ornately designed topper with swirling metal shapes to decorate. On the side, were two small bells hanging down by a small hook, and when Archie moved the handle side to side, they collided with the metal topper creating a gentle ringing noise.

Henry watched as Archie carefully handed him the small object, with a kind smile across his face. Henry found himself lost for words, taking the dainty rattle in the palm of his hand and trailing his finger over the elegant detailing.

"Thank you," he softly uttered to Archie before placing a firm hand on his shoulder, as the two exchanged a tender hug.

Archie had struggled with the speed at which life was accelerating around him. While in the trenches, he felt like a lifetime passed by every day, but when he stepped away from the front-line, watching the lives of his friends unfold, watching Henry's life unfold, the cosy, comforting thoughts of Christmas only a few years ago seemed almost unfathomable to him now.

He had not been the most welcoming to Henry's revelation for quite some time, after he first found out. It took some time for him to realise, that his primary function was to be there, to support Henry, to be a brother to him in all the ways, he could. He could not give him everything in life, nor could he be the only person he turned to.

Coming from the sheltered life they had lived up, until the point of war, they had always only had each other. The emergence of Annie had been an unexpected shock along the way, but he had largely dismissed that as a distraction from the turmoil of war, one he could not blame him for.

However, the expectant arrival of Henry's child was something he had never anticipated, and at first, he thought his place in Henry's life was slowly slipping away; however, after a period of watching the way he was, the way he was with Annie, Archie realised that he was not being replaced by Annie or anyone else for that matter, rather his job was to be there alongside the others, and if he was going to be there every step of the way, he wanted Henry to know that too.

"Thank you," Henry said again, as they broke free from the hug.

As Henry stared down at the small innocent object in his hand he felt awash with fear and panic. This tiny, innocuous item represented the biggest change that was possible in human life. He was only 19 and on top of that, every day he had to be careful not to lose his own life, let alone look after another.

However, as his eyes glazed over the dainty woodwork on the handle, he was reminded that as long as he had Archie by his side, he would not then truly be alone. If he had him there, alongside him in not just the trenches but in life then the deep-rooted feeling of trepidation, simply evaporated out of him, and a feeling of excitement took its place.

An excitement for the pair of them to do whatever it takes, to get out of the Godforsaken cesspit they were sitting in, to take his newfound family back to Cromer, where they could live with his mother and sister while he returned to work for Mr White, a war hero.

Thoughts of home flogged both their brains torturously as they looked up to the Christmas night sky, the stars dancing and twinkling above them. The light of the stars filling the sky innocently with its purity, but what it concealed, the harsh bitterness of the world below and the numbing temperatures that penetrated them, made their harsh reality sting them. The pair of them longed for the sputtering sounds of the fire or a warm Christmas dinner meticulously prepared by Archie's mum.

As they sat, their bottoms firmly frozen in place, Sergeant Parker made his way towards them with two metal dishes in his hand.

"Where are the other two?" he asked them delicately, as Henry and Archie struggled to get to their feet.

"Trying to get warm through the cover of sandbags by the lavatory," Archie chimed mockingly, as the three men shared a snigger.

Since their escapades together in England, Archie felt a newfound connection to Sergeant Parker, he felt he could talk to him as a man, not just as a superior.

"Well, I managed to snag a couple of slices of Christmas pudding from the officers up on the reserve line, scoff it down before the others return," Sergeant

Parker said, raising his eyebrows before turning back to turn the corner out of sight.

"Sir," Archie called out after him, "Any more news on your son?" he asked Sergeant Parker, stopping him firmly in his tracks as his sleeve trailed across his face. He turned back to face Archie.

"Not looking good, I'm afraid, but we can pray for a Christmas miracle," he said, a sombre tone in his voice.

He walked off into the distance before Archie could say anymore.

Archie explained to Henry all about the detailed, private conversations they had while in the convalescent home as they ravaged down the Christmas pudding, discarding the metal dishes in a small cavity in the wall behind where they were sitting, as to not arouse suspicion when the other two made it back.

Archie opened his eyes. It was morning. At some point, he had not known when, but he had clearly found himself slumped back against the trench wall and passed out. As he blinked his eyes several times to adjust to his surroundings, he looked to his left where Henry was in a deep sleep, his helmet over his face, a small and muffled snore escaping from within. When he looked ahead of him, Alan and Frank were locked in a deep conversation, though no louder than a whisper as to avoid waking the others sleeping around them.

It's Christmas, Archie thought. He adjusted his position on the small fire step where he was sitting, his legs numb and frozen together. He stretched them as far as he could, allowing his icy blood to coarse through his veins to the tips of his toes to regain some movement. He looked up, slowly tilting his head back against the trench wall.

It was an uncharacteristically sunny, Christmas morning. However, the sun could not prove much of a distraction to the chilling temperatures, that run underneath it. The wind battered down onto his face as he stared up at the sky.

There had clearly been heavy snow flurries overnight, as the usual blood bath scene of no man's land ahead of him was masked by a thin sheet of white. The wind was kicking it up and settling it all over, thinly burying some unfortunate soul in a temporary, shallow grave.

It was fitting though, Archie thought, *that on Christmas of all days, the day of innocence and purity, the horrors that usually greeted his eyes every morning as the sun rose, were today wiped from existence, replaced with a pure white snow, uncorrupted by the oozing blood of a wounded soldier.*

As much as it distracted from what lay below, Archie's memory was not erased. He still knew that in a day or two, you could look out of a periscope and see the blank stare of lifeless eyes glaring back at you. He sat there thinking of Arthur, as he had done the previous year, and all the other fallen comrades he had lost, who had not welcomed on Christ's latest birthday.

He thought of the disconsolate men who wept for their mothers as they lay with a bullet through their liver or the cries of brothers and cousins watching their family fall by their side.

As his mind meandered down the pathway of reflection, he felt a knock against his knees.

"Happy Christmas, mate," Henry grumbled, stretching as Archie had done moments earlier. Archie smiled and returned the pleasantries.

"Happy Christmas, boys," Alan chimed, shaking the hand of each of his friends firmly and affectionately.

"Another one in the trenches," Frank chimed, rolling his eyes as he rubbed his hands together for warmth.

"And I'm sure, it'll be the last," Henry said to Frank, patting his shoulder as he went on the search for any hot tea to share.

"Go on then, open your package from home," Alan nodded to Archie as he smirked, pulled the parcel out from his kitbag, tore the string from the brown paper, and began unfurling the wrapping.

"Woah, without me," Henry said, returning with no avail.

Archie chuckled before revealing the presents he had expected. Neatly folded on top of the parcel was a small, chequered handkerchief. It had blue and red squares interlocking with one another and was the perfect size to slide inside his pocket.

There were two small bars of rose-scented soap, that Henry quickly snatched from him to allow the fresh aroma to fill his nostrils, for the comfort of home smells, passing it to the other two, to share the same sensation.

"Anyone up for a marzipan fruit?" Archie asked, revealing the last item in the paper.

They all nodded excitedly and spent the next hour sampling the delicacy while in deep conversation about their respective Christmases at home.

Archie found that many conversations in the trenches occurred more than once, such as ways of celebrating Christmases or birthdays, or favourite meals or days out.

At first, he was confused, as to why everyone appeared to have such a short memory, but then he began to realise, by this point, they could probably almost recite every word of the way their friends lived their lives before the war, but it lifted their spirits. It took them back to the safety of their own homes, and their own lives. It made them feel peaceful and distracted them from what was really going on.

There was very little to do on Christmas Day as it happened. They conducted the daily chores they would normally do, but they felt in no mood to attack the Germans, and thankfully they shared the same feelings.

In the evening, a small chorus of, 'God rest ye little gentleman', broke out, unsurprisingly led by Frank, in which the whole line got involved, and there was some leftover rum from the morning rum ration that was making its way around, making the gentlemen in the trench quite merry indeed.

9

The memory of the warming home comforts that had been brought by the Christmas celebration had soon become a distant memory. The vicious clutches of the biting weather had a grasp on them that they could not shake. Archie felt as though he had seen more arms and legs lost to the cold than to artillery since the turn of the year.

Two months had passed, and the fighting, much like the weather, had grown in its incessant cruelty. New technology and new methods of mechanised butchering had been brought in by both sides to hurry the indiscriminate slaughter on the front. The aggressive winds and relentless icy temperatures meant the only thing the men could focus on was giving their bodies enough warmth to function through another day of life.

The engagements they'd had with the Germans in the opening two months of the year, had at least provided them with a rush of adrenalin, that took over their mind, until they were either killed or returned to the torturous task of sitting stationary in the cold, proved a great distraction.

But despite that, the groundhog cycle of being sat out day after day, succumbing to the weather, was so cruel it corrupted the mind, and drained the troops of any morale they still had.

Archie and Henry had a break coming up, they began feeling the worst of the winter was behind them as they moved into March. They knew they just had to get to the end of the month, and they'd be informed that they would receive a few days' leave at the beginning of April. Most of the men spoke of how they looked forward to their first trip home since being out in France, with many talking about where they intended to sample their first taste of home beer.

All Henry could think about, was the opportunity to spend a few days with Annie. He had already written home to his mother, telling her everything. Of course, she had been surprised and somewhat shocked, but there was nothing she could do. Archie then wrote to his parents, informing them, to their great disappointment, that he would be joining Henry in staying in France, as they were entering a time, when he needed him most.

Every conversation about casseroles and pies was cut short when a German heavy bomb dropped metres away from them, spraying the men with tufts of dirt and debris. They realised there was a long way to go until then, and they knew, soon many of them would be sent to meet their maker, over the top before they had a chance to reach British shores.

The men spent their time sitting around impatiently anticipating the order that eventually arrived, the waiting to go over the top was soon to be over. They had been given their latest order. They knew they were to be going over the top to face the Germans once more.

Something about this time, however, felt different, the savage winter was almost behind them, and the men finally became able to feel the existence of their toes in their boots as the ice melted around them. Spring, and its gift of new life, had installed a newfound optimism in the men.

This coupled with the knowledge that survival would bring a return home as a reward was enough for many of the men to feel a rejuvenated confidence in the face of the mission ahead of them.

The morning of the attack, Frank hurried through the queue of men to take the swathing jug of rum in his hands, to feel the cold nectar trickle down his throat, anaesthetising his body from within, for what he was about to do. His legs rolled under his body as he made his way into formation alongside his brothers in arms.

As they stood, waiting for the all too familiar shrill of the whistle to pierce the morning sky, Archie noticed Sergeant Parker leaned up against the rear of the trench wall, his head sunk in his hands, his back turned on his men. Archie peered at the time on his grandfather's pocket watch, which he now carried with him in battle as a good luck token. 10 minutes to go.

He told Henry to hold his place in formation and he waded through the lines of men to get to the shaded figure of Sergeant Parker.

As Archie approached him, he saw his hand trembling as his head rested on it against the dirt. His body vibrates, with short, sharp breaths escaping from his mouth.

"You alright, Sir?" Archie asked, Sergeant Parker quickly shaking himself down and brushing his sleeves with his hand to disguise its flickering movements. He coughed and cleared his throat, the painful, red sting in his eyes the remanence of tears from a not-too-distant past.

"Ahem," he covered his spluttering mouth with his fist. "Not too dandy, I'm afraid, Baxter," he said, barely trying to conceal his emotions from spilling over.

"I received a letter late last night, from my wife. Unfortunately, my poor son, Stanley, passed away a couple of days ago," the Sergeant's lip began to quiver. "It's a terrible business, losing one's child," he continued, trying to regain a sense of professionalism and composure.

"But my wife said, he was here for his birthday with his family, so that's of some comfort," Sergeant Parker continued, before having to break his words to stop the teetering tears from spilling out of his eyes.

"I'm very sorry to hear that, Sir," Archie uttered, the right ones for such an occasion seemed hard to find.

"Life goes on, and besides, he's in a better place now," Sergeant Parker stuttered, as he spoke. "Besides, I might not have long to wait, until I see him again," he said, a strange hint of comfort in his voice.

Archie found it quite out of character for Sergeant Parker. He was never one to address the impending danger of going over the top. He would always reinstate in the minds of the men, that what they were doing was of such grave importance that each and every one of them would live to tell the tales of their successes.

Of course, not all of them did, not most in fact, but Archie knew it set each of them on their way with a self-belief that eradicated the overwhelming fear eating at them from within.

He felt something was not right, he felt a sense of trepidation inside his chest, a sense of foreboding, that something bad was to come of Sergeant Parker, the feeling that for the first time, he was almost willing to die.

"I'm sorry, Sir, things will get better you'll see, you'll see your family soon," Archie knew his words were empty and offered no consolation, but he struggled to know what would.

"Come on, Baxter, positions, not long to go now," Sergeant Parker said, wiping his nose with his sleeve and readjusting his uniform to the correct and proper place, polishing his buttons with his cuff before pacing his way up and down the line.

Henry noticed the change in the way he walked, his legs didn't appear as strong as they normally were, and they were not holding his body up in a way, that exuded the confidence he normally led with, they struggled under the weight of his body, each step a struggle.

"He alright?" he asked Archie, as he returned next to Henry.

"It's his son. He's just passed away," Archie whispered quietly, so only Henry could make out what he said.

His eyes widened and his head drooped. "Poor man," he mumbled, the news had rattled him, but not for the reason it had done Archie.

He thought of Annie, he had not heard from her for a couple of weeks, and he began worrying about her and the baby. He knew the time was upon them when the baby would be expected, and the longer the wait went on for word from Annie, the more fear began to seep into Henry as he wished for news of the safety of both the to-be mother and child.

As Henry's mind began swimming into the depths of his growing anxieties, the bellowing call of Sergeant Parker touched the ears of all the men. His regular rallying cry had less enthusiasm and patriotism than it normally had. Try as he might, he could not completely bury his feelings, he was masquerading an appearance of strength and charisma, but underneath Archie could see the soul deep down crumbling with every word he spoke.

Sergeant Parker was then relieved by the clock as zero hour struck, and his whistle rung out around the trench and the men made their way out once more into the now familiar territory of no man's land.

The ground was rock hard, the scars of winter were trapping frozen molecules in the earth, each step beating down as they ran. The pace they took quickened, they wanted to catch the Germans off their guard, hoping the element of surprise could allow for a quicker victory.

Many men flooded forward ahead of Archie, full of exuding confidence and optimism as they saw, reaching the German trench as the gateway to returning home.

It was these men, who were springing across the plain like gazelles, who were the first to be torn down by the now-mounted German machine guns. Their attack had indeed caught the enemy off guard, and their morning rituals were cut short in order to protect the flooding English attack.

Archie could see bullets flying past him, but this time, the path seemed clearer than most, there were a few hollowed-out shell holes of easy access and the barbed wire defences seemed less fruitful than he had previously seen.

The penetrating night-time temperatures meant, that the Germans had not repaired and restored their barbed wire to its usual maze of invincibility. The rush of soldiers continued to overspill from the British trench to crush the Germans before they could fight back with a full muster of support.

Alan was jogging in line, shouting an indecipherable noise as a way of forcing himself forward with every step, a somewhat animalistic growl as he moved intently.

Archie looked around as he always did, he found that time in no man's land operated differently from time everywhere else. He found himself almost floating out of his body, looking around at all the men around him, flailing and falling.

He would see men have their limbs ripped cleanly from their bodies, their skin clinging on but the force of the German bullet or shrapnel from the surrounding artillery fire left their shoulder joint with a jagged appearance where the arm had been forcibly detached.

He watched pools of blood form around men's bodies as their faces seeped into the earth beneath them. He heard as friends, brothers, and cousins, fought and died together. He became consciously aware of every breath he took as he ran, as though he knew it could be his last. Each step he took he felt a wave of gratitude wash over him that God had allowed him the opportunity to feel the ground beneath his feet once more.

He looked around at the men, he now considered family, the way he valued their lives now, above his own, even Frank's as he watched him, his eyes glazed over with fear and alcohol running blindly into enemy lines.

He turned to his right to see Henry, almost gliding across the treacherous terrain, a calm confidence on his face that had always assured Archie in the darkest of times, and even when they marched into impending death it never wavered.

This time, however, as Archie's legs made the involuntary decision to carry him closer to the German front-line, he found himself looking around for Sergeant Parker. As his head was circling around the thick lines of men falling and running, bodies merging together, he began to lose hope, expecting to hear Sergeant Parker had met an untimely end.

Just as his eyes flickered from corner to corner, still trying to keep himself alive, he saw the blank expression of Sergeant Parker. He was moving calmly, as though he had no fear in his heart, but a willingness and almost an open desire to be hit by the shower of bullets. He was moving slower than everyone else around him, moving in a way that made it appear that no matter what happened in front of his eyes it would not waver him from his course.

The German fire was incessant, but the spirit of the British soldiers, and no doubt an immense hand of luck was allowing them to carve through no man's land and reach the barbed wire.

Archie, Henry and the others threw themselves into a crater just in front of the barbed wire, out of reach of German machine gunners. They saw the fiery mist leaving the metal contraption designed solely for mass annihilation, Archie decided, and they all tossed their grenades the short distance to the depths of the German trench.

A loud explosion erupted, shaking the earth around them. Then silence. The machine gun was silenced but they knew it wouldn't last long before another set of scrambling Fritz took the reins. The men all around Archie who still had use of life and limb began cutting away at the barbed wire, sprinkling grenades over the heads of the German soldiers, who were now shouting a foreign-tongued blue murder.

As they carved the pathway through the wire into the line, a string of soldiers leaped in ahead of Archie and Henry, unloading their fury onto the remaining Germans in the trenches who were half torn between turning and fleeing to safety through their tightly interwoven network of trenches, and standing to the last man, as more British soldiers piled into the enemy lines with a fierce determination to eradicate anyone they didn't consider to be friendly.

Frank leaped forward first, calling out for his king and country, as he delved headfirst over the parapet, Archie could assume his safety, as his slurring voice could still be heard over the melee.

"Come on, Arch, now," Henry called as he pulled Archie up by his arm, who dragged Alan's collar, as the three of them navigated the prickly pathway of wire before encountering a new phase of warfare that Archie had not quite felt prepared for.

As his feet steadied his fall into the deep ditch of German ground, his eyes descended upon a brawl of barbaric fighting. There was no time for bullets to be reloaded into rifles, men were charging at each other with their bayonets poised, depicting some sort of modernised jousting match.

German soldiers scrambled for survival, grabbing knives, rocks and anything in their path to club their way through the quagmire. Archie reared his head to the left where he heard a piercing scream. A British soldier was lying pinned down, his back buried in the dirt, as he was being repeatedly bludgeoned with the enemy soldier's helmet, blood spilling from gashes and gaping wounds in the side of his head.

All around him, men were throwing themselves against each other like some drunken street fights, out the back of a local pub at the end of the night. Fists were flying around as German soldiers crawled their way back. Archie had been caught by a flying elbow, when someone drew back to unleash a punch, sending his body cascading back into the wooden support of the trench wall, sliding down to the ground amongst the stampede of feet.

As he lay there, stars spiralled around his head as he watched a charge of British soldiers pick off any Germans left standing, and the latest support units flocked down into the trenches to drive the Germans back as far as possible.

As the dust began to settle, Archie roamed his body with his hands, trying to detect any signs of injury, other than the blood trickling down from his nose from the swipe from the stray elbow. Henry helped him to his feet, brushing down the copious amounts of dust that had fallen upon his uniform.

"Sergeant Parker?" Archie asked, as he rose to his feet. The memory had just returned to him from a short time earlier where he had seen the vacant figure of Sergeant Parker walking mindlessly toward the German fire.

"Over there," Henry nodded, over to one side of the trench where a medic was kneeling down in front of him assessing any damage beyond the cuts and bruises on his face.

Archie's head fell back with a sigh of relief, he had almost completely expected and prepared himself to hear the news, that Sergeant Parker had not made it. He had looked like a dead man walking across no man's land no more than an hour ago.

Alan and Frank clambered over the rifles and bayonets contorted on the floor beneath their feet, the rats already scurrying over the bodies of the dead, and worse, the undead.

Alan shook one from his boot, cursing, as the four of them joined up together, collapsing in unison against a small step built into the side of the trench. Many of the soldiers they had left the trenches with on Sergeant Parker's whistle, could be heard retching and screaming behind them in no man's land.

After little more than a moment to catch their breath, Archie and the others were given the orders along with a small handful of troops to search no man's land for any survivors and return them to the British lines to receive the medical assistance they required.

As they traipsed their way back across no man's land, Archie found a man coughing and spluttering, crashed up against the stump of a tree, that had been cut in its prime of life, much like many of the men around him.

He knelt down to see the man was missing half his face and a leg. From the skin that remained intact, Archie could see the tears rolling down the man's cheek. He squealed as Archie tried to move him upright.

"You're alright, Sir, I'm going to get you out of here," Archie enunciated loudly, making sure he delivered every word clearly to the suffering man.

"What's your name?" Archie asked as he searched for a way to lift the man to his feet, turning his body revealed a large part of his side had also been blown off by whatever had ravaged him.

"Little, Robin Little," the man replied choking.

"I can't...I can't move, it's no use," he said whimpering, as Archie was trying to prop his body further up the tree stump, but the life was draining out of him and Archie realised there was nothing he could do to save him, except help him be at peace.

"It's no use, I'm going to die, aren't I?" he asked Archie, his body now twitching with fear as he seemed to realise his fate.

"No, I'll get you out of here, don't worry," Archie replied without making eye contact with the dying man, his eyes darting around him for someone else to help him.

Robin grabbed Archie's arm, his head instinctively turning to meet the eyes of his mortally wounded comrade.

"My pocket, take it," he uttered, his sentences becoming broken as he struggled through the pain.

Archie did as he was instructed and hastily filed through his pockets until he came across a notepad with a small fountain pen clipped neatly in the corner.

"Take it," he whispered, the tears seeping out of his eyes, washing the blood from his face.

"Write to my family, tell them, I was brave, tell them, I wasn't crying, tell them, I was laughing on the wrong side of my face," he choked, before coughing blood that sprayed across Archie's uniform.

"I will, I will," Archie replied, comforting the man who sat, slumped against the tree.

He nodded and smiled as Archie reassured him, before his eyes rolled back, his eyelids closing, his body away from this world, entering him into the next.

Archie sniffed and tucked the notebook in his pocket, before carrying him back to the trench to allow him to be buried with dignity, unlike many of his fallen comrades, before spending the rest of the daylight hours fishing for survivors in the great ocean of blood and bodies.

That night, the moon rose high into the sky, and more stars lit up the great abyss above them. Archie wondered if it was a sign of all the good men they had lost that day. He had written a letter to Robin Little's family and instructed it to be attached to their telegram.

The air was cool, but there was a change in the air, spring was on its way. Despite the weather beginning to improve, the day's events and horrors of close combat had chilled them all from within. Alan lit up a cigarette and they all huddled around it, catching any sparks of heat or light they could muster from the small stress reliever.

"Henry Longley, letter for you," a tall soldier came over to them, dropping a letter off with Henry before turning and making his way out of the cluster of men and vanishing as quickly as he arrived.

Henry sat there and peeled the envelope carefully open, prizing the letter out from within.

Dearest Henry,

I am sorry for not writing these last weeks, but it is with the utmost joy and happiness that I write to inform you of the birth of your son.

It has been a troublesome couple of weeks, I fell rather unwell when he was first born, but thanks to the great care of Madame Soignant, I have made a full recovery, and both I and the baby cannot wait to see you.

I do hope you are safe and well, where do you find yourself now? Do you think you will be able to see us soon? I do understand it is not quite as easy as that, but I would so love for you to meet your son.

I have decided to name him Stanli, after my father. His name was Stanislaus, but my uncles always called him Stanli, so, I wanted his memory to live on through our son. I hope you love the name, and our son, the way I do.

Sending you my warmest wishes of love,
Annie

Henry's eyes left the paper and looked up in shock. He stared right through his friends, who by this point, had crowded in front of his face to hear the contents of the letter.

"So?" Archie asked, anticipatively.

"I've got a boy," Henry mumbled, his eyes still stricken with a look of disbelief.

Archie leaped onto him embracing him tightly, followed by Alan and Frank who formed a small bundle on top of him cheering and ruffling his hair as they all laughed jovially.

The excitable sentiments lasted a few moments longer before Alan and Frank broke away on the hunt for any leftover rum they would be able to smuggle back through to celebrate the announcement.

"A boy," Archie stated, with a smile looking into Henry's eyes before the two broke out into a chuckle and tightly gripped hold of each other.

"A boy," Henry repeated, softly and calmly.

"Has he got a name?" Archie asked, curiously.

"He's called Stanli, after her father, thankfully he had an easy English name to say," Henry beamed, his cheeks rosy and flushed from the excitement.

Archie's eyes widened when he heard the name. He jolted his head to the side, where he saw the sullen figure of Sergeant Parker looking up to the sky sipping a mug of tea. Archie watched him with a soft, warming smile.

"What is it?" Henry asked, confused as to why Archie's attention had shifted.

"Nothing at all. It's a perfect name," Archie's face was alight with joy and the two shared another tender moment in the time they still had alone.

"These next weeks can't come quickly enough, will you come with me, come and meet him?" Henry asked Archie, urgently.

"Of course, I'd be honoured," he replied sentimentally. "Only if, I get to be Godfather," he joked and the two ripped out into laughter once more.

"It's gonna get me through now though. I have to get through these next weeks, for him," Henry said, his face turning serious very quickly.

He had found a new purpose and a new reason to go on and Archie could see the onset of tears forming in his eyes.

"Come on, let's see, what's keeping the others," Archie said, hauling him to his feet. "Can you believe it, you're a dad?" he continued, as the two walked away round the corner of the trench on the hunt for their comrades.

They paused reflectively for a moment before breaking into raucous laughter and walked around the safety of the trench roads, arms around each other's shoulders, Henry whistling gleefully, and Archie with a newfound determination to keep his best friend alive.

10

Henry's eyes opened. They flickered and darted around the room, dancing around the small tremble of the candlelight in the corner of the room. His eyes were red and raw, he had mustered very little sleep for the last couple of nights. He swatted the hair at the back of his head, beating away the scratchy particles embedded in his locks from the coarse pillow.

He sat up, resting his head against the rickety headboard of the bed. He trailed his fingernails over his body, itching at the small flea bites that spread across his legs, resembling a hilly region of the Lake District. The small red hives tormented him, and the blood that oozed from within when he tore away at them mocked him. He sat restlessly.

The morning light was breaking through a small crack in the shutters. The dilapidated windowsill took its rightful place in the ramshackle room. The wood was chipped in all the corners, the paint barely smeared evenly across the exposed, moulding oak. A corner of the shutter appeared to have been broken with some force, allowing for a trail of the morning light to escape into the room like an unwelcome guest arriving far too early to the great discontent of its host.

In this case, Henry was the host. And in this case, he was a welcome host. The discontented host was lying in the bed beside him.

A stone's throw away, across the dusty floorboards, the second bed was erected, with one leg slightly shorter than the others, leaving one's body at a somewhat awkward sleeping angle. That didn't seem to deter the occupant from enjoying a deep slumber.

Curled up underneath a thin, rough blanket, Archie was sailing away in a deep sleep. His snores echoed around the room as his head was sunk deep into the small pillow, enjoying the most luxurious sleep he had, had for some time.

Henry, on the other hand, did not find the same opportunity to rest. His body was still lethargic and exhausted, but his mind was as active as if it were the middle of the afternoon. His brain was juggling a multitude of thoughts. As he lay there, he was no longer the man he was, when he left home.

His body, motionless, on the rickety mattress reminded him of the same squeaking bed he used to occupy at Huckerby Hall. He wondered who now would be there, would the bed be empty, lying in wait for his return?

Or would the imprint of his body on the sheets be wiped clean and replaced with that of a new occupant? When he thought of his old life, it seemed like it was an impossibility, that it was but a couple of years ago. Now he had a child. A son.

He sat, his head tilted back against the headboard, his eyes gazing above him, seeing through the cobweb-adorned ceiling and out into his past. As his mind retraced the memories of years gone by, he realised, he would never be able to return to that life. At least, not in the way he left it behind. He could not see a life beyond the war, for, it was impossible to know if and when the war would end.

And should he indeed be fortunate enough to survive the war, he now had a son to look after. He knew as soon as the war finishes, he would marry Annie. Not only because he deemed it the correct thing to do, but because he loved her dearly. He had grown to love her in a way he had not been able to fully comprehend.

Every morning his eyes would open hoping to see her, and his mind would paint the image of her body when it welcomed in a new day. He found he could not sleep for thinking of her, he could not turn a corner without hoping she would be there, despite knowing she never would be.

Then there was his son. As his mind contemplated the new realities in his life, he still struggled to fully grasp the magnitude of his latest revelation. He was a father. He had been so for a few weeks now, but he often found himself, in the dark corners of the night, wrestling with the realisation that he, in fact, was a father. The idea filled him with such joy and elation, but the nature of living his life at war meant he could very rarely allow himself to wander down the path of optimism and dream of a life raising his son.

However, he was setting himself up for the dream to soon become a reality. He had woken at the crack of dawn with no more than two hours of sleep due to the excited and nerve-wracking anticipation of meeting his son.

He knew how excited he was, he couldn't wait any longer to behold the innate beauty and innocence of the small child he could call his own. However, the same feeling of fear and nervousness that fills the heart and mind of every first-time parent, occupied his own in the same vein.

Henry turned to look at Archie, his eyes closed, in a way that reflected total peace, rather than the state of semi-consciousness they had all grown used to when trying to capture a minute's sleep in the trenches.

The apprehension he felt subsided when he saw Archie next to him. Just as he had been by his side in every major moment of his life, Archie was once more Henry's accomplice. Henry thought of the peculiar turn of events, on reflection, that had led them to where they were.

His whole life had changed in the course of the war, the journey to foreign lands had brought him more than a few scars and life experiences. It had brought a new family into his life. Yet, the decision to come to war was the last intention Henry had in 1914. It had been Archie who had driven him to sign up.

Though having never explicitly asked him to be there alongside him, Henry, always knew he would not rest as long as Archie was out of the reach of his protection. He saw his course of fate as the hand of God, rewarding him for his loyalty, by giving him the greatest gift of all.

Archie stirred, his fists wiped across his sore eyes, as he winced at the beam of light cascading through the crack in the shutter. He stretched out his limbs, his feet trickling over the edge of the bed, his toes euphoric to feel a release from the soggy socks and battered boots.

His hair was messy and his eyes barely open wide, but he saw Henry sat as though he had been awake for hours. He checked the time on his grandfather's pocket watch, fearing he had wildly overslept. 6:10 a.m. He had not.

"Not tired?" he asked Henry mockingly, stretching his arms out wide as he yawned.

"Couldn't sleep," Henry replied, his brain evidently still not present in the conversation.

"Today's the day then," Archie smiled, finding a spring of morning energy as he sat up. "How are you feeling?"

"I'm excited," Henry said, turning his body over to face Archie. "And nervous," he added, his head drooping slightly.

"It's natural, I'm sure. But you're about to meet your child, your very own son," Archie's words were filled with optimism and kindness.

Henry did not reply, he simply nodded and tore the sheets off himself, getting changed.

Within an hour, they were washed, shaved, and dressed and out of the small hotel. It had been far from luxurious but had provided them with the essential bed rest they needed to stop over on their journey.

They had left the rest of their friends and comrades who made their way home to England, and they set off on their own path back to the small village near the River Somme.

hey had been dragged across different areas of the war-torn French countryside in the subsequent months since Henry last saw Annie, and they were faced with a sizeable journey to be reunited.

They had split the journey up by stopping over in a couple of small roadside hotels in relatively untouched regions. The hotel workers spoke little to no English, and they seemed surprised, to say the least, at the arrival of British soldiers.

They had been navigating a quiet path, one which they were given by a fellow Norfolk man, whose Aunt resided in a townhouse not far from where they were headed.

He provided them with some rough outline of the path to take to stay out of trouble, and it seemed to be adequate enough, as they had avoided any confrontation, which coming from where they had just been, it seemed as though they were in another world.

The French countryside astounded Archie. He would stare and gaze across vast fields, the grass always a luscious green, healthier and more fruitful than at home. The trees were great and tall, their old trunks riddled with the scars of hundreds of years. He often thought of the battles they had witnessed down the centuries, whether the conflict they were fighting now was the worst they had seen.

When they got far enough out of the clutches of war, the vibrant landscapes caught the sunset so perfectly no matter the time of the year, but as the spring sun fell behind the hills, it kissed every blade of grass, and it would be the only time Archie felt truly peaceful.

He had enjoyed the travelling, however difficult and enduring it was to traverse their way back to a place of torturous memories, he found their wild surroundings a great comfort.

They had a few hours ahead of them still to walk, they had set off before breakfast and had to make do with a few bread rolls and a slab of cheese the hotel staff generously gave them as they set out on their way. The day was a warm one, with a pleasant breeze tickling the leaves around them as the rising sun illuminated the path that carved through a small forest ahead of them.

"Have you got the rattle?" Archie asked as they reached the rear of the wooded area.

Henry brandished the small contraption from his inside pocket.

"Good," Archie stated. "The weather is nice, maybe we will be able to take him down to the river, what's her face, the lady that owns the café, she can pack us all up a picnic?"

Archie too was beginning to feel excited; Henry had already promised him the title of Godfather and it was one he was ready to live up to.

"Maybe. But at first, I want to take him on a walk, just me, father and son. I want to be there for him, the way my father couldn't be, while I have the chance," Henry replied, almost a hint of bitterness in his tone.

"Your father was a brave man, just like you are. I have no doubt you will make it through to watch him grow old," Archie said, he knew Henry had longed for his father's presence as a child, how he detested war and blamed his father's death on the greed of the men in charge.

The men he was now fighting for.

"Funny how life works, isn't it," Henry muttered.

"What do you mean?" Archie asked curiously.

"My father left for war while I was a baby and never came home to us when the war ended. When I was old enough to understand, I blamed him for going, I hated war and everything it stood for. Now, here I am going to see my son, before having to leave him to go back to war, not knowing if, I will return to him or not. Like my father. I'm a hypocrite really," his tone was sombre and his voice quiet.

"You're not," Archie replied instinctively. "Your father was a great man who gave his life for his country and for you. To protect you. Now you're fighting to make sure your son can live in a peaceful world. You will make it through, I'll make sure of that," Archie continued, his final words softer as he looked up to the sheet of blue draped overhead, the rays of sun touching every corner of the horizon.

"I never thought of it like that," Henry answered, a look of realisation fell across his face.

"See," Archie started, "your father was never to blame for fighting for your protection, and when you're older, you will be able to explain to your son how brave he was. How brave you are now," he smiled at Henry as he patted his shoulder.

"How brave we are," Henry reciprocated the sentiment.

"Do you miss it? Home?" Henry asked, as he watched the leaves dancing in the breeze, remembering the same sights in the small lakes and rivers of home.

Archie paused for a moment.

"I don't think, I do," he replied to Henry's shock.

"Why? Nothing at all, not your family, not anything?" The surprise came through in Henry's voice.

They so often spoke of life in Cromer that it seemed somewhat unbelievable to know Archie didn't miss it.

"When I was home, as I said to you, when I came back, your mind doesn't ever settle, it's only ever here. People go about their daily lives, bumping into you in the street, as though you've never been away, almost questioning your absence. They have no idea. And for as long as this war goes on, they won't understand."

"You feel an outsider in your own home. I miss my family, of course, and yes, my father has been to war, but this is different from anything even he could comprehend. His stories tell nothing of the horrors we have faced. It feels as though no one understands but the people here, and you miss that when you're at home," Archie's head dropped, his chin almost touching his chest as the pain was evident in his voice.

"I'm sure, your father saw things he never spoke about, the same way we cannot find the words to say what we have seen. Only those who share your experiences can truly understand," Henry offered encouraging words in response.

"Perhaps. But this is no war you read about in books or learn about in history. There is nothing of these great guns that tear away at life and limb, or the scale of tanks and artillery guns rolling their way through the earth wiping out any signs of life that cross its path. Nothing of gas and screaming men," Archie was growing distressed as he spoke, and Henry latched onto it, grabbing hold of his shoulders and pulling him in.

"I know, I know," Henry put his hand on Archie's cheeks, it was as though now the two of them were together, alone, there were no pretences, the walls of which they had built to block out what they saw could afford to crack in each other's company.

Like so many things in their lives, they knew exactly how the other felt without needing to ask.

"When we're finished here, we'll go home, together. Annie and Stanli too. We'll take over the shop together, leave all this in the past," Henry's voice was calm as ever.

He had a niche that Archie still could not understand, where he made him feel as though his problems, really weren't problems at all. That they could solve them together. His words instantly brightened Archie's face who, tore a leaf of a branch of a tree and felt the spine with his finger before letting the cool spring air elevate it from his hand and out into the French wilderness.

"So then, you intend on bringing them home with us?" Archie asked, referencing Henry's new family.

"I do. I haven't told Annie yet, but her mother wants nothing more to do with her, she has nothing holding her here, and I could give them a better life at home, so I'm sure she wouldn't oppose," Henry spoke as visions of his future glided past his mind's eye.

"What will your mother say?" Archie queried.

"You know mother, she works hard, and it can be a stretch to feed who lives under the roof anyway, but she would welcome them both with open arms. Course until we can find a place of your own," his face was light as he spoke, his eyes shining on his post-war euphoria.

"You've thought it all out then?" Archie chuckled, as they marched through the countryside.

"We have a lot of time to kill," they both shared a warming laugh. "But in truth, yes, I have, I just can't wait for this blasted thing to be over," Henry's voice was stern as he finished his sentence.

The pair continued their walk with more discussions about their future life plans for when the war finished and all their hopes and dreams. Archie listened, as Henry seemed to have worked out every intrinsic detail of his life, which included working with Archie in the book shop which brought him great joy.

Henry's once dream of being butler in Huckerby Hall seemed to have dissipated since the major change in his life and viewed the job he wanted to support his family, was to help Archie in taking the reins of the bookshop off his father.

They meandered the many narrow pathways and tight networks of dust tracks until they began closing in on their destination. They passed through several small towns and villages and many places where they were reminded of the real prominence of war, be that through the familiar sound of the barrage or the scars drawn on the walls of tall buildings and small family homes.

"There it is," Archie said as the chequered roofs came into view over a barren hilltop.

"I'm feeling nervous now," Henry uttered, a quaking in his voice.

"Brings back a lot of memories here," Archie said, as his ears could almost hear the deafening memory of the weeklong artillery bombardment before he fought and fell at the Somme.

"Come on, this way," Henry took control as they entered the heart of the town and the café fell into full view.

Henry felt his heartbeat cascading against the wall of his chest. His breath quickened, it was a contorted emotion of nerves and exhilaration. They followed the path up to the outside of the café, where they stood for a moment up against the rope, separating the outside tables from the open expanse of road.

"Henry," a strong voice called out.

Henry looked up, alarmed, as Madame Soignant marched with intent out to them.

A sudden wash of calm filled the air, and Henry smiled at her presence as she closed in on them, her arms wide to greet him with a tender embrace.

"It is so wonderful to see you, we have been expecting you," she chimed cheerfully.

Henry found the woman's greeting rather extravagant for someone he had only met once before.

"Madame Soignant, it is lovely to see you again, please let me introduce my best friend. Archie, Madame Soignant, Madame Soignant, Archie," He beamed, as he spoke.

"Pleasure," Archie said, cheerfully as she swiftly moved on to embrace him also.

"Come, we cannot leave her waiting any longer, she is anxious to see you," Madame Soignant said leading the way through the café, past the only two customers civilly drinking their cups of coffee and opening the door that led to the stairs up to where Annie and the baby were lying in wait patiently.

"Are you excited to meet your son, Monsieur?" she turned to look at Henry, whose face was showing no sign of emotion either way.

"Yes very, quite nervous too in fact," he answered, anxious to get up the stairs.

"There is no need for that, you'll see," she replied with a friendly tone as they reached the landing where the door, behind which contained Henry's future.

There was no more waiting to be done, the moment he had been patiently waiting for was upon him.

"Meet your son," Madame Soignant spoke softly as she opened the door to Annie's bedroom where she sat in bed, the covers up to her waist as her elegant night dress draped over her shoulders, her dark hair bouncing against the skin of her collarbone.

Delicately held between her soft, sun-kissed arms, was her small, innocent baby. Henry's baby.

Henry instantly locked eyes with Annie, and then down to the sleeping child cradled in her arms. He instantly removed his hat when entering the room and took the soft, slow steps over to the head of her bed, where he looked down, his eyes full of tears, at the pure, unblemished, dozing face of his son. His eyes tightly closed and his cheeks plump and rosy.

"Your son," Annie spoke softly, her voice almost quieter than a whisper, as she raised him up to hand over to Henry, who wiped the tears from his eyes and carefully took Stanli in his arms.

"My son," he exhaled, no louder than a sigh as he looked up across the room at Archie, whose eyes were also glistening in the light.

They shared a tender smile as Henry looked back down at his son. He planted a soft kiss on his head. His precious skin and fine hair were tender against Henry's lips as he rocked him side to side.

"You have done marvellously," he said turning to Annie, who also seemed to be affected by the contagion of tears spreading throughout the room.

"I have missed you," she said softly, everyone doing their utmost to make sure Stanli did not wake from his slumber.

"And I have missed, you," Henry said, leaning over to plant a delicate kiss on her lips.

"I can't believe, he is my son," Henry broke out into a small chuckle, his body still in a state of feeling as though it existed in a parallel universe as he held the infant in his arms.

The child of his own creation. He was perfect, Henry thought.

"And he is named after her father. Stanli Henry Longley, it is all official," Annie smiled at Henry seeing the way the news spilled more tears out of his eyes.

She watched him, she loved him truly, more than she had loved anyone before. She knew it was unconventional and complicated, however, she had never thought beyond the moment she lived in. She knew his safety was not guaranteed but it did not stop her from allowing herself to fall deeply in love with him.

"Would you like to hold him?" Henry said, looking at Archie, as they both made their way over to one another, meeting in the middle of the room.

Archie took control, feeling the gentle rise and fall of the baby's breath against his arms. "He has your nose," he said as they all laughed, the joy in the room bursting out of every door and window in sight.

"I shall go and make you up some drinks, and bring you some food," Madame Soignant said, as she left them to settle their things in.

Henry was to share the bed with Annie and a small, dusty mattress was placed in the corner of the room for Archie.

Henry slid under the covers next to Annie, whom he held in his arms, caressing the silky skin of her arms with his fingertips. He stared out of the window in the far corner of the room and watched the sun beating high in the sky. He felt as though in that very moment, all of the worries in the world evaporated into nothing.

He felt his life to be perfectly happy, though he needed nothing more than the people who were in that very room with him. He knew his leave would not be indefinite and like all good things, it would come to an end, but until that point, as he stared out into the warm afternoon sky, he vowed to cherish every second of every day.

The good fortune of warm weather did not last long, the next few days were all met with the same torrential downpour of rain, limiting them from being able to do much more than play card games in Annie's bedroom and enjoy copious amounts of free food and drink downstairs. Archie could almost feel his body grow in size as he munched his way through pastries every hour of the day.

One morning they woke, however, with only a couple of days leaves left ahead of them, and the clear skies had broken through. There was not a single cloud blotching the morning sky, and the heat could be felt from within the room.

Archie woke first and rushed over to the window, flinging it open and allowing the pleasant temperatures to sink into his skin.

"It's sunny, it's finally sunny," he called out, unaware the other two were still yet to rise from their night's hibernation.

Stanli had also still been enjoying the comforts of his small blankets and let out a subtle cry when Archie's voice reverberated around the room.

"Quick, we should have some breakfast then head down to the river for a picnic, seize the day while the weather is on our side," he continued, as Annie had sat up in bed and begun to share Archie's enthusiasm.

"What a perfect idea, I'll get Madame Soignant to help me pack up a basket and we can all go for a picnic," Annie beamed, as she spoke, curling up to Henry in bed, who enjoyed watching her in the mornings, as he found her skin shone and her eyes were at their brightest when she woke to welcome in the new day.

She hurriedly got herself ready and told Madame Soignant their plan, who felt quite over-excited by the announcement and decided to close the café for the day so she could join them.

Before long, they were on their way through the town, Annie in a floral dress for the spring, and Archie and Henry in a shirt and trousers they had bought from the local tailors to give them a welcome break from their uniform.

Henry was pushing Stanli in a small navy-blue pram, with wheels considerably bigger than the body of the contraption. The baby was sound asleep and unaware of today is much different from any of the others that preceded it. His daily schedule consisted of mainly eating and sleeping at this stage and whether that took place inside or outside it really made little difference to him.

Madame Soignant was carrying a large hamper which she had filled with cutlery and crockery, while Annie was holding another containing pastries, jams, breads, salads and more food than was worth noting.

Before too long, they found themselves at an open clearing, where the clear blue river ran down ahead of them, embanked by two green areas filled with trees and wildflowers. They picked a large oak to settle themselves under, where Henry could sit with Stanli under the shade to keep themselves out of the heat.

Madame Soignant and Annie unfurled some blankets and delicately placed all the goods that had been prepared out in front of them.

"There is plenty of food, so tuck in it, all must go," Madame Soignant announced, as she finished her organised arrangement of food.

Henry handed Annie the baby who took him down to the riverbed to watch the dragonflies rattle between the reeds and sail past them into the maze of greenery.

"Thank you, Madame, for everything you have done for her, for them both," Henry said, sincerely to Madame Soignant as he indulged in a thick slab of cheese. "I am forever indebted to you," he smiled.

"Please, call me by my first name, Juliette," She replied, her cheeks rosy from the heat as she simpered at Henry.

"You know," she began as the pair of them had their eyes locked on mother and child. "When I lost my daughter, I never thought I would find purpose again in my life, she has…they both have brought that into my life and for that, I thank you," the two of them took hold of each other and the gratitude exuded between them.

Henry finished his handful of cheese and trotted down to the riverbed to join Annie.

Madame Soignant stood watching the proud parents, bundling up their child in the fresh, spring air as Archie made his way to stand next to her, mopping his brow with a handkerchief with a jam-filled croissant in the other hand.

"Look at them, so happy. They have so much love there," Madame Soignant stated, as her eyes welled up with a sense of pride looking out on her newfound daughter with her child.

"Indeed, I agree," Archie replied, chomping his way through the fresh pastry.

"I pray every day for his safety, that he may return to them when this is all over," she spoke softly, turning to face Archie who could see the gloss of tears sat on her eyes.

"So do I," Archie replied, nodding as he too watched them playing in the tall grass and reeds, ignorant to the rest of the world's troubles, revelling in their momentary bliss.

"What's it like out there, on the battlefield? Answer me truthfully, I can take it," Madame Soignant asked, her voice both curious and serious.

"It's cold. Muddy. And very boring for most of the time," Archie replied, feeling himself suppress the darker truths within.

"Are you ever scared?" her tone, is sympathetic now.

Archie stopped and thought for a moment, he contemplated lying but felt there was no longer a need to conceal the truth. Especially not from those who lived within touching distance from the front lines that she would no doubt be able to see straight through the lies.

"Yes," he said simply. "Sometimes you cannot move for fear, cannot speak, think. Even breathe. To be quite frank with you, I'm not sure, I'd have made it this far if it wasn't for him," Archie nodded in the direction of Henry whose beaming smile could be seen from under the tree where they were standing.

"When will this madness end?" Madame Soignant asked, with full knowledge, that there could be no answer that could be given with surety.

"Whenever it is, it can't come soon enough," Archie responded, filling his mouth with the end of his croissant, tasting the burst of flavour from the vibrant jam within.

Down by the riverbank, Henry had taken a seat under the soft, natural blanket of thick grass, with Annie coming down to join him, the baby in her arms. Henry put his right arm around her, pulling her tightly into him so their hips met at the joint, his index finger on his left hand slotted delicately in between Stanli's small grasp.

"I wish, I never had to go back," Henry uttered as he watched little fish leap above the surface to catch a glimpse of the changing seasons before delving back deep into the blue.

"How is it? Truthfully, I know you don't really tell me what it's like," Annie asked, a hint of sadness in her voice as she spoke.

"You know, the thing is. I couldn't even begin to tell you. I wouldn't know where to start," Henry answered, his eyes narrowing as he looked to the other side of the bank and beyond. "But I have Archie there and I couldn't do it without him, he keeps me safe, so you have no need to worry my love," he concluded, kissing Annie softly on the cheek.

"I want to enjoy this moment, here, with my boy," he added, taking Stanli into his arms and raising him high into the sky, the sun bouncing off his round, innocent head.

Henry spent his afternoon down by the river and under the confines of the sheltered tree, tickling Stanli and letting him sleep in his arms, sapping up every moment with him he possibly could. He had grown instantly attached, inseparable like many fathers and sons, the way he had seen Archie be with his father.

He knew it was crazy, but knowing his safety and his life were not guaranteed, he was intent on maximising every minute with Stanli. So, if the worst was to happen, he would be content with the fact that his son had spent as many precious moments with his father as God would allow.

The light in the day drained quickly and before they knew it they found themselves in the dimming light of sunset. They watched the orange glow of the sun fall behind the horizon, they watched the way it cast its delicate reflection across the river, the way its beams of evening light touched every corner of their surroundings.

They savoured their last moments of sunlight, and happiness down by the lake before Madame Soignant and Archie furled the blankets and packed the scraps of food back into the hampers with the used plates and cups. Then, regrettably, Henry loaded Stanli back into his pram and the small familial unit turned their backs on the calmness of the river and headed back to the café, the sun not just beginning to set on their day, but also their time away from the battlefield.

Henry fastened his top button, straightening the creases out of his uniform with his palm. He grabbed his hat off the coat rack in the corner and fixed it firmly against his set hair.

"Keep this here for me, for when I return," Henry said softly, as he hung his new shirt and jacket on a hanger in the wardrobe.

The room was unusually quiet. It was the morning he had been burying deep within his mind but could not escape the reality anymore. It was the day they had to return to the war. Leaving a life of peace and tranquillity and return to one of conflict and violence.

Annie nodded and smiled, Stanli in her arms as she sat rocking on a small chair in the corner of the room.

"Here," Henry started, walking over to Annie to collect Stanli from her loving grasp. "I want to take him outside, have a moment with him before we go," his voice was demoralised and uninspired.

Henry gathered his son in his arms, Stanli's plump face pressed up against his father's chest, as Henry made his way down the stairs and took a seat on one of the outside café tables, sitting Stanli on his knees, and toying with his small hands with his own.

"He will miss you both. Very much," Archie said to Annie, as he gathered their things ready for their imminent departure.

"And us him. And you too," Annie said, with a compassionate smile which Archie returned.

He too had enjoyed the trip more than he had anticipated. He did not solely feel he was there to serve the benefit of being Henry's accomplice, but a true member of the small family.

"Can you do something for me?" Annie asked, her voice gentle.

"Anything," Archie replied, placing the bags down on the floor and dedicating her his full attention.

"Bring him home to me. Whatever it takes, he must live, please," Annie's voice was less composed than when she first spoke, a plea in her tone.

"I will lay down my life to protect him. Whatever it takes," Archie replied, with a gulp, nodding sympathetically.

"Everything all set?" Madame Soignant bellowed as she entered the room, her hands on her hip, her pinafore dusted with flour and icing sugar, her question slicing through the momentary silence in the room.

"Yes, all set and ready to go. I'd like to take this opportunity to thank you for letting me, as well as Henry, stay in your home," Archie tipped his hat and smiled warmly.

"You are welcome, anytime," beamed the friendly lady, whose gaping arms wrapped themselves tightly around Archie's frame as she planted a delicate kiss on both cheeks.

"Right, are we ready to head back?" Henry's assured voice broke through the room, as his footsteps were heard climbing back up the stairs, Stanli's whimpering muffled by his father's strong voice.

Archie nodded to Henry as he entered the room. His eyes darted across every crevice of space to allow his brain to capture everything for when he was away.

"Just taking a photograph of it all in my mind for later," he smiled, recognising the peculiarity of his twitching head movements.

"Speaking of photographs, I want you to have this, to keep it. So, one day you can bring it back to us," Annie remarked as she rummaged through a small handbag beside her bed.

Henry went over to meet her, Stanli now beginning to drift off to dreamworld in his father's arms.

Annie handed Henry a small rectangular photograph. It was a photograph of the three of them. Their small family. On the left, Annie was sat with Stanli in her lap, his eyes awake but barely decipherable in the photo. Henry was sat on the right, his strong posture and arm around Annie showed him off as the patriarchal figure he was.

The day before, Annie had led them to a photographer not far on the outskirts of town to get it done so that Henry could take a small piece of their family to the front-line. He had not known it was Annie's intention to give it to him.

He had been led there under the pretence it was to sit by her bed until he returned to her at the end of the war. As it happened, that was never her desire and she kept it neatly inside a Bible for this precise time to pass it into the possession of her beloved Henry.

Henry took the photograph in between his fingers, tracing his index finger over the delicate lines of Stanli's face. He raised the photo up to his face and softly placed his lips against the ink. A small, oval tear crowned in the corner of Henry's eye.

"I will keep it with me always," Henry mumbled, his words merging into a long block of sound as he sniffled away the tears.

"Just bring it home to us," Annie wept as the two clung hold of each other, the tears streaming down both their cheeks. They held each other for some time, Henry repeatedly planting kisses on any part of Annie he could rear his head to find.

When they broke from their embrace, Henry had one final moment to hold his son, to feel the soft rise and fall of Stanli's small lungs against his arms. He pulled Annie in with his spare arm and the small family held onto each other, clutching at all the precious seconds they could grasp in each other's company before the inevitable, cruel claws of time would snatch them away once more.

"Come on, we better get moving," Archie said softly, cautious to not upset anyone more than they already were.

Henry tore himself away, his fingers unwrapping themselves from Annie's as he moved further away, their fingertips being plucked apart as he stepped away from the bed and blew both mother and son a final kiss before taking his hat from Archie and tucking the photo inside his chest pocket and collecting his bags from the floor.

"You'll always be in my heart," Henry spoke placing his hand over his chest where the photograph now sat, following one more kiss sent fluttering through the air to Annie and Stanli, Madame Soignant escorted the two soldiers down the stairs and out of the front of the café.

"You boys look after each other and do take care," Madame Soignant uttered, as she placed the palm of her hands on each of their cheeks respectively.

"We will, thank you, for your hospitality," Archie replied, turning to make his way out onto the sunlit path.

"Look after them for me until I return," Henry requested, as he looked deep into her eyes.

"I will. Just make sure you return to them," She answered, a stern tone in her voice, almost demanding his safe return.

Henry tipped his hat and made his way to meet Archie who was standing waiting for his friend to join him, as he stared down the road they were waiting to embark on.

"Ready?" Archie asked, tapping Henry on the shoulder, seeing the emotion written across his face.

"As I'll ever be," Henry replied, closing his fists around his kitbag and slinging it onto his back as they set off on their long journey back to join the rest of their comrades.

Annie stood, watching them walk off into the distance, Stanli twitching in her arms, as the innocent tears trailed down her plump cheeks. She thought of calling after them but did not want the hurt for herself or for Henry of locking eyes once more, only for their gaze to be ripped apart from each other once more.

So, she watched, silently suffering as his footsteps got further away. It had seemed only yesterday their steps were echoing around the walls of the street for their arrival, now they were walking with their backs turned to the town they had both grown to love, unsure if and when they would ever lay eyes on the patchwork roofs or delicately painted facades of shops and restaurants ever again.

As they meandered the path out of the town over the familiar green hill Archie made a realisation, the way he had seen Henry, with Annie and Stanli, he realised he may never find something like that, no matter how many years he walked the earth. However, Henry had already found it, and there was no one person on the planet he cared about more than Henry.

He realised it was his mission to make sure Henry made it through, he returned to his small family, and he lived a long and happy life with them. He had always been willing to lay down his life to protect Henry but now he knew, as he had promised Annie only moments earlier, that Henry had to survive, however, long they had left in the trenches, whatever it took.

"Right, come on then, we've got a long journey ahead of us, get the cards out, we'll pass the time just like we used to at home," Archie smiled as he spoke, trying to raise Henry's mood as he had barely lifted his head from the ground since they left.

Archie's words brought him some solace and comfort and a grin crossed his face as he reached inside his pocket and began shuffling the cards.

"King of Hearts?" Henry asked mockingly as the pair of them broke out into a rapturous laughter, a newfound spring in their step carrying them across the dusty terrain.

"Nice try, just deal me the cards," Archie quipped, as he threw an arm around Henry, and the two locked eyes momentarily.

Archie could sense the comfort in Henry's eyes, they both felt at peace with whatever fighting their bodies had left in them, as long as they took it on together.

11

Dearest Annie,

I cannot believe, six months have now passed since our visit. It seems another lifetime ago as I sit here now in the wind and rain. How are you, my love? How is little Stanli? Oh, how I miss his perfect face when he looks up at me.

I had a dream last night; we were back down by the river; he was in my arms and the grass was blowing past us in the wind. How I would give anything to be free from this place and return to you.

It's not all bad here though, I have Archie and the boys with me, and we keep each other going. They always ask for updates on you and the baby, I think they will all be very keen to meet you both when all this is over.

I do so hope you are keeping yourselves safe and well. I keep you close to my heart as always. I look forward to your next letter, hopefully, I will not be waiting long.

God bless you, and all my love,
Henry

"Longley, here now," Sergeant Parker's voice was loud and bellowing.

Henry swiftly tucked the letter into the envelope and stood to attention.

"The rainwater is flooding the trench; I need you to help Baxter and Howells pump it out down there," he instructed, waving his hand down the trench to wear Frank and Archie were busy slaving away at the quagmire.

"Yes, Sir," Henry nodded in agreement with his commands and scuttled down to join them.

"Another letter to Annie?" Archie asked as he recognised Henry being a latecomer to the trench maintenance team.

"I had a dream last night we were back at the river and Stanli was back in my arms," Henry recounted, as he began working as the thick layers of mud threw themselves up onto his uniform.

"I'd quite like to meet this baby of yours," Frank said, throwing his sleeve across his nose as he sniffed.

"Well, when we are done here, you can come back with us and meet him," Henry smiled, and put his head down to work.

"Yeah, I'd like that," Frank responded.

His time in the trenches had mellowed him and he had valued the friends he had made, since being there, the brotherhood the four of them had formed over the last years of fighting.

The weather was calm, and the winds were settled, there was a gentle breeze, but the clouds were thick with a dark grey colour. They held promises of rain yet to be delivered. The men were all working in the trench, finding ways of reinforcing them and keeping them strong amidst the growing adverse weather conditions, capitalising on the best day of weather they had to flush out all the water.

As they were scurrying around, busying themselves with tasks and routine duties, the sky began to change colour. The light that was breaking through the clouds had been engulfed by a thick fog. This cloud, however, was not stationary, occupying its place in the sky, rather it was moving toward them.

"GAS!" a monstrous, bellowing voice, tore its way through the trench, repeating the shrill, deafening cry consistently in every direction.

The men dropped everything and scuttled, hurrying together, grasping and clutching for their gas masks before the impending sheet of mustard-coloured fumes fell upon them. A melee of shouting broke out, and fear was rife among the soldiers, either attempting to fix their protective masks firmly in place or grappling at their guns, loading them and preparing the ammunition for a German attack.

"Soldiers, incoming!" cried a small, round soldier whose voice was muffled by his gas mask.

Amidst the swathes of yellow emerged a horde of German soldiers, already masked and equipped, primed for attack. When they had realised their position from the piercing wailing from the British trench, they began unloading their bullets, round upon round, on anything they could make out to be moving ahead, throwing grenades and moving with intent.

Henry had swiftly recognised the danger, attached his gas mask efficiently, and scanned the frantic faces around him to find Archie.

"Arch! Arch!" he called out but to no avail, his voice was lost in the abyss of pleading, choking victims.

The sudden reality of impending doom had locked Archie in a state of shock and confusion. He had been unable to prize his gas mask free to protect himself, and now the waves of poison were fast approaching them. There were men rushing all around him, prioritising their safety over the protection of the trench. In the midst of it all, Henry had been separated from his side.

He clicked back into a sense of consciousness and realised; he must find Henry; he must protect him. He turned to his right where Frank was standing, staring at him, paralysed with fear. He too, was yet to feel the relief of the mask on his face.

Just as Archie held the protection in his hand, ready to adorn his face with it, a commotion occurred, with German hand grenades exploding all around them. One such explosion shuddered the ground where they stood, Archie's legs trembling beneath him and his right arm shooting out to the trench wall to support his stance.

In doing so, the gas mask cascaded to the floor, submerging itself in the mud below, the rampant legs of petrified soldiers trampling over it as they moved. Archie stared up, the cloud of gas almost drooping over his head, ready to engulf him. He turned to Frank, who held his mask over his head, ready to deploy it over his face. Archie's eyes were full of panic and dread. He was not ready to die.

As the fumes tickled the parapet, Frank darted over where Archie stood, transfixed in one spot. He took hold of Archie's head, pulling his own gas mask down over his friend's face, and fixing it in place. Archie's eyes widened at the realisation of what had happened, Frank stood there by his side, exposed to the fate that would soon wash over him, a small, contented smile almost written on his face. A contentment that he had given salvation to a friend whom he had grown to cherish so dearly.

Henry spotted Frank's naked face in the crowd, hurrying over to him, spotting Archie next to him, recognising his all too familiar frame. He grabbed Archie by the arm instinctively, ready to follow the masses in retreating to the support line to get the means to counteract the German attack. As he turned with

Archie, it dawned on him. Frank. He had not comprehended what was happening.

"Frank. Frank, quick we've got to go," he screamed, praying his voice escalated above the noise of the rattling gunfire and incessant explosions.

"Go," Frank uttered, softly and calmly, nodding them in the direction of the stampede of soldiers retreating ahead of them.

Before he had time to respond or reach out an arm of support, the yellow mist had engulfed the trench. Henry turned back as they became swept among the circling legs fleeing the scene.

The Germans were arriving through the barbed wire, unleashing bullets into the trench. Archie and Henry both moved with their heads reared back, Archie's eyes locked on Frank, who was being lost in the clouds. As his eyes settled on his flailing friend, he saw his body shudder and shake, twitching side to side.

Several flying German bullets had hit him, sending him tumbling to the ground. As they turned the corner of the trench, Archie's eyes said goodbye to his fallen friend, whom he had left sprawled across the muddy cesspit of the trench floor.

Henry and Archie reached the breathing space of the support line where their nostrils clogged up with the scent of fresh, somewhat clean air. They found Alan huddled in a corner washing water over his face. They approached him, their faces downcast.

"Frank?" Alan asked, the truth already a known reality from the look in Archie's eyes.

The pair of them shook their head and they all hung their heads to the ground, a few solitary tears escaping the strong eyes of each one of them.

There was very little time to grieve and mourn as the troops were rallied to push the Germans back out of their trench, a mission they were determined to succeed in, for Frank.

The sun set on a bloody day of barbaric brutality, as the stars began rising in the sky. They had succeeded in their mission. After hours of fighting, they had reclaimed what was rightfully theirs, and in doing so, had the opportunity the bury their deceased with honour and dignity.

Among them, Frank, his skin blistered from the gas, and his body was riddled with bullet holes; however, as his body was taken away to be buried, his face looked more at peace than it ever had done in any of his living days in the trench.

The three of them now sat on a small fire step, their faces cut and muddied.

"It's my fault," Archie muttered, as their sullen eyes watched the rats scurry along past them without the energy to fight them off.

"It's not your fault," Alan responded, swiftly.

"It is though," Archie snapped back, "there was an explosion, my mask flew out of my hand, and there was no way I was getting it back. Frank came to me, saved me, and gave me his mask, he knew what would happen to him. It all happened too quickly; I couldn't do anything—" Archie continued, talking hurriedly.

"You are not to blame," Henry took Archie's head in his hands. "I grew to love Frank, he was one of us, but when I saw it was him and not you without the mask on, I was relieved," Henry said directly into Archie's eyes, the distress riddled on his face.

"You don't mean that," Archie sniffed.

"I do. I'll miss Frank, I'll miss him a lot and he didn't deserve to die, not here. But I can't do this without you and that's more important than anything else," Henry took Archie in his arms, embracing him and pulling him close to his chest.

"I'm terrified," Alan started, a slight quivering in his legs. "There's all this dying around us, surely, it's only a matter of time. I'm scared because I don't want to be next," His voice was shaky and weak.

"Listen, we're all scared of dying. You just have to find something worth dying for," Archie responded, his eyes turning to face Henry, and his mind filling with images of him and his small family.

That morning Archie had found himself overcome with fear and trepidation when staring into the jaws of death. However, when he reflected on it, he knew, that he had to wait, he could only allow death to take him from this world when he had guaranteed Henry's safety.

The seasons were changing once more, there was a bitterness in the air that they had grown to recognise. They had become well accustomed to the transformation of the world throughout the year while at war. It had almost taken over and replaced the memories of anything that came before.

They were huddled around, tightly packed together living through their third autumn at war. When they began their first, there were five of them, as they sat under the starlit sky there were just three of them with a fighting spirit left in their body.

Frank had been ready to die, Archie thought. He lived every day with a festering fear that today could be his day. It had become bordering on torturous for him to wake up each day, to fight every day watching the lives of good men fall around him as the bullets missed him, teasing him.

It had become almost too much for him to take. He would drown his endless angst in as much rum as he could delight in himself. It was purely a way of deterring his mind from the spiralling serpent eating away at his brain day after day.

It had become so immense, that when the opportunity had presented itself to save Archie and finally be released from the world he was living in, he was willing to welcome it with open, fearless arms.

The three of them had become accustomed to life without Frank, it seemed quieter and calmer. Yet, once his incessant chatter had left their lives, they longed for it back.

Archie watched the moon as it shone bright in the dark sea above. They were approaching the end of another year, another year closer to the end of the war, whenever it was to be Archie had found solace in the knowledge it could not last forever.

As he watched the moon and the stars dancing in the sky, he prayed. He rarely prayed and had found himself feeling distanced from the God, he now questioned the existence of. He found it impossible to comprehend how a God, who loved all people could let this level of suffering happen under his watch.

Despite his conflict in faith, he prayed. He prayed that when the new, upcoming year was delivered upon them, it would bring a change in fortunes. It would bring relief from the violence of war, and it would bring a return to the peaceful life he had once known and loved.

He did not believe his praying would have any bearing on the outcome of the war. He did not even know why he turned to God when he had grown to realise the only ones responsible for the mass genocide between men were the men giving the orders.

He did not know what to believe anymore, whether to have faith or abandon it. However, he knew he had to hold onto something, hold onto a hope that Frank, Arthur, and all his fellow comrades had not fallen in vain and that the peace they gave their lives for, would soon be upon them.

12

My Dear Henry,

I hope this letter arrives to find you in good health. We both wish you the happiest of Christmases. It fills my heart with sadness that we cannot be together celebrating, but I pray next year will bring us better fortune.

You would not believe how fast Stanli is growing up, he is smiling all of the time, and his smile reminds me of you for which I am eternally grateful and brings me so much joy.

I hope it will not be long, until we can be together, as a true family, but, until that day, I shall pray for your health and your safety.

Be safe my love and happy Christmas,
Annie

Henry read the letter with a warming feeling in his soul. It felt as though the months were passing quicker the longer, they were there, they had been resting in the reserve and support lines for some time and they had felt the bitterness of the December frost build around them.

Another year was drawing to a close, and Christmas had arrived once again. Sure, as the night followed the day, Christmas had once again descended upon them. 1918 was around the corner.

Archie had ceased to predict what the new year might bring, as each time they had welcomed in a new year with optimism and hope that the war would end they had always ended resigned in defeat that they would have to plough on into another calendar cycle on the front lines.

It seemed better this way to allow the months to play out in front of them, focusing on survival rather than a return to a life that seemed to be one solely of the past, not the future.

Christmas morning brought with it a sense of higher spirits, the reserve line was more relaxed and the mundane duties that graced each day were allowed to be put on hold in their trench for the day. There was a light flurry of snow to bring in the daylight hours and the morning was uncharacteristically slow, followed by a trench-style Christmas dinner.

The dinner in truth, was far from the comforts of England, and in fact, varied very little from their daily meal. They sat around a small stove keeping them warm where they indulged in a mixture of bully beef and some additional vegetable comforts which they had not received in their previous Christmases when on the front-line.

"Another year over then," Alan chimed, as they munched their way through the already cold serving of food.

"And to think, they said it would be over by Christmas, three years ago," Archie quipped, leaving them all in a state of ironic hysterics.

"It feels another world away, I feel used to it here now, it would be weird to go back I think," Alan added, a reflective look on his face.

"I don't think it will be long until we are home," Henry responded, with a mouthful of bully beef.

"What makes you say that?" Archie asked curiously.

"I don't know exactly. I just have faith that this year approaching will get me out of this place and back to my family, all of them," Henry said, referring to his newfound French as well as his English family.

"Well, I hope you're right," Archie said. "I don't know how much longer I can go on," He continued, blowing into his closed fists to try and generate some heat around his fingers.

"We've seen some things," Alan said, his eyes looking up. "Do you hear it, when you sleep?" He asked, almost hesitantly.

"Hear what?" Archie asked in return.

"The screams. The explosions. The pain." Alan's legs shook, as he spoke, and his voice was strained.

Archie and Henry nodded in unison. Henry would try his utmost to focus his brain's energy into thoughts of Stanli rolling around in the long grass, or Annie's long flowing summer dress. However, the reality was every time he shut his eyes on the world, he would hear the men he ran alongside, crying for their mothers, begging for death to come swiftly.

Archie shared the dreams. He had become accustomed to the long nights without sleep, he had almost found them a relief. When he was awake, he did not have to fall victim to the cruel conscience of his dark mind. He would relive the day of Frank's death; he would feel overcome with guilt again and again. He wondered when God would relieve him of such a burden when he would set his mind free.

While they were awake, however, and while it was Christmas Day, they were determined to focus on their future in a positive light, not a negative one.

"When the war does end, what will you do then Alan?" Henry asked inquisitively.

As much as their conversations continued to revolve around their lives at home, they only ever spoke of their dreams and wishes, what they missed, and what they longed for, never the reality of returning to their old lives.

"Well, it'll just be the same old, I suppose," Alan replied, his voice surprisingly downcast. "I expect, I'll go back to the shoe shop and pick up from where I left off," his voice was uninspired.

It was as if being at war had given him a higher purpose, and as much as he longed for his home comforts to return, the once exciting day-to-day life of shoemaking now did not seem quite so exhilarating after several years of war. He wondered if he would fit in with the life he left behind, knowing he was no longer the same person he was when he left.

"You should move to Cromer, and set up a shoe business next to our bookshop," Henry exclaimed.

He had referred to it as his bookshop, rather than just Archie's ever since he had expressed his heart's wishes to join a partnership with Archie.

Alan's face lit up, and the light in his eyes returned.

"I think, I'd like that. I think, I'd like that very much," he smiled, as he replied.

"It's settled then," Henry chimed, as the three of them clanked their mugs of tea together in a celebratory fashion.

Archie and Henry opened their Christmas packages from home after they finished their food. They were unchanged from the last two years, and they indulged in their sweet delights, sharing with Alan as the three of them spent the night talking into the quiet hours of the morning.

After several marzipan fruits and a number of long yawns, Alan curled up beside them, placing his head down on his kit bag and slipped off into a slumber, leaving Henry and Archie alone in the world, the stars in the sky seemingly their only company.

"I'll miss some stuff about life here, but I certainly won't miss Christmases here," Henry joked, as they reduced the volume of their voices, as Alan snored beside them.

"Are you really so confident we will be home by next Christmas?" Archie asked him tentatively.

"I pray for it every day, surely soon, God has to answer my prayers," Henry replied, Archie only wishing that was how simple it would be for the war to end.

"Besides," Henry continued. "We have spent long enough in this stinking cesspit that I have to keep telling myself we'll be out of it before long," they laughed ironically, as several rats rattled past their feet, feasting on the scraps of lunch that had missed their mouths and become cemented in the ground beneath their feet.

"The seasons are changing once more, before we know it, spring will be upon us, new life, a new dawn. I pray it will bring one final push to end this blasted thing once and for all," Henry unleashed his rallying cry with gusto and Archie slung an arm around him, patting his shoulder firmly.

"We've come this far we can't give in now," Archie smirked, as he pulled his helmet firmly down on his head and saluted firmly.

"Exactly," Henry started, rolling over onto his side to close his eyes on another Christmas. "Just imagine, this time next year, I'll be sitting by the fire, my son in my arms, without a care in the world," Henry's voice was soft and calm, his tenderness shining through as he tucked his hand under his cheek.

"Indeed, you will," Archie said, patting his brother on the back and slumping down against the trench wall tilting his helmet down.

His eyes could still just about make out the starlit sky. Thousands of sparkling diamonds illuminate the dark world below. Archie was cold, he tucked his hands inside his uniform to offer them salvation from the cold. He longed for the long evenings and the birds filling the sky with their familiar spring song. He closed his eyes. He imagined the warm sun beating down on his back as he sowed the seeds of a new flower bed with Mr Humphrey in the rolling green acres.

His mind drifted off into sleep, for once, it was not the clatter of machine guns or the commotion of artillery that he heard, but rather the busying of Mr Humphrey's shovel in the fresh earth, and the sweet song of the larks overhead, and he slept, at peace.

The sun was high, its golden rays stretching across every particle of scorched earth and every blade of damaged grass. Its long limbs reach down, heating the earth below. Archie swept his sleeve along his forehead mopping up the dangling beads of sweat under his eyebrows.

There was a firm breeze, the birds were high in the sky in chorus with one another, their song only briefly interrupted every time a shell detonated in no man's land. They had become so accustomed to unexpected explosions and artillery barrages that they no longer quivered at the magnitude of noise or the shattering of the earth around them.

An explosion occurred a few metres ahead of the British barbed wire and Archie wiped away some flying debris that had clung to the sweat on his face. He patted down his uniform and took a seat on a duckboard to keep his trousers as clean as possible.

Another booming noise rattled through the centre of the front-line, clusters of battered earth showering themselves over the heads of the unwavering soldiers, with one such sprinkling of dirt scattering itself over the paper Henry was attempting to write across. He shook the paper dry before returning to his task.

Annie darling,

I pray, that my latest letter continues to find you both in good health and high spirits. How is Juliette? I find myself so often forgetting to ask of her, but, I do hope she is well.

I hope Stanli has started sleeping better and stopped keeping you up, I speak from experience when I tell you a lack of sleep does not do well for your mood!

I cannot believe we are but a few weeks away from it being a year since we were last together. The time seems to have flown by and I miss you both terribly. I cannot believe our son is now a whole year old, it is terrible really how I have spent such little time with him, but by God's good grace, I hope to change that very soon.

Things have been very busy here recently and I apologise for not sending him a present, we have been stretched in numbers and spent the last while on the front-line with no rest, I have had no time to find a small village with anything to buy him, but I hope to soon enough.

It appears that the Germans are throwing everything at us, we have been pushed back but I believe we are soon preparing to force them into a retreat of their own. Hopefully, we can kick them back once and for all, and before you know it we can be back together soon.

What a wonderful thought that is.

My warmest wishes and all my love to you and our boy,

Yours always,
Henry

Henry sealed the letter carefully and planted a soft delicate kiss on the envelope before preparing it for its delivery. The beginning of the year had presented itself as rather dull in comparison to their previous months on the front-line; however, in the last week or so they had found themselves caught under a heavy German bombardment losing several men and several yards of ground in the process.

Archie, Henry and Alan had been in the support line when the original attack began, however, they were locked in a bloody scramble to reclaim their front-line trench but became overwhelmed once more by the might of the powerful German onslaught.

After being forced to retreat again, more men were drafted into the reserve trench to prepare themselves for mobilisation to push back the German army and strive forward. They were preparing themselves for the attack for a day or more and Archie felt it was only a matter of time before they were given the orders of striking the heart of the Germans and pushing them back across the barren landscapes.

Later, that afternoon, such an order was delivered. The amalgamation of new and old troops launched themselves over to reclaim their front-line trench. The German numbers were strong, but the rejuvenated spirit of the British troops proved too overwhelming and after a couple of hours of torrid fighting, the depleted German numbers retreated, allowing Archie and Henry, along with their fellow surviving troops to reclaim their front-line.

That evening the sun settled finely on the horizon. As they sat polishing their guns and their buttons, and they huddled together strapping up minor wounds and cuts, the orders were delivered that the following morning at dawn, they would be going over the top, aiming to crush any German resistance across no man's land and attempt to push them as far out of France as possible. *It was a rather large task in one day's work,* Archie thought, *but they were determined to stop the recent German barrage and were planning on attacking while they suspected the German numbers to be weak.*

Sergeant Parker delivered the news to his soldiers in a lauding speech that filled every man with the confidence and self-belief to fulfil such a task. Archie, Henry and Alan had grown accustomed to their sergeant's antics before a battle, but it never ceased to inspire them and they spent the evening sat watching the stars in the sky, just like every other night, but this night, they felt a buzz that they may be on the verge of pushing the German's back for good.

Alan had left Henry and Archie on their own momentarily, while he had scurried off to find some more water, leaving Henry the perfect time to turn to his oldest friend.

"Do you still get nervous the night before, the way you used to?" Henry asked tentatively.

"I'm always nervous," Archie replied sincerely.

"Do you ever worry tomorrow might be your day?" Henry asked curiously.

Archie thought silently for a moment, since returning to the front lines almost a year ago, every time they faced the enemy, he had prepared himself to die so long as it meant protecting Henry. He felt no different, he knew, he must ensure Henry's survival no matter the cost to himself.

"I worry that it must not be yours, I worry that it is my duty to protect you, to the very end. So, in truth, I know it won't be our day, our day will be many, many years from now," Archie spoke gently and calmly, as Henry put an arm around his shoulder and the two looked deep into each other's eyes, only for a moment, before Alan returned wiping the excess water from his top lip.

In the short glance exchanged, both Henry and Archie felt calm about what was to come. Henry believed in Archie, as he always had, he believed he was right, tomorrow would not be their day.

"We refuse to die," Archie said quietly smiling at Henry Alan's eyebrows raised in confusion as he took another sip of water before the three of them sat gazing up at another night sky.

Another night that was to pass them by and make way for a new dawn, a new fight.

The darkness of the night drifted into a low blue light as a new day was being welcomed in once more. There was a calmness in the air, the breeze was still and swirled around the trenches, the cool air tickling the hairs on the back of Archie's neck. Strings of birds darted across the sky, waking up the earth below with their songs of morning glory, breaking the night and greeting the day.

They were well used to the rituals of the morning before an attack. No matter how many times they had faced the guns, they still always struggled to sleep in the night building up to it. There could be no guarantee of safety, and should a bullet have their name written on it they would have an eternity to rest.

Archie scrunched his eyes with his fists, he had managed an hour or two of sleep when his mind shut off from the world around him and his eyes closed encasing him in his own shell.

Henry, however, had managed a little while longer while Alan had been up and down all night frantically busying himself and polishing his boots, which was rather a thankless task, as every time he finished, he was cementing them back within the thick layers of mud and grime.

The rum rations were handed out and there seemed significantly more to go around in Frank's absence, it gave them something to laugh about as time moved in its characteristically stagnant fashion, before going over the top. Henry wiped the rich nectar from his lips and wandered over to Archie's side, who was stretching his back.

"Alright?" Henry asked, no more words seemed to fall from his mouth, but the solitary worded question seemed adequate in the circumstances.

"Think so. You?" Archie returned the question his voice as strong as he could muster.

"Yeah. Yeah, I'm alright. Just gotta make sure, you, get back," Henry said, raising his eyebrows and brushing what appeared to be a rat dropping from Archie's shoulder.

"Likewise," Archie smiled, and the two readied themselves for the next part of the ordeal.

Archie walked off with Henry to stand guard by a ladder leading up to the butcher's graveyard. He had promised Henry, he would bring him home and he promised Annie, he would reunite them.

If this was indeed, as they had been told, to be their great push of getting the Germans out of France—though they had been told it many times—Archie had to ensure any bullet that may be inscribed with Henry's name would take a deflected path to him. He looked up to the sky. He closed his eyes. And he prayed. He prayed for his safety, that God would watch over him, but that above all else he must allow him to guide Henry to safety.

Alan meandered over to them, slightly swaying from his rum intake as they naturally fell into formation without being instructed. Sergeant Parker's strong, confident voice delivered the news they had two minutes to go. Henry reached inside his breast pocket and pulled out the photograph of his small family. He held it close to his heart before raising it to his face, planting a kiss on the face of Annie and Stanli, before laying his eyes on it once more, and then tucking it back inside to safety.

One minute remaining.

"God speed, my friends," Alan uttered calmly, as he exchanged looks with both Archie and Henry.

"I'll see you on the other side," Henry said, patting them both on the shoulder as he looked across to the other side of no man's land he was referring to.

"Until we meet again," Archie chimed finally, nodding at them both.

"Positions men. Fix bayonets. For the king and country, God be with you," Sergeant Parker bellowed, as his voice reverberated around the trench.

"Be safe," Henry whispered to Archie, clutching tightly onto his forearm.

"And you," Archie replied, as he took his position ahead of Henry, as opposed to alongside him, to feel the force of any attack they face going over the top.

Sergeant Parker's whistle broke through the narrow avenues of the trench and a powerful rallying cry broke out from all the soldiers throwing themselves up the ladder and out into no man's land.

"Behind me," Archie called out to Henry as he slung him onto the ladder he was on, behind his own position to protect him.

Alan scuttled off next to them and shouted inaudible nonsense to pluck up the courage to face the enemy as he broke off ahead of them. Archie's eyes watched him go with terror, fearing for his safety, before his mind deferred back to Henry who was tightly behind him.

They fell out onto the vast wasteland scattered with bodies and trunks of trees that had been uprooted in their prime, like the men that lay around them. There were helmets and limbs littering every step they took as they strode further, delving deeper into unknown territory.

When they set out, they had been expecting little resistance, they had been expecting the same depleted forces that they had forced into retreat, only the day before, to be scrambling themselves together to protect their trench from the mass of spirit British soldiers descending upon them. What they found however, were great numbers of machine guns primed in position, ready to spray bullets out onto the sacrificial lambs marching towards them.

It was clear to Archie that they had reinforced their numbers and were no longer there for the taking, as had been pledged to them the night before. He gulped heavily as they took great strides through the great swathes of battered earth.

He looked to his left; Henry was marching confidently alongside him, as he always had done. The British artillery guns began peppering the German defences, at the same time the German's heavy guns began breaking up the advances through no man's land, dropping bombs and mortars in their path, sending great heaps of dirt flying through the air, bodies and limbs merging with the earth as it sailed through the sky.

They heard the blood curdling screams of the victims laying in their path, crying out for their mothers, begging to be relieved of their immense pain as their thighs hung virtually detached from their body. They passed men clutching at the skin of their cheeks, the ground beneath them splashing under foot, and not from puddles of absent water.

Archie looked to his left; Henry was ploughing over any obstacle that fell in his path as the sight of German barbed wire grew closer into view. Archie had lost sight of Alan, his eyes had wandered the scene in front of him, scanning and surveying the bodies as they fell, but he had not recognised any to be his rampant friend. He prayed for his safety somewhere in the midst of the indiscriminate attack. His body kept itself moving, step after step, breath after breath.

He looked to his left; Henry was there, close under his protection. He turned to his left again, Henry looked across at him, smiling. Despite the bloodbath bubbling around them, Henry managed to freeze the world for just a moment to exchange a moment of tenderness with his best friend. Archie smiled back, moving closer in front of Henry, knowing what he must do, the closer they got to the enemy lines.

Archie looked to his left; Henry was not there. Archie frantically threw his head around in every direction before looking behind him. He saw Henry laid out on the ground a step or two behind him.

"Henry!" he cried out, piercing through the air.

Instantly, he threw himself to the ground and crawled to Henry, the world stopping around him.

He reached Henry and looked down at him. A small pool of red was oozing its way out of Henry's midriff and Archie stopped breathing. He froze.

"Arch. Arch," Henry mumbled, his voice shaking anxiously.

Archie scooped Henry's head up in his arm and pressed his hand deep into his body above his lung.

"You're alright, everything's alright," Archie said, trembling as he scanned the area around, his eyes pleading for a medic to rush to his aid.

"Is it bad?" Henry asked coughing.

"Just a scratch," Archie laughed, trying to joke to put Henry's mind at ease as he felt his hand fill up with blood as he began pushing down harder on the bullet hole.

"It doesn't feel like a scratch," Henry started. "I'm scared," his voice trembled as he spoke.

"There's nothing to be scared about. I'm getting you out of here. I'm getting you back to Annie, Stanli," Archie pleaded with his friend who was lying quivering in his arms.

Henry looked up, seeing Archie's face dart about the battlefield, he had known his best friend long enough to read his feelings and expressions.

"It's not looking good, is it?" Henry asked, the tears circling in the corner of his eyes.

"I've got you. Best friends for life remember, stick together like glue." Archie was growing desperate as he shook Henry in his arms, brushing his hair out of his face.

"I don't want to die," Henry wept slightly.

It was the first time in 20 years of life that Archie had ever seen Henry show anything other than his oozing calmness and confidence. He felt lost, he could feel his heart shattering inside him as he searched for ways to help his best friend.

"You're not going to die," Archie said, looking down at Henry who had turned his face to one side to disguise his tears from Archie. "Look at me, you're not going to die, I'm going to get you out of here, I'm going to get you home," Archie continued, trying to masquerade a strong voice as he spoke.

"Can you do something for me?" Henry asked, choking slightly before he spoke.

"Anything," Archie replied instantly.

"Look after Annie and Stanli for me. Protect them and keep them safe," Henry pleaded, as he lay there, a paleness about his skin.

"You will do that," Archie responded, reluctant to lose faith in Henry.

"I think we both know, I cannot. Please, for me," Henry said, his natural surety and calm demeanour that Archie had only ever known had returned even in the darkest of hours.

"Of course, I will," Archie said, the tears beginning to wash with the dirt on his cheeks.

"Take these," Henry started reaching inside the pocket by his chest, close to wear his skin had been torn apart by a cruel German bullet. "Take them, take them back to Annie," Henry smiled up at Archie as he handed him two small objects.

The first is the perfectly pristine photograph of his cherished family. The second is a small rectangular box. His deck of cards. He placed them delicately in Archie's hand and furled his fingertips around them keeping them protected.

A singular beam of light broke through the thick grey cloud of smoke and fumes, reaching down to Henry lighting up the path above him. Henry looked up, his eyes settling on the ray of light touching his face.

"It's beautiful," he uttered quietly, as a small smile adorned him.

The colour was draining from his face like a painting left out in the rain, sinking into the earth below.

Henry winced, the pain was getting to him, and he could feel the grasp of God reaching out to him. He looked up at Archie, their eyes locking, both swollen with tears.

"Thank you, for everything," Henry said softly, as his head rested on the crease in Archie's arm.

"I cannot go on without you," Archie's voice lost his sense of control, and he sniffed as the tears fell down his face.

"You can and you must. You must finish this, for me. Take them home for me, introduce them to Mother and keep them safe," Henry instructed Archie, reaching his weak arm up to hold onto Archie's hand as he felt the life drifting out of him.

"I will protect them with my life," Archie promised Henry, clutching deeply onto his hand in his.

"I know you will," Henry's voice was growing softer and quieter. "I know you will…my brother," Henry whispered softly, as he exhaled, loud enough so Archie could hear every syllable that left his lips.

Archie looked down into his deep eyes, taking in every memory they had shared together flashing in front of his eyes as their eyes were locked on each other's for a few precious moments longer.

Just as Henry finished his gentle words to Archie, he exhaled deeply and his hand loosened in Archie's grasp, his eyes softly closing on his best friend and on the world.

"Henry…Henry," Archie whispered, shaking Henry's still body to no reply.

He closed his eyes, his head tilting back to the sky as the tears streamed down his face. He leaned his head over Henry's body kissing his forehead as he slipped the cards and photograph tightly inside his pocket. He looked around, the men he fought alongside were retreating back to their trench under the weight of the German defence.

Archie lay there with Henry until darkness fell upon them, savouring the last hours he would ever live in his best friend's company. When the blanket of the night dropped overhead, he shuffled along the scarred landscape with Henry on his back carrying him to the safety of the British line, the place they had grown to call home over the last few years.

He reached the parapet with Henry still firmly attached to him and slid into the safety of his familiar confines. As he slumped down against the trench wall, Henry, still in his arms, and his body drained with fatigue and exhaustion, the tears streamed from his face.

He could see the stretcher-bearers making their way around the trench and Archie looked down at Henry and placed his hand into Henry's pocket removing a small chord, on which was a red tag with Henry's name on. He tucked it into his pocket alongside his own and held Henry with him until the stretcher-bearers came to take him away.

They could see the distress on Archie's face as they loaded Henry onto the stretcher.

"Friend?" a tall, gangly stretcher bearer, asked Archie.

Archie shook his head.

"Brother," he replied as he held onto Henry's still hand until they moved him away and around the corner, out of sight but as long as Archie lived, never out of mind.

Archie sat there as he watched them carry his best friend out of his eyeline for the last ever time, watching his peaceful face turn the corner to the promise of a better life, a better place.

He huddled himself up in the corner of a fire step and took the items out of his inside pocket, he gazed down at the photograph of Henry's family, his eyes so full of light and life. He knew it was his lasting duty to return to Annie, take them home with him, and keep them safe as long as he lived.

Then he turned his attention to the small box of cards, of which the corner had become slightly tainted red from Henry's blood spilling through his uniform onto it. He opened the deck, the same way he had done for years before the war. He tipped the cards out onto his hand and flipped over the top card on the deck.

The king of hearts. Archie chuckled to himself and felt a warming feeling inside as he tucked the cards back inside their safe sleeve and returned everything to their new rightful home, the pocket over his heart, where he would also keep Henry, and their endless memories together.

He leaned back against the trench wall and gazed up to the stars. *There seemed to be more stars in the sky that particular night,* Archie thought, as he noticed one shining more brightly than all the rest. He smiled as he saw it, for he knew Henry had found peace and safety in the next life, in heaven, alongside Frank, Arthur, and all the good men they had lost along the way.

He leaned back against the trench wall, gazing up to the stars, and closed his weary eyes on the world.

The sun rose on the following day, Archie found he had slept quite sometime during the night, the exhaustion had taken its toll on his body and his mind welcomed a night's salvation.

When he woke to the early song of the birds overhead, his eyes instantly darted around to find Henry, before the crippling reality returned to him and he dropped his head between his knees, without the energy to do much more than lift it into his hands.

When he heard familiar tones, his ears pricked, and he raised his head with his palm on his chin. It was Alan. He waded his way through the people, sliding down the sides of groups and hobbling over uneven duckboards.

"Archie!" he exclaimed slumping down onto his knees, barely protected by the wooden flooring separating him and the cesspit below.

He threw an arm around Archie's shoulder and raised his head up with his other hand.

"What is it? Where's Henry? I thought I'd lost you both," Alan spoke at a rapid pace, as though the words had been waiting to tumble out of his mouth all night.

"Henry's gone," Archie mumbled, his voice barely decipherable.

Alan's knees sunk, drowning in the mud, but he did not seem to care, his face was expressionless and pale. He pulled his hat from his head and held it in front of his chest.

"Oh no, no, no, no," he uttered, shaking his head, his voice despairing but angry.

Angry at the fact he could keep losing his friends and the world was unwilling to give him anything in return for his hardships.

"Archie, I'm so sorry," he shuffled along the floor of the trench to seat himself alongside Archie, where he wrapped his arms around his sole surviving friend and the two of them sat silently for a moment, not saying anything, not knowing what could even be said.

"Were you with him, when it happened?" Alan asked curiously.

Archie nodded softly.

"He died in my arms. There was nothing I could—" Archie stopped and turned his head away to the side, sinking his teeth deep into his bottom lip to stifle the tears.

"It's never your fault," Alan spoke softly and reassuringly.

"It was my job. My duty was to protect him. His family, he had a family, a new family to go home to," Archie's valiant efforts to hold the tears back could no longer be upheld and the walls caved in.

His words merged together as Alan wrapped his arm around Archie's neck and tipped his head downwards to shield him from onlooking eyes.

"You could not protect him, no one can protect anyone out here," Alan whispered gently in Archie's car, as he could feel his body vibrating as the tears rolled down his mud-stained face.

"But what now? What am I supposed to do now? I owe it to him to see it through," Archie questioned his eyes slightly raw and red as he looked at Alan.

"We fight on for him. And for Frank. For everyone. And when we fight for him side by side, we pray we make it out alive and we let the names of every single man we have fought alongside who has not made it home live on," Alan spoke poetically, as Archie's head bobbed along with every word he heard.

"Henry was a great man, and a great friend to me and a brother to you. You will miss him, and I will miss him. But he did not die for nothing, he died so me and you could be sitting here now. So that we can do all we can to be stood here when someone goes, you know what fellas it's time to go home," Archie remained transfixed on Alan's every word.

"And when that time comes, we go home, we go to Cromer," he started with a smile, seeing a small twinkle return to Archie's eyes at the sound of his hometown. "And when we do, I have no doubt, you will make sure his son and his family and all those who knew him, will never forget the man he was," Alan concluded his monologue and Archie's eyes were heavy with tears.

"But how can I go back home without him?" He was flushing all the questions he had out of his system along with all his overwhelming emotion.

"You'll have to do it because there is no other choice. It'll be hard but you'll have to face it, live your life from now on for you and for Henry. That's all you can ever do," Alan finished with a slight cough, as the scars of sorrow were still stricken across Archie's face, but with a streak of determination in his eyes, as Alan rose to his knees and then to his feet.

"I'll go and get you some tea," Alan said warmly, before striding off with intent.

Archie prized himself to his feet and looked around. The spring sun was dazzling above them, the birds spiralling overhead. The sun in the sky did not care for the bloodshed occurring beneath its watchful gaze, it did not care for the slaughter it witnessed, it only cared that each day it would bring new life, and allow new plants to grow into magnificent trees. Unlike the narrow minds of men on earth, it did not waste its time on taking life, it focused on creating it.

Archie took in the clouds rolling their way from one bank of blue to the other. As he looked across the horizon something caught his peripheral gaze. He saw something out of the corner of his eye. He settled his focus down on the parapet just ahead of him. Sprouting its way through the thick, dense mud, was a solitary poppy. A small, innocent flower struggling through adversity to show a sign that when all seems lost, life will prevail over death.

Archie stopped and stared at it for some time, he watched the individual petals whistle and waltz in the breeze. He closed his eyes, his mind carrying the image of the flower. It transported him back and made him think of being stood in the gardens with Mr Humphrey, four springs earlier, sowing the seeds of a new, promised beauty.

He thought, *Not of how the world had transpired since he was last shovelling his way through the rich, English soil, but of how throughout it all the beauty and modesty of nature had not faltered, and while the men of the world were adamant on tearing it apart, mother nature was doing her bit to help sew it back together.*

Archie smiled as he opened his eyes and watched the flower once more. He felt Henry's presence with him as looked upon it, he knew from that moment on, no matter how many days, weeks, months, or years the war still had to live, he would not be alone.

Henry would be watching over him, guiding him to his destiny and to his survival, to carry him over the line. He had a duty to Henry, an order to fulfil, and as he stood there watching the one sprouting of new life in the world, he knew in his heart, that he was going to deliver what he promised Henry, and he knew he would see it through.

13

Alan scampered across the rickety wooden flooring underfoot, his boots knocking against the surface, elevating the noise of his presence. He slid and scurried past bodies surrounding him, dipping and ducking to avoid clanging mugs and flailing hands.

His breath was heavy as he mazed his way through the crowd of exhausted, pale-faced men. He stumbled, his hands launching to the sides of the trench to adjust his balance before he regained composure and continued on his mission through the network of tunnels.

"Archie!" he exclaimed, calling out with a heavy pant.

Archie could not hear him; the raucous noise of the troops Alan was bombarding through, mellowing the sound of his voice.

"Archie!" he called out again, this time pricking the ears of his friend, whose head fizzed from side to side searching for the origin of the call.

Archie broke through the final barrier of men before reaching Archie.

"Archie," he said, this time with slightly less enthusiasm and gusto than the previous shouts.

"What is it?" Archie asked puzzled.

Alan rested bent double, his hands on his knees his head facing the ground as he panted and breathed heavily, his tongue wagging slightly out of the corner of his mouth like a stray dog. He looked up, tilting his head upward so his eyes locked onto Archie's.

"It's over," he said, his voice calm and gentle. "The war is over," he continued, a smile breaking out across his face.

"What?" Archie scoffed.

He couldn't quite believe his ears. He had felt they had been close for some time but confirmation that no more blood would be spilled across the permanently tarnished countryside did not seem real.

"They've signed the ceasefire. We did it," Alan stated, standing up and resting his hand on Archie's shoulder.

Archie removed the helmet from his head and slid his back down the trench wall sliding his fingertips through his wet hair. He could not believe it. All they had grown to know was fighting and within the click of a finger, it had all disappeared.

Their purpose was over, and what had always remained to them, a constant thought of an unattainable future of returning home, suddenly became an imminent reality. Archie let out a sigh, reaching the arms of his lungs out to inhale all the oxygen he could find before exhaling it all back out again.

"Wow," he uttered, before letting out a scoffed chuckle.

It did not seem a reality, they were no longer to be walking around as marked men, men with a death warrant hanging over their heads. They would once again feel what it would be like to walk the English streets and eat the local food they dreamt about every night.

Archie and Alan looked at each other and laughed, and then they embraced each other, wearily. They only had each other to embrace. There was no Arthur. There was no Frank. There was no Henry. Only them.

They had stayed standing while all those they held dear had fallen. They held onto each other, unsure how to feel. The relief washed over them like a powerful wave crashing into the shore.

"We've done it," Archie said, before tilting his head up to the sky and smiling.

He felt Henry with him, he had done this for him. He had survived for him. He had not died for nothing, his life and the lives of all of their friends which had been cruelly snatched from their youthful hearts had not been in vain.

"Now what?" Alan asked ironically, the future they had dreamt about now becoming one they could plan for.

"Now we're free," Archie replied, grabbing the shoulder of his close comrade and shaking him where he stood a grin on his face. Alan chuckled and smiled.

"What will you do now? Will you go straight home?" Alan asked softly.

"I will go home," Archie said slowly, the words seeming unfathomable that they had left his lips.

"And I shall join you there, I have decided," Alan said, making Archie smile, knowing the life Alan had told Henry, he would lead in Cromer, could now blossom into fruition.

"But there's something I have to do first," Archie said, looking Alan in the eye and fixing his hat firmly on his head.

After a few tiresome weeks had passed and the order of their discharge had been delivered, Archie found himself traversing the narrow French pathways alone. He had left the rest of his fellow comrades behind and with his kitbag attached to his back, and all his most valued belongings tightly fixed in the pockets on his uniform he marched over the hills and across the rivers of the now peaceful French countryside.

As he walked, he intently listened to the chirping of the birds high in the trees, the only noise blanketing over them being the subtle whistle of the breeze through the leaves. There was no longer the commotion of bombs and bullets flying through the sky and cascading into life and land.

He walked contented with a smile on his face. In the months that had passed since Henry's death, he had often felt alone, and scared. He found he could not ever look forward, as he felt it would only be dangerous to tempt a fate that may be taken away from him. He would only be able to clutch onto the memory of Henry in the forefront of his mind while he focused on ensuring his own survival.

Now, after the weight of the world had been removed from his shoulders and the burdening crown of survival had been removed from his head, he walked freely, and his mind clogged and overflowed with memories and images with Henry.

He remembered the exact steps he had traced with Henry, not more than two years earlier. Yet it felt like a lifetime ago. Henry's life had been taken from him in that time and he now was forced to relive the life they lived and walk the steps they took together, but now alone.

He had spent the last months of his life upset, but now he felt happy. He missed Henry, terribly, but he finally was able to live life for the both of them. He could lead a life that Henry would be proud of, lead a life worth living.

He approached a hill he knew all too well, a familiar hill he had meandered over many a time, with Henry by his side, filled with different emotions every time they reached the peak, this time, those emotions lived through Archie, and he felt ready and excited to take on life. They had spent long enough at war living in the shadows, now he was out in the light, he was excited to live life, with Henry in his heart for many, many years to come.

Archie trotted over the peak of the hill to the sight of patchwork roofs, and the sun breaking through the chimneys. He hurried down the other side of the hill using his momentum to let his legs run freely through the grass, the cool winter wind rushing through his veins.

He stepped foot onto the stone pathway, his boots touching down on familiar soil. He looked around him, there was a change in the air from when he had last been there, the faces he passed were smiling not sad, the children were running and laughing freely not hidden away for safety.

They were wrapped up for winter with their cheeks rosy and their noses a comforting red. Their parents watching them with beaming smiles, the only sounds that filled the air that of joyous laughter. The horrors of the past four years were washed away by the simplicity of a happy smile and a jolly cheer.

Archie passed them all, walking through the courtyard until he reached a familiar building. A small but quaint café. The outdoor tables were tucked away for the winter and the door was shut. Archie looked up to the windows above the ground floor.

He held fond images and memories from the rooms behind the small panes of glass he looked up at. He took a deep breath before walking through the heart of the entrance, past the stacks of outdoor chairs and upturned tables until he reached the front door.

He stood there for a moment, breathing slowly and gently. He reached inside his pocket and pulled out the small rectangular photograph. He looked down at it. Henry, Annie and Stanli all looked back up at him. He smiled and looked up to the sky. He had done it.

He had kept his promise to the person he cared for more than any other. In that very moment, all the sacrifices and bloodshed had not been for nothing. He had made it. He looked down at the picture once more, smiling down at the picture of Henry who was smiling back up at him.

"I made it," he said softly, looking down at Henry, a small tear neatly fell down his cheek.

Archie took a deep breath and knocked on the door.

14

Steam ploughed into the air and the train chugged and whistled into the station.

"Ah, this is my stop," said the old man, his voice soothing and gentle.

He picked up his small flat cap from beside him and placed it neatly on his head. He took the old, wooden walking stick that was balanced up against his knee and used it to push himself up off the soft bench in the carriage.

"I have very much enjoyed our conversation, do take care of yourself," the old man spoke delicately to a young woman who had been sitting opposite him.

They were the only two people in the carriage and the door was firmly closed. She appeared to him to be in the realm of her 20s or 30s. He picked up a leather bag that had been occupying the space next to him where he sat and made his way slowly toward the door of the carriage.

"Wait a minute," the young woman called out, as the old man was reaching for the handle of the carriage to slide the door out to his release. "How do you know that story?" She asked him curiously, raising an eyebrow slightly.

The man stopped in his tracks and turned round to her, a smile on his face.

He said nothing, rather, he rested the curved handle of his walking stick on his forearm, and adjusted the tie on his shirt, loosening it and pulling it down slightly. He then unbuttoned the top couple of buttons on his shirt and pulled his jacket and shirt down and over to the side revealing his skin beneath.

As he stretched it across to his shoulder, the young woman sitting opposite him saw a small, round, and painful-looking scar where mangled skin had been reattached together. The young woman's eyes widened, as the old man smiled at her and tipped his hat before sliding open the door and making his way out of the carriage.

The young woman sat startled; she pressed her face up against the window watching the old man step off the train, gingerly to a small crowd of people waiting for him. As his feet made contact with the platform, a little girl, no older than seven or eight darted over to him, throwing her arms around his waist and clutching on. The old man placed a tender hand on her head and ruffled her delicate, dark hair.

Stood just behind the girl were a man and a woman hand in hand, who the woman on the train deduced to be her parents. The man was tall and slim with dark hair and a familiar look about his face. Standing next to the couple was an older lady. She was standing with a smile on her face, watching the little girl warmly embrace the old man and take his hand in hers as they broke from their hug. The older lady was standing elegantly, dressed in a long dress and a knitted cardigan, and adorning her dark hair was a soft, cream beret.

The couple led the way walking hand in hand, with the elder two walking behind with the little girl still clutching tightly onto the old man's hand. The man reared his head back over his shoulder and made eye contact with the lady on the train who was still watching him. He smiled and nodded at her, and she reciprocated, her head nodding at him, as he turned to walk down the platform.

As he began walking away, the young woman sat on the train and noticed something catch in the light of the sun. She focused her eyes on two disks that had been stitched onto the old man's leather bag. The two tags each had a name inscribed delicately on them. The first tag read A. Baxter. The second positioned tightly next to the first read H. Longley.